Praise for Ann W;

The Babbling Brook Naked Poker Club Series

The lush character description and the dialogue was splendid. The setting in a retirement home was an unlikely and zany choice. Mystery, nosy old biddies, liars, cheats, romance, intrigue...all wrapped into one wonderful read. Janet Tunget

Beautifully written in Warner's trademark clean, eloquent prose, this light-hearted mystery set in a retirement community is very fun to read. The quirky members of *The Babbling Brook Naked Poker Club* will charm and inspire you, as they band together to catch a thief. Gail Cleare, author of *The Taste of Air*

The Dreams Trilogy
Dreams for Stones, Persistence of Dreams
Unexpected Dreams

...incredibly vivid and emotional tale of love and loyalty, friendship, loss, and faith...*Booklist*

...a lovely story about life changes and love lost and found. *Romantic Times Book Review*

Stunning! Juli Townsend, Author of *Absent Children*

A compelling page turner. *Romantic Times*

Excellent characters and dialogue drive the romance and suspense...great reading. *Romance Studio*

.....another wonderful story from a terrific author...a romance filled with mystery... (and) the power of love. *Coffee Time Romance*

Love and Other Acts of Courage

Love and Other Acts of Courage is...beautiful. The plot is engaging...and the ending very satisfying. Lorena Sanqui for Readers' Favorite

...a love story woven within an engaging mystery with twists and turns, believable villains, and enough tension to keep you turning pages. Dete Meserve, author of *Good Sam*

...the characterizations of Max, Jake, and Sophie are done so delicately, so perfectly, that each alone would be worthy of a separate story. In short, *Love and Other Acts of Courage* is *so* much more than a love story. Kate Moretti, NY Times Bestselling author of *I Thought I Knew You*

Memory Lessons

The storyline in the book will draw you in, and you will think you know what is going on...but it has surprises awaiting you...don't miss this inspirational story. David Johnson, author of *The Tucker Series*

A lovely and compelling story. The characters are multidimensional and real. The plot contains some genuine surprise twists...and stuck with me a long time after I had put it down. Michelle Lam, author of *The Accidental Prophetess*

...delivers high-stakes drama with real characters and an understanding of how women process memory and guilt. Ms. Warner does another fine job, tying both plot and subplots together in a completely atypical, but convincingly logical story that left me satisfied. Patricia Macauliffe

Absence of Grace

The writing is perfect. Absolutely smooth and divine. Like the best bar of chocolate in the world. Fran Macilvey, Author of *Trapped*

Love the way this book flowed back and forth like the tide bringing in new finds. Wonderful story of healing and forgiveness. Karen Daniel

Look for these titles by Ann Warner

Absence of Grace

Counterpointe

Doubtful

Memory Lessons

Vocabulary of Light

Dreams for Stones

Persistence of Dreams

Unexpected Dreams

Vocabulary of Light

The Babbling Brook Naked Poker Club Series

Love and other Acts of Courage

by

ANN WARNER

Silky Stone Press

Silky Stone Press

Love and Other Acts of Courage

Copyright 2014 Ann Warner

http://www.AnnWarner.net

ISBN: 9781720258520

Editing by Pam Berehulke of Bulletproof Editing

Cover Art by Ann Warner

Published in the United States of America

Library of Congress Registration TXu001904750

This book is a work of fiction. Names, characters, and incidents are either the product of the author's imagination or are used fictitiously.

Dedication

To all those who have lost someone they love at sea.

Prologue

AUCKLAND, New Zealand - May 17, 1994

AMERICAN WOMAN RESCUED

Search and Rescue forces today reported the rescue at sea of an American woman, Sophie Suriano. The Suriano yacht with two aboard had been reported overdue from Nuku'alofa, Tonga.

Mrs. Suriano was evacuated by helicopter to Whangarei Base Hospital, where she is undergoing treatment for injuries suffered during and subsequent to the sinking of the yacht Sylph. Still missing is Mrs. Suriano's husband, Samuel.

The cause of the sinking is not known at this time.

Chapter One
San Francisco - November 1994
MAX

The client, a woman of slight stature and sharp edges, walked into my office with the aid of a cane and the hesitancy of the recently ill.

She was a referral from Ben Talbot: "Max, have I got a case for you."

"Last time you said that, I ended up on the wrong end of an oil tanker collision."

"Hell, the *Alejandro* made your reputation."

"What is it this time?"

He'd given me a summary. A hit-and-run, in international waters off New Zealand, involving a Chinese freighter and an American yacht. Two people aboard the yacht, only one survivor.

Not my kind of case, and Ben knew it.

"The fact is, Sam Suriano wasn't just a client. He was a friend," Ben said.

It was the one approach I couldn't refuse out of hand, which was why Sam Suriano's widow was currently being ushered into my office by my assistant, Cassie.

The contrast between the two women was startling. Cassie, dark-skinned and regal versus Mrs. Suriano, pale, gaunt, and looking much older than her forty years. Further proof of what else Ben told me—that severely injured, she'd been cast adrift on the Tasman Sea with no food or water and with little protection from the elements. Seeing her now, it was difficult to imagine how she'd managed to survive.

"Mrs. Suriano, Max Gildea," Cassie said.

The woman lifted haunted eyes to mine. I nodded, and after a brief hesitation, she lowered herself into the client chair. Cassie set a cup of tea on the table next to the chair and left the room without giving me a signal, although Cassie never brings in a new client without letting me know her opinion.

There's the eye roll (thinks he's a comedian), the flapping hand (won't stop talking), the smile with a thumbs-up (this one's a keeper), and the grimace with a thumbs-down (turkey, pass him on to someone else).

Her instincts are excellent, so I always pay attention. This time, however, if she made a judgment, she wasn't sharing.

"My condolences on your loss." I spoke the formal words acknowledging the death of Mrs. Suriano's husband with a proper solemnity, and she inclined her head in response.

"Ben Talbot gave me only a summary of your situation. Perhaps we might start with you filling in more details." I picked up a pen and waited for her to begin.

"First, I'd like to ask you a few questions." Her voice was clear and firm without the tremor her appearance suggested would be there.

"Ben didn't discuss my professional qualifications with you?"

"Indeed. He said you're...relentless."

Not bad. I'd have to remember that. I nodded, encouraging her to get on with it.

She tipped her head, examining me. "Tell me, do you handle many wrongful death cases?"

"No, I avoid them whenever possible."

"I see." She tightened her lips, and a small crease appeared between her eyes. "Then why did Ben say you were the best person for this?"

"You'd have to ask Ben."

She continued to examine me. "Do you sail, Mr. Gildea?"

"No."

"And yet all your cases are associated with ships and the sea."

11

"I know a successful attorney whose practice involves the thoroughbred industry, and yet he's afraid of horses." Brother Andy. A Gildea family trait perhaps—to deal with fears sideways. Our father was afraid to fly, but nonetheless spent twenty years in the Air Force.

"Are you afraid of the water?" she asked, her expression and tone intent.

"No." Always the exception.

"What are you afraid of?"

What the hell? "Snakes and spiders. Nuclear weapons. Meteors."

"You're not taking my questions seriously."

"I usually ask the questions." I returned her steady look with an effort.

"And it makes you uncomfortable to answer them."

"Yes." That yes represented a degree of personal candor I rarely grant, even to those closest to me. I shifted, trying to clamp down on the discomfort her questions had elicited.

She had been leaning forward as she questioned me. Now, she sat back. "Where do you want me to begin?"

Her more relaxed posture suggested I had passed muster, although damned if I had any idea how I'd done it. "Start wherever you like." I leaned back as well, relieved to be once again on familiar ground.

As she began to speak, Mrs. Suriano looked past me, her eyes losing their focus. Her voice dropped to a monotone, and her body began to rock.

The most useful part of her story? That the ship responsible for the sinking of the Suriano yacht had been identified as the Chinese freighter, *Nereus.*

The ship was first implicated by New Zealand authorities, based on shipping schedules and satellite tracking, then its involvement was confirmed by Japanese authorities in Yokohama, the ship's first port of call. Fresh dents were found in the freighter's bow, and they contained traces of anti-fouling paint. Anti-fouling paint is used on boat hulls to prevent barnacles, algae, and other types of marine growth.

"The anti-fouling paint on the *Nereus* was matched to what we'd used on the *Sylph*," Mrs. Suriano said.

"I didn't realize the yacht had been recovered."

She shook her head. "It hasn't been. A friend used the same batch of paint we did. He provided the samples for the matching." Mrs. Suriano turned her gaze back to me, and in that moment, I had the totally absurd urge to pull her into my arms, pat her on the back, and tell her everything would be all right. Like one would a child.

It wasn't an impulse I could easily indulge from a wheelchair, and it certainly wasn't my usual response to a client. My clients are, at any rate, mostly men with well-camouflaged paunches and perfectly barbered hair. Men who tap manicured fingers against the arms of my guest chairs, directing me to speak quickly and to the point about their situations. Men who refuse sympathy and consider compassion a sign of weakness. The sort of men we would be up against in this case.

All I had to work with was Mrs. Suriano's insistence that the reason she didn't see the freighter approaching was because it was running without lights, something the freighter crew denied.

But no matter how the accident happened, there was no excuse for the crew's subsequent action—sailing off without attempting a rescue. They'd subsequently claimed they had no idea they'd even hit the yacht, but Mrs. Suriano disputed that.

"Sam and I saw several of the crew looking down at us as the freighter turned away."

"What exactly do you want me to do for you?"

"I want you to help me sue the ship's owners and the officers in charge at the time of the accident for the wrongful death of my husband and for my pain and suffering, property damage, and anything else we can tack on."

Right. That was what it always boiled down to. Money. Even with a case as horrific as this one.

"Why?" It was brutal, but I needed to check how committed she was.

She gave me a kitten-backed-into-a-corner look, but the intensity was pure tiger, and I braced for the angry words to follow. Instead, her tone was controlled. "You think it's all about the money? That's what you're thinking."

I waited.

She looked away then straightened. "I have plenty of money. More than I can ever possibly need. What I don't have any longer is my husband." She stopped speaking abruptly and took several deep breaths before continuing.

"The *Nereus* was running without lights. She hit us, and her crew knew they hit us. They left us to die. And then they denied it. They didn't even have the humanity to say they were sorry we were hit." She took a shaky breath.

"I want them to regret that, and I want to stop them from ever having a chance to hit anyone else." She closed her eyes, and her hands clenched. Then she opened her eyes and met my gaze. "It's the only weapon I have. To force them to pay so much it hurts."

It's my experience that whenever someone says it isn't about the money, that's usually exactly what it's about. But the emotion in Mrs. Suriano's eyes and voice convinced me. This case wasn't about money. Worse. Much worse. It was about justice, something I gave up on years ago.

"Unfortunately, there's a law that affects this type of case." I watched her as I spoke. "It's called Death on the High Seas Act or DOHSA. It will restrict any financial settlement you might receive to compensatory damages only. In other words, your husband's estimated lifetime earnings, the loss of the yacht, and your medical expenses."

Her posture stiffened. "It's the only reason I survived. To stop them. To make them pay."

"I'm afraid DOHSA will make what you want impossible."

"I don't understand."

I spoke gently, although I have strong feelings on the subject. "DOHSA was passed in 1920, and at that time it was ground-breaking. It represented the first time compensation was provided for widows and children of men killed at sea. Now, however, it works more in favor of the shipping industry since it doesn't allow for punitive damages."

"So, you're saying...because of this...DOHSA, they're going to get away with murder?"

"Only a criminal case would effectively address the question of their guilt. All a civil case can accomplish is to find them at fault and require them to pay a compensatory settlement. Unfortunately, I doubt that will affect them as much as you would like."

I gave her a moment to consider that before delivering the final blow. "If you decide to proceed, you need to know this firm cannot accept a case like this on contingency."

Her chin came up, and her eyes flashed with a return of the anger she'd suppressed earlier. "Of course I intend to proceed. If they lose the case, at the least it will prove they were responsible. And I'm willing to pay whatever that requires."

Money again. With a sigh, I bowed to the inevitable. "I'll need a retainer of twenty thousand to begin. Making it to court will likely cost in excess of a hundred thousand."

She opened her purse, pulled out a checkbook and pen, wrote quickly and then leaned forward to place the check on my desk. I left it sitting, but the number she'd written was clear. One hundred and twenty thousand dollars.

I wouldn't want to play poker with her.

I didn't doubt the check would clear.

~ ~ ~

Mrs. Suriano left, and I wheeled over to the window. On a clear day, I can see all the way to Sausalito, and this was a clear day. I picked up the binoculars I keep handy and watched a freighter heading out under the Golden Gate.

After a time, I put the binoculars down and buzzed Cassie. She seemed unusually subdued when she came in.

"What's going on?" I said.

"What do you mean?"

"You don't have an opinion on Mrs. Suriano? Correct me if I'm wrong, but I don't remember that happening before."

"She was wearing a Dellagracia," Cassie said, avoiding both my gaze and my question.

"I thought she was wearing a nice blue suit."

Cassie propped her hands on her hips, the distracted look gone. "Lordy, Max, a nice blue suit? Dellagracia doesn't do *nice* suits, he does *amazing* suits." Cassie has needled me about fashion ever since I criticized the too-short skirt and too-tight top she wore when I interviewed her.

I gave her what she calls "my look," and she settled back to business. "So, are we representing Mrs. Suriano?"

15

I didn't argue with her use of "we." When I take on a client, that client gets not only my best effort and the firm's, but Cassie's as well.

"We're going to do the prelims. See how it goes."

"Why the lack of enthusiasm?"

"The case hinges on a she-says-they-say scenario that will be impossible to prove. She says the freighter was running without lights. The freighter crew denies that. And DOHSA limits our options. Bottom line, Mrs. Suriano won't get what she's seeking."

Cassie's chin came up, a dangerous sign. "Why not tell her that?"

"I tried. She's not ready to hear it."

"So, you're going to take her money and string her along? That stinks, Max."

"As long as we're representing her, we'll do our best to make sure she receives whatever compensation we can get for her."

"I always thought deep down you was rooting for the underdog, Max. Even when you defend oil tankers."

When Cassie's upset, she slips into old habits. It doesn't happen often, at least not with me. Along with how to dress, she's learned to choose her battles, and after more than ten years of working together, she and I can read each other's moods with a glance. That familiarity helps us avoid conflicts, although if it's one thing I can count on, it's that Cassie never minces words.

~ ~ ~

That evening, as he did every evening, Roosevelt Hawkins, a cousin of Cassie's, picked me up at the office and drove me home.

"Cassie tells me your given name be Franklin Delano," he said, when we met. "I'm Roosevelt. Reckon we can be one helluva team." And we are.

Before Rosie, I'd been finding the daily tasks involved in living without legs time-consuming and exhausting. But with Rosie running my household, driving me to and from work, and cooking most of our meals, that aspect of my handicap was lifted.

Rosie's also my workout partner. Tuesdays, Thursdays, and Saturdays we do his favorite activities—swimming laps and doing weight circuits at the health club. I prefer circling the SeaSide College track, which we do Monday, Wednesday, and Friday.

This being a Wednesday, he drove us to the track, and as I settled into my racing chair, he pulled off his sweatshirt.

"What's for dinner tonight?" I asked.

"Got a deee-licious cass'role perking away. Smelled real good. And a flirty little mousse just sitting in the fridge waiting for us." He chuckled, a sound as rich and warm as a bowl of his chili. "Course, you know, Max, before I met you I say we having us stew and pudding."

"A stew by any other name would taste as sweet."

"Don't make no sweet stews, no way. Mousse is where that's at." While Rosie might not recognize literary allusions, he handles word play quite satisfactorily.

"How long you figuring on tonight, Max?"

"Let's try for an hour."

He nodded in agreement and jogged off. I moved into my lane, set my timer, and started rolling. Usually it rests my mind to settle into the rhythmic movements that propel me around the track in the special chair my brother Jeff designed for me. Tonight, though, my mind, full of Sophie Suriano's story, was spinning as fast as my wheels.

Chapter Two
New Year's 1995
MAX

My brothers and their families always spend the holidays in San Francisco. Christmas we celebrate at the folks', and New Year's everyone gathers at my place.

When I first bought the two acres on a bluff overlooking the Pacific, my folks worried about me choosing to live in such an isolated spot, but after Rosie moved in, they stopped fussing.

After dinner, as was our tradition, everyone went out to my meadow to play a softball game. I wheeled myself onto the terrace, surprised when my favorite sister-in-law, Kelly, pulled up a chair and joined me. Kelly, a tomboy at heart and one of the family's best athletes, didn't usually sit out the games.

A breeze blew in from the sea smelling of saltwater and kelp and flipped a lock of Kelly's black hair into her face. I watched as she smoothed it, along with the rest of her hair, into an impromptu ponytail that made her look as young as her thirteen-year-old daughter.

As the happy bantering of the others faded, she gave me a troubled look. "I need to tell you something, Max."

"Must be serious, if you're willing to sit this one out."

"It is. I..." She stopped, took a breath. "I may have ovarian cancer."

I took her hand and held it between both of mine, trying to think what to say to comfort her, to lift the heavy weight of fear suddenly pressing down on us both.

"You said, *may*. That means you might not."

She closed her eyes. "That's what we're hoping. I'm having surgery in two weeks. Then we'll know for sure."

"What can I do to help?"

"Just pray."

I hadn't prayed since my accident. Didn't see the point. That wasn't something to share with Kelly under the current circumstances, however.

"And..." She paused and looked up to meet my eyes, "start living."

"I'm living." The words came out sounding more harsh and defensive than I'd intended.

She shook her head. "When I found out that I might have this..." She gestured with her free hand, then dropped it back in her lap. "I was so scared, I couldn't think straight. Then I realized. We never know, do we? We always think there's going to be plenty of time. Only sometimes, there isn't."

Her voice wavered, and she took a steadying breath. "But I knew that no matter how this turns out, I needed to talk to you."

"What? Just because you *may* have cancer, you think you can say anything you want?" It was an effort, but I managed to make it sound like a tease. At least I thought I did. "You don't need to worry about me. I've got a terrific life."

She shook her head. "It's half a life, Max."

"Half a life for half a man." I meant it as a joke, but I nearly choked on the words.

"Please don't..." Her words were cut off by a sob.

I fished out a handkerchief for her, then looked away—at the rest of the family spread across my meadow, calling out taunts to each other, running the makeshift base paths, their legs flashing in the sun, while I sat on the sidelines with a woman who'd just told me I wasn't living and she might be dying.

My nieces and nephews scored on their parents, and the younger ones shrieked with the joy of it. I took Kelly's hand gently between mine and rubbed it, the smoothness of her skin sliding against the wheelchair calluses on my palms.

When she spoke again, it was almost dreamily. "Do you remember when we met?"

Unlikely I would forget. Jeff brought her over shortly after Susan decamped.

"If I'd met you first instead of Jeff..." Her voice trailed off, then she roused herself slightly. "Dear Max, the legs wouldn't have mattered to me." Slowly she shook her head. "It's time for you to let it go."

If she meant let go of my bitterness toward Susan, she could relax. I did that years ago. After all, the breakdown of our marriage wasn't all Susan's fault, even if I did let my family think it was. After the accident, I saw how she looked at what was left of me, and I pushed her away with my remaining strength. I could hardly blame her for actually leaving.

"You need to find someone," Kelly said. "To love. Life's too short to lose that chance." She fell silent, and if it was my turn to speak, damned if I knew what to say. I sat staring across the meadow, no longer seeing it.

"I'm sorry, Max."

The softness almost did me in.

I blinked to clear my vision. Kelly's hand was still tucked in mine. As the others continued their game, we sat, the quiet gathering between us.

~ ~ ~

I've always been closer to Jeff and Kelly than to my two other brothers and their wives. Geography has a lot to do with that. Jeff and I both live in the San Francisco area, while Link and Andy live in Seattle and Louisville, respectively.

There's more to it than that, of course.

Jeff found his purpose in life as a result of my accident. He designs aids for the handicapped, particularly those confined to wheelchairs. Those designs have pulled me out of despair and gave me back my mobility and independence.

Now, it appeared, I would be given a chance to pay back that support.

~ ~ ~

Prior to my second meeting with Mrs. Suriano, I reviewed what I'd learned about the freighter responsible for the sinking of the Suriano yacht.

It was the *Nereus,* a 170-meter, 30,000-ton bulk carrier, owned by Helice Shipping Limited, offices in Hong Kong. In all, the company owned ninety-five freighters that cycled among ports in Asia, Australia, New Zealand, and the States, all of them flying the Liberian flag of convenience.

Cassie attached a note to the list of ship names in the report.

> Max, All these names appear to be Greek. Weird!! Have included approximate meanings. Of course if Helice (he' li see) was Helices that would make it the plural of Helix. Since it isn't, it must refer to the sacred city of Poseidon. Looks like someone has an Oedipus complex. CQL

I skimmed the list of names and translations—*Halcyon* (seabird), *Tethys* (wife of Ocean), *Nereus* (sea god). Cassie was right, and given the Chinese ownership, it was unusual.

Setting that puzzle aside, I turned to the reports we'd obtained from the maritime authorities in New Zealand and Japan, since Yokohama was the freighter's first port of call after New Zealand. The Japanese report verified what Mrs. Suriano had told me about the damage found on the bow of the *Nereus.* The authorities concluded, based on the freighter's schedule and the damage to the bow, that the *Nereus* did indeed strike the Suriano yacht.

As a result, the crew of the freighter was cited for failure to follow international navigation rules that require a motor vessel to give way to one sailing under wind power. However, the board also noted there had been a failure to maintain proper lookout aboard the stand-on vessel, *Sylph.*

Thus blame was apportioned to both vessels. Reprimands were placed in the files of the *Nereus* captain and the mate on watch at the time of the accident, and as far as Japan was concerned, the case was closed.

One of our firm's researchers had compiled copies of all the news reports written about the accident for me. Reading them, I learned Mrs. Suriano was rescued fifty-six hours after the sinking, not the twenty-four to thirty hours I'd inferred from her account.

I already admired the woman. This information deepened that admiration. It also increased my outrage at the crew of the freighter. But despite that outrage, today I was meeting with Mrs. Suriano to inform her that she would be better served if I passed the case to a colleague who had more experience with wrongful death suits.

I straightened the pages into a neat stack. If I managed to finesse it, Mrs. Suriano might even believe it was her decision.

"I expect Cassie explained the purpose of this meeting is to update you on our progress," I said, after Mrs. Suriano was seated. I focused on the pile of documentation, which was easier than looking at the woman and knowing I was about to add to her distress.

As I summarized what we'd learned, she sat straight and still, apparently listening intently. "None of that is new, is it?"

"Correct. But our first step was to collect existing documentation, and that process has helped clarify matters." I straightened the referred-to documentation and returned it to the folder.

A tiny crease appeared between her eyes. "What does that mean? Clarify matters."

"There's no question DOHSA will apply. And it isn't good news that after their investigation, the Japanese authorities assigned blame to both vessels and declined to fine the captain."

Her lips tightened.

"You need to…" No. I had no idea where that statement was going. I paused and tried again. "If you choose to go ahead, this is going to be a very difficult case. It's unlikely you'll get even a small measure of the satisfaction you're hoping for."

Her expression turned fierce. "There's no question of my going forward."

Okay. Something less direct, perhaps? "The attorneys for the *Nereus* are going to fight hard against the evidence she sank the *Sylph*. And they may be successful, particularly with regard to the matching of the anti-fouling paint."

She followed my words with an intent look, her hands clenched in her lap.

"Getting a jury to accept that the paint on the *Nereus* is

22

the same paint that *would* have been found on the *Sylph*, well, it gives them a lot to work with. But what's even more problematic is the issue of how the accident happened. We have only your word that the *Nereus* was operating without lights."

She lifted her chin and gave me the tiger look. "It doesn't sound like you're interested in proceeding."

And there it was. The perfect segue. "I proceed with cases, not because of my interest, but because my clients choose to continue. But when they make that choice, I want them to have realistic expectations." Not what I meant to say.

"So, they aren't surprised when they lose?"

"Sometimes a case isn't winnable."

"Is that how you view this case?"

"It will be difficult." *It will be difficult?* Did I just tell her it would be difficult? What the hell was I doing?

"But not impossible?"

"That's not a question I can answer, yet." *Damn it. Tell her!*

She continued to give me a steady look, while I tried to figure out why I couldn't do it. All I had to say was, *"This isn't my kind of case. You'll be better off with..."*

Maybe it was the haunted expression she had until something pricked her, and she turned fierce. Or maybe it was knowing what the *Nereus* had taken from her. Or maybe it was the memory of Kelly, telling me I wasn't living. If I turned this case down, I might have trouble looking my sister-in-law in the eye.

But whatever the reason, I was unable to say those few simple words that would allow me to get back to my usual cases.

The meeting ended, and I was still Mrs. Suriano's attorney.

Chapter Three
CASSIE

When Sophie Suriano showed up, I had a feeling that this was a case Max shouldn't turn down. But after she met with him the second time, things were not looking so good.

"Tell me." Her voice was low and angry. "How do you manage working for that insufferably arrogant man?"

"Who? Max? Max is a sweetie." This was not good. Not good at all.

"He sits there like some kind of potentate behind that huge desk and never even offers to shake my hand. I don't care whether he's sweet or not. With those manners, he'd better be damned good."

Well, Sophie and I might not look anything alike on the outside, but I swear, on the inside we're sisters. I had exactly the same response to Max the first time I met him. Wanted to chuckle thinking about that, but right now, even smiling was out. I needed to stay solemn as a white church lady, or Sophie would walk out of our lives, and I didn't want that to happen. I had a mighty strong feeling about Sophie.

So I spoke real careful. "Max is extremely good at what he does, and he has an excellent reason for the state of his manners."

"What? He's paralyzed from the waist down?"

"Better than that. He has no legs."

That stopped her. She stood there, her eyes wide and her mouth frozen in the shape of an *O*, and I wondered if that was how I looked when I found out Max didn't have legs.

Sophie finally realized her mouth was hanging open. She shut it and blinked. "You've got to be kidding."

"I never kid about Max's legs." Maybe not strictly true, but close enough.

Her eyes narrowed. "You mean to tell me when we go to court he'll be in a wheelchair, and I'll hobble in with my cane? Well, we should certainly ace our artistic impression scores."

I couldn't swear who began it, but the next thing I knew, we were both laughing like someone sprinkled us with chuckle dust. At the same time, I was breathing one huge sigh of relief.

~ ~ ~

I first heard how Max lost his legs right after I started working for him. Not from him, of course. It's not a subject he ever mentions.

He was only a few years out of law school, newly married, and starting at Stedman Richards and Micelli when he had a run-in with a drunk driver. When he woke up in the hospital, his legs were gone. Not long after that, his wife left too.

Far as anyone knows, he's never tried to add a new lady to his life, even though he's a fine man. There isn't anything the least bit parsimonious about Max. He has all his hair, and it's almost as curly and dark as mine. And he has kind eyes, although they can turn as hard as marbles when he's provoked, and a nice mouth a person has to watch close, to catch when he's jiving. He's not one bit like Ironside, if that's what you're thinking. Max is a lot leaner, considerably younger, and much better looking.

Personally, I think his wife had to be a real sorry excuse for a human being, walking out on Max that way. No doubt in my mind after knowing him less than a week, he was worth sticking around for.

It's my theory that after his wife reacted the way she did, Max convinced himself no other woman was going to see beyond those empty pant legs either. Even with clients, Max hides behind his desk as long as he can, so by the time they discover he doesn't have legs, they know him well enough they won't make the mistake of thinking no legs means he's deficient in other ways.

Personally, I think he's a man who just needs a good cry, but he sure won't get it working on his usual kind of case. I'm not exactly a tree hugger, but I swear it's hard working on some of the cases Max takes on.

I've stuck with it because I care about Max, and because I keep hoping one day he'll recognize the good in himself that led him to hire a smart-mouthed Black woman and defend her against all comers.

Chapter Four
SOPHIE

When I first met Max Gildea, frankly, despite Ben Talbot's glowing recommendation, I wasn't impressed. But I liked his assistant, Cassie. She didn't look at me as if she was seeing a freak, and she seemed to understand how much help I needed and the proper tone to use in speaking to me, so that she sounded neither uncaring nor overly solicitous.

That day she was wearing an elegant dress. I asked her what the color was called, because to my eyes it appeared to be a light gray.

"The saleslady called it tropical tangerine, but my momma would say, 'That's a nice orange dress, Cassie.'"

We smiled at each other, and I tried to picture smooth chocolate skin against warm orange. She stood and ushered me into Max's large, airy, and perfectly appointed office that confirmed his status as a senior partner in the firm.

I walked in slowly, leaning on the cane Philip carved for me out of rimu wood. After I was seated, I noticed the bonsai tree lit by a spotlight, sitting on the credenza behind Max. The light should be one of those purple ones that help plants grow.

Well, perhaps it was.

I studied him as Cassie introduced us, baffled that he didn't stand to greet me or come around the desk to shake my hand.

Although seated, he looked to be a tall man, with broad shoulders and big hands. His dark eyes were alert and intelligent, and his hair looked crisp, wiry, and perfectly barbered. In summary, he had one of those faces that gets more interesting and good-looking as its owner ages, although he might not have the character to deserve that.

As we spoke, I felt the scar pulling at my cheek. Sam's mother has told me she knows a surgeon who can remove it, but it's my scar. I'm not giving it up to please Sam's mother. She wants me to color my hair as well. She says forty is too young for a white streak. But what difference does that make when I'm never going to see Sam again.

I took a breath and refocused. I didn't want to lose my composure in front of this man. This Max Gildea. This solid, prosperous man who appeared to have never lost anything. How was he going to understand what this case was about?

Then I found out about Max's legs. Everything I thought I knew about him...wrong.

It was easier in some ways, more difficult in others, once I discovered he was also fluent in the language of loss and pain I now speak, a language we share by simply looking at each other.

Because of that, I took advantage of him, probing to find his tender spots as a way to distract from my own. He was patient with me, only occasionally reminding me my questions had the power to hurt. But I felt nothing.

I think I've become like one of those robots in a science fiction story. I walk, I talk, I look human, but I'm devoid of human emotion. Or maybe not completely devoid. There is one emotion that remains.

Anger.

I hug it protectively. It's the only assurance I have that I might one day feel something more.

Chapter Five
MAX

I summarized the Suriano case at the monthly partners' meeting. Twelve perfectly groomed men, and three equally well-groomed women, who comprised the senior ranks of Stedman Richards and Micelli sat around the conference table listening. A faint scent of tobacco, coffee, aftershave, and expensive perfume drifted over the assembly.

"Did I blink and miss a change in our policy on contingency?" Todd Wermling asked, when I paused.

Todd and I were hired the same year, and we'd got along, more or less, until our definitive encounter in the men's room a month after I hired Cassie. "Hey, Max," he'd said, drying his hands. "I keep forgetting to thank you."

"For?"

"For hiring the affirmative action babe. Saved me from busting my balls justifying why I didn't hire one. I owe you, man. Big-time." He turned toward me, a grin plastered across his vacuous face.

"That's not a very enlightened attitude." I'd never been able to quite put my finger on why I didn't care for Todd until that moment.

"My ass. You know the drill." His lip curled. "No offense, but I want an assistant who'll assist. Now, I got to admit, that one you hired is a looker, that is if you go for one of those people." He'd leered at me and made a snorty noise, his usual reaction to something he found amusing.

My clenched jaw was beginning to ache. I unclenched and took a deep breath. *The bastard.* "Those people? I doubt you'll get far using such imprecise language."

He smoothed his hand over his hair, giving himself a satisfied look in the mirror. "Call them whatever you like, just don't expect me to work with one."

That did it. "You know, Todd, I'm reaching this inescapable conclusion that you're an idiot and a bigot. While I can't do a damn thing about your intelligence, I can sure as hell make you think twice before you repeat your smarmy racist innuendos to anyone else."

"What can you do? Run me down with your wheelchair?" The snort again. Not only did the man need a heart transplant, he was in desperate need of sinus surgery.

I spun my chair and blocked the exit. "Let me *run* something by you, Todd, old buddy. Sitting in this chair, I'm at the perfect height to reach out and give your balls a good squeeze."

Todd winced and moved back a step.

"Just mentioning that to get your attention. What I will do is make you a promise. If it gets back to me that you've made any more of your just-between-us-guys comments about my assistant, you'd better invest in a codpiece."

Todd and I stared at each other, until his eyes dropped. I waited another second before moving my chair out of his way. He sidled past, speeding up as he reached the door.

Although I doubt he provided the specifics of our interaction, it wasn't long before word got around that questioning my personnel decisions was ill-advised. Cassie, my major personnel decision to date, heard, of course.

"Hey, Max, did you know Todd Wermling's been acting real peculiar since yesterday morning? Came back from the men's room and asked his assistant to get him a dictionary. After she did, he stomped out and threw it on her desk and told her to find out what an effing codpiece was. Course, once she discovered that's the part of a sixteenth-century man's getup that protected certain, shall we say, vital organs, it got her to thinking. And she remembered seeing you come out of the men's room right after Todd. She's put two and two together, and she has this real interesting theory. Want to hear what it is?"

I sighed. I'd quickly discovered nothing stopped Cassie in full spate. One simply had to wait it out.

"She thinks you two had an argument, and you straightened him out. Well, maybe not straightened exactly.

He did spend the day kinda hunched over. Apparently misplaced his codpiece and wasn't taking any chances." She chuckled. "'Course, I have my own theory."

"Of course, you do, and we have work to do."

"Sure, and we'll do it. Soon as you comment on my theory."

"You know I don't listen to office gossip."

"Sure you do. You just don't want to admit it."

Irrepressible. But I'd known what I was getting into when I hired her. No one to blame but myself.

"I'll bet Todd was being his usual sweet self," she said. "Talking 'bout all the riffraff taking over the country. Likely, you tried to reason with him. When that didn't work...oh my. I've seen you maneuver that chair, and I surely wouldn't want to tangle with you." She grinned at me.

I kept my expression neutral. It didn't pay to encourage her.

"I'm right, aren't I?" she asked.

"More or less. Now can we get to work?"

Hiring Cassie was one of the smartest things I ever did, even if it did turn Todd into an enemy. The short answer to why I hired her? She has guts and personality. The longer answer is that she made me laugh after she told me the only acceptable excuse for me not standing to greet her was if I had no legs.

Now, I turned to Todd, to respond to his comment about contingency. "Client's paying the bills. Incidentally, the client's name is Sophie Suriano. She's the widow of Samuel Suriano, the eldest son of Charles and Dorothy Suriano." I'd just aced Todd in the prestigious client sweepstakes. If he'd been using a pencil for his doodles, he would have snapped it.

Pleased at Todd's reaction, I continued. "Anyone here ever deal with either the Surianos or Helice Shipping?"

I looked around the table. No nods.

"Never even heard of Helice Shipping," Anthony Micelli said, pursing his lips.

"It's a privately held company based in Hong Kong. Ships are all registered in Liberia."

"Who owns it?" Anthony asked.

"A man by the name of Shaoming Wong."

"Who insures them?" someone else asked.

"PacTran." Most of us had dealt with PacTran, in one way or another.

"I can understand representing a Suriano is a plus for the firm, and the financials are in order." Anthony frowned at me. "However, there's a big downside. The case. There's little chance of a decent payout."

"I disagree. Sam Suriano had significant earning power. And Helice Shipping is going to have a very difficult time finding jurors who won't sympathize with what Mrs. Suriano went through. They're going to want to award every cent they can." It was my strongest, hell, my *only* strategy.

"The woman's richer than God," Todd said. "Who can sympathize with that?"

I felt a burst of anger that was equaled by my determination not to let him know he'd scored. I pulled out the pictures. I hadn't intended to show them, but Cassie made sure they were in the file when I left my office. The top one was of Sam and Sophie Suriano, their arms around each other, standing on the dock with the *Sylph*, pristine and white, moored behind them. The second was a recent one of Mrs. Suriano, leaning on her cane and looking nothing like the vibrant young woman in the first picture.

I passed the pictures to Anthony, who examined them before handing them back. "Okay, Max. I concede your point."

It meant I was stuck with the case, and I had Todd to thank for it.

~ ~ ~

After the partners' meeting, I stopped second-guessing the decision to represent Mrs. Suriano and went to work.

Shortly after that, she called and asked for a meeting. There was only one reason for us to meet. She was going to fire me. An assumption that was strengthened when she walked into my office wearing bright pink. As if she'd chosen her outfit to mirror her intention.

It should have been a relief. Instead, I felt a sharp and surprising regret.

"Good morning, Mr. Gildea." She sat in my guest chair and raised her eyes to mine. "I asked for this appointment because I owe you an apology."

The good news? It didn't sound like she intended to fire me. Although when, why, or how that became good news was a mystery. The bad news? She'd discovered I didn't have legs and had decided to comment on it. I'd already heard Cassie's version of this particular event, and I had no desire to relive it. I nodded, hoping that would end it.

"I thought your manners were atrocious and shared that with your assistant. I let myself forget things are often not what they seem."

"I accept your apology, although I don't consider it necessary."

She met my gaze, and for the first time in our acquaintance, she smiled. It softened her face, and even though the scar that crossed her right cheek pulled the smile off center, it was still a good smile.

"Can I ask you something?" she said.

"Of course."

"Your name is Franklin Delano Gildea, so why are you called Max?"

As a subject, it was a vast improvement over my lack of legs or questions about what I was afraid of.

"When we were kids, my brothers took the good superhero names. Mom told me I could be the Maximum Hero. The Max stuck."

She examined me. "You do look more like a Max than a Franklin. Or a Delano."

"Thank God. How about you? You have a nickname?"

The frown was so fleeting I would have missed it if I hadn't been looking at her. "Oh." She ducked her head. "I got teased when Sam and I decided to marry." She looked up and with a finger tapped out the rhythm in the air between us. "Sam and Sophie Suriano."

"Nice alliteration. But no nickname, then?"

"No." There was a dead end in the answer. Her hand dropped and then she gave her head a shake and looked at me with a partial smile that didn't reach her eyes. "Tell me about your brothers."

She was clearly still trying to figure me out. I wasn't totally comfortable with the conversation, but if she needed the reassurance of knowing more about me, I was willing to go along, at least for the moment.

"Thomas Jefferson, Andrew Jackson, Abraham Lincoln, and yours truly, Franklin Delano. Gives you a bit of a feel for my folks' take on history."

Sophie smiled at that.

"Link's a neurosurgeon. Lives in Seattle, wife and three kids. Andy's an attorney. Specializes in the thoroughbred industry. Lives in Kentucky. Wife and four kids. And Jeff's an inventor. Lives here in San Francisco. Wife, two kids."

"And Max, otherwise known as Franklin Delano, does he have a wife and children?"

"No." I knew a thing or two about dead ends myself. Still, I'd been too abrupt. "I'm divorced," I amended, hoping that would end the topic.

"Is Andy the lawyer who's afraid of horses?"

"Yes." It surprised me she remembered that. "One of his first cases, he asked to see the animal involved. It stepped on him, wouldn't move. He was in a cast for a month. He still represents trainers, jockeys, and owners, but he stays away from the horses." I stopped talking, but Sophie wasn't done with my family.

"And what does Jeff invent?"

"Items to help the disabled. I use chairs he designed for work and for racing."

"Racing?"

"Marathons."

"Do you race often?"

"Three, four times a year."

"You must train all the time, then."

"Rosie and I hit the health club or the track every night."

"Rosie?"

"Roosevelt Hawkins. My live-in assistant."

"You have an assistant named Roosevelt." Her lips curved in amusement. "Don't you think that's funny?"

"Precisely the reason I hired him. I keep him because he's a good cook."

"Do you have any other hobbies besides racing?" she asked.

I turned and pointed at the tree sitting on the credenza behind me. "Bonsai." I'd been given a tree after my accident. Keeping it alive had been one of the few things that had lightened the awfulness of that time.

"That's quite a contrast," she said.

"Which is perhaps what appeals to me."

"Thank you," she said.

"For?"

"For answering my questions." She dipped her head and gave me one of those cockeyed but still appealing smiles. "You can be a bit intimidating, you know."

"I hope only to our opponents." That gained me another smile.

After she left, I sat back, surprised to discover I, too, was smiling.

Chapter Six
MAX

It had been six months since Sophie Suriano first walked into my office and five months since Kelly's diagnosis of Stage III ovarian cancer. As proof that life goes on regardless of what happens to each of us personally, it was once again time for the spring bonsai show in Golden Gate Park.

Kelly and Jeff always came, and we made a day of it, examining the trees, eating a picnic lunch, crossing our fingers as the judges approached the winning trees holding ribbons. I've won Best in Show twice in the past, and Kelly was there both times to laugh and hug me and do a victory dance with Jeff.

With a quick, unexpected flash of awareness, I wondered whether she would be with us for next year's show. It was the kind of random thought I tried to suppress, although that was increasingly difficult to do as the effects of Kelly's chemo became obvious.

When she first started losing her hair, she began wearing hats. Today, it was a pink straw affair with flowers on it that, from a distance, appeared quite gay. She hadn't lost much weight, but she had a frail look that hadn't been there at New Year's and in spite of the warmth of the day, she was bundled up like someone going ice fishing.

My entries in the show this year, chosen with Rosie's stamp of approval, were an azalea, a juniper, and a grove of birch trees planted on a flat piece of slate. The birch grove was my personal favorite. After ten years, the black and white complexity of the intertwined branches was like a pen and ink drawing.

Kelly smiled when she saw it. "I predict another Best in Show, Max."

It no longer seemed very important.

After we examined the other trees, Jeff got lawn chairs out of the van, and Rosie went off to get lunch for the four of us. I glanced at the crowd walking through the exhibit and saw Sophie. She still used a cane, but her gait had improved, and with that change, she appeared more her real age. She stopped in front of each tree, looked at it, then consulted the label that listed the kind of tree, its age, length of training, and owner. When she reached my birches, she read the card and then looked around until she spotted me. She walked over.

"Sophie, what a pleasant surprise."

"Max. I wondered if you might be here."

I introduced her to Jeff and Kelly.

Rosie arrived carrying hot dogs, popcorn, and drinks, and I introduced him, as well.

She shook his hand, her lips quirking into a smile. "Franklin Delano and Roosevelt."

Rosie threw back his head and laughed in his rich baritone. "Yes, ma'am. We're a team."

"Would you like to join us for lunch, Sophie? As usual, Rosie got enough food for a dozen people. If you don't help us out, we'll have to do extra laps."

"I'd love to."

Jeff got another chair out of the van and added it to the circle, while Rosie passed out the food.

"So, Roosevelt, how long have you and Franklin Delano been a team?" Sophie asked.

"Thirteen years, two months, and five days. Not that I'm exactly counting. But when you got it good as I do, you naturally want to keep track. Alls I got to do is a bit of cooking, driving, and cleaning, and I lives like a king."

I glanced at Kelly to find her examining Sophie. I knew what that meant. I was in for a grilling the next time I visited.

After Rosie and Jeff cleaned up our trash, Sophie reached for her cane. I wanted her to remain sitting beside me a while longer. If Kelly was right, and my birches won, it would be pleasant to share that with Sophie.

No future in it, though.

"It's time for another meeting," I told her. "I'll have Cassie give you a call to set up an appointment."

She nodded then thanked us for lunch, saying it was nice to meet everybody. I watched her walk away until the crowds wandering through the exhibit blocked my view of her.

Kelly didn't wait for the next visit. "She's a client, Max?"

"Yes."

"Her name seems familiar."

"Her father-in-law is Charles Suriano."

"Of course. Did she have an accident?"

"Yes."

Kelly cocked her head. "Client confidentiality?"

"It's a long story. I can tell you the public part next time I visit. Okay?"

"Deal. Come soon."

~ ~ ~

Working on Sophie's case while fitting in frequent visits to Kelly and Jeff began to take on the aspects of a surreal ping-pong match. I was the ball becoming steadily more dented and flattened as I moved back and forth between the two women, watching one regain her vigor, while the other faded—as if the two were walking the same path, but in opposite directions.

Kelly never let me talk about her illness when I visited. Instead, "Tell me how Sophie is doing." Since meeting Sophie she'd read the newspaper accounts of the Surianos' ordeal. "See, Max, once you decided to look for meaning, it found you."

Yeah, right. I hadn't decided, and I certainly wasn't looking. Sophie's case was happenstance. But I couldn't tell Kelly that. Anything to distract her from what she was going through.

"I've been re-reading *To Kill a Mockingbird*," Kelly said. "Do you remember the part where Atticus says it's the nature of the law that every man will get at least one case that will affect him personally?"

"It's been a while since I read it." But I remembered it. That book was a big part of why I picked the law as a profession.

"There's a scene where he talks of the courage to take that on. Let me see if I can find it." She picked up the book and paged through it. "Yes. Here it is. He's talking to his son."

As she read, I stared at the delicate lines of her face, the near translucence of her eyelids, the looseness of the wedding band on her finger.

The part she'd chosen to read was where Atticus talked of how real courage was taking something on because it was the right thing to do and sticking with it through to the end, even when you knew you were licked before you began.

I listened to the words, but I was thinking about Kelly. Gallant. Brave. Knowing she might be licked, but facing it head-on. She was the only person who believed I was capable of that as well.

She stopped reading and raised those eyes that were still so beautiful and smiled at me. "I believe Sophie is that case for you, Max."

Chapter Seven
CASSIE

The way Max works a case is this. He assembles a team to collect facts, but he expects everyone to pay attention to what is going on around those facts. Sometimes that pays off when we find what I call a niggle and Max calls a piece of the jigsaw. I catch some of my best niggles out of the corner of my eye, so to speak.

I'd already found one in Sophie's case, although we didn't yet know whether it was going to help unravel a big snarl later or just trail off into nothing. It was the oddity of a Chinese man using Greek names for his ships and his company. Another niggle I picked up during a conversation at a church social. I wanted to call Max right away to tell him what I'd found out, but my Melvin said why'd I want to bother the man on a weekend when ain't nothing he could do about it till Monday.

I had to admit Melvin had a point. So I waited. But as soon as Max arrived Monday morning, I took in two cups of coffee and made myself comfortable. When I did that, Max knew I had something to say, and he kind of perked up and paid attention.

"Did you know Egyptians only turn their car lights on when they see another car?" I said. "Even when it's pitch dark. They think the lights run down the batteries."

"And your point is?"

"I'm sitting right here in front of you. Isn't it plain as that?" Usually Max recognizes a niggle almost as quick as I do.

He frowned. "Sorry, you'll have to help me on this one, Cass."

"The lights, Max. Sophie's case. If Egyptians turn off their lights except when they see another car, although, Lord knows how they manage that, maybe Chinese are real careful with lights too. Maybe even lights on ships." I saw the old bulbs begin to pop then.

He sat back, sipping his coffee with a thoughtful look on his face. "Yeah...that's not bad. If we could prove the *Nereus* was running without lights the night she sank the *Sylph*, we'd be halfway to winning the case. Unfortunately, that's an impossibility. Not to mention, the way Egyptians use, or don't use, car lights would hardly be considered relevant."

"'Course not. Got to be more specific than that," I said.

"Crew's already said lights were on."

I knew Max was just pulling on it a bit, trying it on. "You have a suggestion?" he said.

"I think we need to get someone on board to observe how things are really done."

"You don't think they'll have learned their lesson?"

"Oh my word, Max. They left two people adrift in the middle of the ocean and barely got their hands slapped. I very much doubt they've changed their ways."

Max put his coffee down and tapped his finger on the desk. I knew what that meant. He was running through the possibilities. "Get Sophie on the phone, Cass, and tell her what you're thinking."

Now see, that's typical Max. Usually he dials his own calls. Told me early on he wasn't missing any fingers, and they all worked just fine.

I put the call through, spoke briefly with Sophie telling her about how Egyptians run around without car lights, and then listened while she and Max talked.

"I'm not sure how that helps us," Sophie said.

"What Cassie's suggesting is we try to prove the *Nereus* routinely runs without lights. The ship's due in New Zealand in three weeks. If I can arrange to get someone on board, you willing to pay for it?"

"Yes."

"Okay, I'll see what I can do."

See what I mean about Max being a sweetie?

Chapter Eight
MAX

In order to implement Cassie's idea, I called Gerald Cameron, a solicitor with a New Zealand firm we'd worked with before.

"I need to hire an investigator to spend time aboard a ship in order to determine how they operate at sea." I gave him the specifics of the case and what I wanted the investigator to accomplish.

"If this ship did what you say, I'd bloody well like to see them pay for it," he said.

Yeah. Me too. "The investigator will need to be Asian."

"Not a problem. I have contacts in the community. Let me see what I can arrange, mate."

Gerald called a few days later with a name, Alex Wu. If Wu was successful in infiltrating the crew, we'd have to wait until the *Nereus* arrived in Japan and we received his report before we'd know how good that part of our case was going to be.

While awaiting word about that, I was notified the attorneys for Helice Shipping were taking steps to get the venue shifted to Liberia.

They had an excellent shot at that since the *Nereus* sails under the Liberian flag. But if they were successful and the venue was changed, it would end our chances of any settlement.

~ ~ ~

I'd been having trouble sleeping, and the best remedy for that is a long race. I found one in San José the following weekend. Only a 30K but better than nothing.

When I crossed the finish line and braked to a stop, I looked around for Rosie. He's usually real easy to spot. Not only is he big, he favors bright colors. Today he was wearing a neon yellow shirt and black jeans. When he came toward me out of the crowd, he was also wearing his widest grin.

"Look who I found, Max." He stepped aside, and there was Sophie.

Clearly, she'd made a conquest. Rosie's a friendly, easygoing man, but there's an underlying reserve that doesn't usually crack quite this fast.

"Sophie. What are you doing here?" My face stretched into a grin of my own.

"I was visiting my...a friend. I saw a poster announcing the race, and I thought...well, I'd never actually seen one." She shrugged and gave me a tentative smile. "And then, I ran into Rosie. He said you were competing, so I had to stick around." She moved closer. "That's a racy-looking chair, Max." She reached out and touched one of the wheels.

"It's Jeff's latest design. It knocked five minutes off my time." Rosie finally remembered to hand me a towel and a fresh water bottle. "Would you like to join us for lunch?" I asked Sophie.

She cocked her head and smiled. "Hot dogs?"

"Nope. We always indulge after a race. There's this bistro Rosie knows about. Parsley, Sage, Rosemary, and Thyme. Although they shortened it to Parsley and Sage when they found out the sign painter charged by the letter."

"You're pulling my leg, Max?" Then her eyes went wide.

I gave her a solemn look. "I make it a rule never to mess with other people's legs."

She responded with a smile, and I realized that the people I'm most comfortable with are the ones who find comedy as well as tragedy in my legless condition.

"I'd love to join you," she said.

After she sent her car and driver home, Rosie drove us to Parsley and Sage, which is located on the coast, nearer San Gregorio than San José. After lunch, Rosie left us sitting on the deck with glasses of iced tea, while he went off for a tour of the kitchen.

"This could take a while," I said.

"I didn't realize Rosie was such a serious cook."

"I've been remiss. You'll have to come to dinner on a night when Rosie's cooking."

"I'd like that." She looked away from me toward the lazy breakers catching the sun as they spread sparkles on the beach. I watched her, worrying a little. She'd seemed distracted during lunch, barely attending to the conversation at times.

I reached out and touched her hand. "You okay?"

She jumped and shook her head. "Sorry. I was..." She stopped, sighed. "I just visited Gibby. It's...it makes me remember."

"Gibby?"

"My daughter."

"I didn't realize you had a daughter." I spoke in a neutral tone to let her know it was okay not to tell me more, although I hoped she would.

"Gibby has Down Syndrome, but she's determined to be independent. She...she has her own apartment, with a friend. And a job. She gets seasick when it's calm, so she didn't want to go with us..."

The hand that lay on the table clenched. I laid my hand over hers and tucked her fingers into mine.

"I miss her, but I can't ask her to come home just because... But she doesn't...she doesn't really understand why Sam doesn't come to visit. I told her he died, but she can't...it's just so hard."

Sophie had her head down, talking convulsively. "I had Gibby when I was seventeen. Her biological father couldn't take it. Gibby being...he called her defective. She's not. She's beautiful, and I love her so much. I couldn't have children after that, but Sam always said Gibby was enough for him..." The words trailed off as Sophie gulped and blinked back tears.

Usually, when a woman starts to cry, I want to wheel as fast as I can in the opposite direction. Not this time.

"It's okay, Sophie. Don't beat up on yourself." I picked up the hand I'd been holding and rubbed it gently between both of mine. "Look at me, Sophie."

She closed her eyes briefly, then raised her face slowly to mine.

"What you went through. It's going to take time."

She looked away. "I...I think I'd better..." She pulled her hand away and pushed her chair back.

Helplessly, I sat as she rushed away. If ever a woman needed to be held while she cried, Sophie was that woman, and there I sat, trapped in a wheelchair, unable to offer even that simple comfort.

Rosie returned before Sophie did, full of enthusiasm about what he'd seen in the kitchen and the rousing debate he'd had with the chef over the relative merits of grilling versus sautéing, or some such thing. Usually I find Rosie's descriptions of his kitchen sojourns entertaining, but not today.

When Sophie rejoined us, her eyes were red, but she seemed calm. Rosie looked at her and then at me and raised an eyebrow in question. I nodded, and he excused himself, saying he'd go get the van.

"I'm sorry, Max. I ruined your celebration."

As if that mattered.

"It gets better eventually," I said. I wanted to pull her into my arms so badly, my whole body ached with it.

"Does it?" She sounded lost.

I knew something about that. Being lost. Words didn't ease it. Only time could, and it was a damn slow process.

~ ~ ~

The lunch at Parsley and Sage marked a change in my relationship with Sophie. I now had to struggle to keep it strictly professional. I told myself it was natural to feel deeply sympathetic toward someone who'd gone through what she had. But what I felt for Sophie was more...

No. I neither wanted to label nor examine too closely what Sophie meant to me, although it could have been as simple as this: talking to Sophie, being with Sophie made me feel less hopeless.

~ ~ ~

"Were you depressed after it happened?" Sophie asked the day I had her in for an update and told her the Helice attorneys had requested her medical records.

"Yeah." I didn't need to ask her which "it" she was talking about.

"Did antidepressants help?"

I shook my head. "I refused to take them."

"How did you manage?"

"Read. Worked jigsaw puzzles. Slept. Tried not to think." No one had ever asked me such specific questions before, and I didn't care for it much.

But Sophie wasn't asking out of idle curiosity. "Why do they want my medical records, Max?"

"If I were representing Helice, I'd use the records to make you out to be an unreliable witness."

She looked away. "I see."

I didn't think she did. "Sophie?" I had to clear my throat to get the word out.

She shifted her focus to my face.

"You don't have to do this."

She looked at me a beat longer, and when she spoke, her tone was weary, as if she were repeating something she'd been forced to say far too many times. "The only reason I survived was to do this. To stop them from ever hitting another yacht. To make them pay for what they did to Sam."

"Okay, Sophie." I felt as weary as she sounded.

~ ~ ~

I'd had her records evaluated by the firm's medical expert early on, of course. He identified one area that required a specialist's review. That was the disagreement between the original attending physician in New Zealand and the psychiatrist currently treating Sophie for depression, anxiety, nightmares, and insomnia.

The physician in New Zealand considered Sophie's inability to see color after the accident a result of her head trauma, while the psychiatrist labeled it a form of hysterical blindness. The neurologist I subsequently consulted had the following comment:

This patient's color blindness is likely an extremely rare condition caused by bilateral damage to the V4 location in the visual cortex. In the present case, the patient had several small hemorrhages in that area as a result of her head injury. It is not an hysterical condition as alluded to in her psychiatrist's notes. My current fellow, who is studying visual pathways in the brain, would be able to testify about this if necessary.

Although I was relieved to know Sophie's color blindness had a physical rather than emotional cause, her records were still going to cause us major problems in court. After what she'd been through, she had a right to her nightmares and depression, but I could easily imagine what Helice's attorneys would do with that information, as well as with the fact she'd sustained a head injury and blood loss at the time of the sinking.

Likely they would argue, as I would in their place, that her injuries, followed by her lengthy ordeal, left Sophie too severely traumatized for her memory of events immediately before, during, and after the sinking to be considered reliable.

Sophie was tough, but I didn't know if she could withstand the attack coming her way in court—an attack that would be hard to simulate, even if I got someone as lacking in empathy as Todd Wermling to question her the way Helice's attorneys would.

The uneasiness I'd felt from the beginning of the case deepened.

Chapter Nine
MAX

The New Zealand solicitor, Gerald Cameron, called to tell us Alex Wu had succeeded in getting aboard the *Nereus* despite the fact they'd already had a full crew.

"How'd he manage it?"

Cameron chuckled. "Wine, women, and song."

"Be sure he sends me the bill."

"Wu said that part's on him."

While I waited to hear from Wu, the court ruled in our favor on the issue of venue for Sophie's case. The trial would take place in a U.S. court, not a Liberian one. It was a major victory, but we couldn't celebrate for long.

"Before a judge takes the case, we'll be required to attempt to settle out of court," I told Sophie. "We need to talk about our bottom line."

She shrugged. "Refuse to accept whatever they offer."

"That isn't how it works. It's a negotiation. That means we need to name a figure we find acceptable."

"Fine. Make it large enough it forces them into court."

"DOHSA may prevent that."

Her posture stiffened, and with increasing discomfort, I continued. "Of course no amount will ever be enough. But with DOHSA, it may not be possible to push them into court."

She shook her head as if my words were pesky gnats. "Pushing them into court is what I'm paying you for. A monetary settlement won't mean a thing unless they're also held accountable for the wrongful death of my husband."

~ ~ ~

Because of Sophie's insistence, I had continued to keep my focus on preparing for trial rather than a settlement. Our witness list would include the friend who provided the paint samples that were matched to those found on the bow of the freighter, an expert from the testing laboratory to talk about how the paint was matched, a couple of experts to testify about ship lighting requirements and how right-of-way is determined, and the maritime officials from Japan and New Zealand who carried out the accident investigation—they would testify by videotape.

We would also have financial experts testifying about Sam Suriano's lifetime earning potential, and we might add Alex Wu to our list, depending on what he learned about lighting procedures on the *Nereus*.

I was still debating what to do about the freighter's crew. We'd retained an attorney in Yokohama to interview them. What or who we might ultimately include in the trial awaited review of those depositions.

The problem with the crew's testimony was that it would have to be passed back and forth through a translator. That meant there was little chance lies would be obvious to a jury. Probably the best we could hope for would be contradictions and inconsistencies.

The final witness on the list would be Sophie. She would be the pivot point on which the case would turn, and although that was also her preference, she had no idea how difficult testifying was going to be.

It would be tricky for the other side, of course. If they attacked her directly, they'd come off looking like thugs. They'd need to be subtle. Come at her sideways. Get her to question what she remembered, until she started to sound uncertain.

Although I planned to prepare her for every question I could imagine Helice's attorneys asking, if they were good, they'd eventually find a chink and start chipping away, hoping to get her to implode.

There was really no way to fully prepare her for that and only a few maneuvers available to stop it once it started.

~ ~ ~

Sophie made one of her periodic trips to my office.

"I can't delay sending your medical records to Helice's attorneys much longer," I told her.

"It isn't good, is it."

"No. Competent attorneys, and my sense of these guys is they're very competent, will take you apart. Head injury, nightmares, depression, medication. They'll play on that for all it's worth."

"I see."

"I'm not sure you do." I looked at Sophie—at the premature white streak in her hair, the scar on her cheek, the haunted eyes. It wasn't only color she was blind to. Frustration at her refusal to understand what we were up against sharpened my tone. "They didn't get you the first time. This time they're going to make damn sure they don't leave any survivors."

"How much longer before we hear from the man on board the ship?" she asked.

"It should be any day."

"Can we put off sending the records until we hear from him?"

"I can try." But it wouldn't matter. If Sophie was determined to go ahead, the records would eventually have to be sent.

~ ~ ~

I was visiting Kelly after another round of chemo. She was pale and much thinner than she'd been at New Year's.

"How is Sophie doing?" she asked. It was a standard question since she'd met Sophie at the bonsai show.

"Okay, I suppose. Hard to tell, though. She doesn't say much."

"Like someone else I could name," she said, giving me a look.

Kelly didn't talk any more than I did about bad stuff. No point in mentioning it, though.

"I hate to admit you might have been right about my taking on Sophie's case. It's making a difference in my life," I said.

She smiled at me. "Trying to do something that matters. It's the quickest way to happiness, Max."

I shook my head. "Happiness is an illusion."

She leaned toward me. "No. Happiness is real. I know it is. And I have a feeling—"

Jeff walked in from the workshop, and I didn't get to hear what Kelly's feeling was. But I didn't need to. I knew what she was going to say.

It was all spitting into the high wind of reality as far as I was concerned.

~ ~ ~

Alex Wu's report arrived from Japan three weeks after he boarded the *Nereus* in New Zealand. Although handwritten, it was neat and easy to read.

> Esteemed Mr. Gildea,
>
> Here is report of voyage of freighter *Nereus* from New Zealand to Japan. I am position of second cook. I take walks, every night. Mate asking what I do. I say needing fresh air, exercise. Kitchen too hot. He laughing, pay no more attention me.
>
> I finding using of lights at night is choice of mate on watch. Third mate always using lights. First mate and second mate always turning off lights when on night duty. First mate yelling at third mate one night. Ask why wasting money that way, on lights, he mean. Third mate say, "You want we run down another boat?" First mate shuts up. Lucky they not see me. After that, third mate sometimes using lights, sometimes no using.

There were more pages detailing Mr. Wu's observations during the voyage, including several additional comments by the crew that showed they had been aware at the time that they'd hit the Suriano yacht.

At the end of the report was a daily log listing whether or not lights had been used. Wu also included time and date-stamped videos of the dark ship and audio recordings of some of the crew comments, but since all the conversations were in Chinese, we would need to arrange for a translation.

The data Wu had collected on the lights was exactly what we needed. The crew comments about the sinking were an unexpected bonus. I decided to bring Wu to San Francisco in order to evaluate how best to use the information he'd gathered.

Rosie picked Wu up at the airport and brought him to the house. He was a man in his fifties with a short, stocky frame and graying hair. I asked if he had the original record of his observations aboard the *Nereus*. He pulled several cheap copy books, like those used in schools, from his duffel bag. I flipped through one and saw it was full of Chinese symbols interspersed with pages of English.

"Didn't you worry someone from the crew might look at the books?" I thought he'd taken a hell of a risk.

"Oh no. They can look. I write every day. Many words. In Chinese, I write about weather, how I miss family, many pages, same thing. I very careful. Very boring. I also practicing my English. I have books, I copy words and English letters, same thing over and over. They try to read, they go sleeping. I show you how I keeping track of information."

He'd used a simple code embedded in his English practice. While he explained, I took notes. Then using the notes, I went through the books, picking out the information. While I did that, he sat drinking coffee and looking out at the ocean. I handed him my results and then watched the sun move toward the horizon, while he checked my work.

After several minutes, he looked up from the pages with a wide smile. "Very good. You finding all code."

"How did you manage being a cook?"

"My family has restaurant. Very good restaurant. I cooking there many years."

I questioned him about the videos and how he'd managed them. "I get reputation for many walks during night. I telling them, can't sleep. Need fresh air. Soon they don't bother with me. It dark, so they don't notice small camera. And I very, very careful. Always keep camera in place they not think to look." He leaned back with a satisfied expression and took a sip of coffee "I don't think they happy, you have this information."

"No. And I'm going to keep it under wraps as long as I can."

"Under wraps. What that mean?"

"I won't let them know about it until I have to."

"Ah, under wraps." He chuckled. "Is good way of saying. I learn something new."

Chapter Ten
MAX

"Sophie on line two, Max," Cassie said. "And she sounds upset."

"I'm being followed," Sophie said. "The last few days, wherever I go, I see the same Asian man watching me. He doesn't even attempt to hide. I think he wants to be seen."

"You're sure it's not a coincidence?" I spoke calmly, but my gut had tightened.

"Yesterday, he was standing in the back of the church as I walked out. He made eye contact and saluted me. Max, it's making me nervous."

It was making me more than nervous.

"Tell you what, I'll arrange to have an investigator escort you tomorrow. See what he makes of it."

~ ~ ~

The investigator, Tommy Dorset, called the next afternoon to report. "I had Sophie go to the mall. I waited outside the store we'd picked, and after a few minutes an Asian guy showed up. Sat next to me. When Sophie finished in that store, she went to another one, like we'd agreed. The Asian got up, followed her. I followed him, and when he got settled, I moved in real close. Held a piece of pipe I just happened to have in my pocket against his side and asked him real soft why he was following my friend. Man fell apart. Gibbered like a turkey right before Thanksgiving." Tommy chuckled.

"Said his name was Nishizaki. A man he didn't know offered him a hundred bucks a day to follow an old lady with a white streak in her hair. Claimed the guy gave him a choice. Get paid to follow her or get turned into immigration. Said he gets a call telling him where Sophie will be. Church on Sunday, mall today. He was also told to make sure she knew he was watching her."

"The guy who recruited Nishizaki, you get a description or a name?"

"Both. Not going to be much help. Chinese, medium build, name of Wong. I suggested to Nishizaki he leave town for a while, and he said he would."

I had Tommy arrange additional security for Sophie, then all we could do was wait to see if whoever set this up would try something else when Nishizaki stopped taking calls.

~ ~ ~

"Max, it's a Mr. Conroy on line one," Cassie said.

Robert Conroy was the name that had been most prominent on the motions filed by Helice's Texas-based attorneys during the attempt to get the venue changed to Liberia.

I picked up.

"Gildea, got an offer for your client. Three big ones. All the little lady has to do is sign an agreement that no other legal action will be taken and no details of the settlement will be made public." The accent was a lazy Texas twang, but there was nothing lazy in the approach.

I pictured him sitting back, boots on his desk, wearing western pants accessorized with a big silver buckle, picking his teeth with a toothpick. More likely he was wearing a thousand-dollar suit and a stiffly starched shirt, although I'd still be willing to wager on the boots and the toothpick.

"How many zeros you proposing to put after that three?"

"Six. Helice has decided to be generous, so they don't have to waste any more time on a frivolous suit. This way, everybody wins. The little lady can buy herself a new boat and still have money left over for that expensive shrink, and we can quit killing trees over this thing."

Conroy didn't sound like the type to be much concerned about killing a few trees, but what was most

55

interesting was that he was offering a settlement so soon after Sophie had been followed. My conclusion? We were being bullied. As for the crack about Sophie's psychiatrist, I'd sent the medical records a week ago. Conroy was letting me know how he intended to use them.

"Even with seven zeros after that three, my client isn't going to go for it," I said.

"Thirty mil? Hell. That's way out of line, and you know it. But if you want to deal, we can deal. Helice Shipping has authorized me to go as high as five mil. The little lady might be interested in hearing that."

"You better get authorized for more than five million, Conroy. The little lady isn't a chump, and neither am I."

"Five mil's our final offer."

"That doesn't begin to compensate Mrs. Suriano for her husband's earning power. I guess we'll see you in court."

"You haven't talked to your client yet."

"I have her instructions."

"A real gold digger, huh?" Conroy guffawed in my ear.

It was a tactic designed to push me off balance—the kind of tactic only assholes used. I'd used it myself on occasion.

Talking to the man, I felt like a fine layer of oily dirt was slowly coating my skin, and the down-home, folksy drawl was getting on my nerves.

"I'll get back to you, Conroy. Leave your number with my assistant." I put him on hold without waiting for a response and rang Cassie to pick up. Then I dialed Sophie's number. I should probably have calmed down before I called her.

"A settlement? You mean no trial," Sophie said.

"Yes."

"I already told you no." She sounded as angry as I felt.

"Do you want to know how much?" I asked.

"No."

It was what I expected her to say, what I'd told Conroy she'd say. And for ten seconds after I hung up, I felt pleased she'd responded the way she had. It meant we still had a chance to make the culprits who abandoned her and her husband pay a price that involved more than money. What the sick bastards really deserved was to be dropped off on a raft in the middle of the Pacific without food, water, or a paddle. See how they liked it.

But there was another part of me that knew it would be better if Sophie agreed to a settlement.

~ ~ ~

I called Conroy back to formally decline Helice's offer.

"Hell, if you can't convince the little lady her suit ain't worth it when you got a nice offer on the table, how you expecting to convince a jury the *Nereus* had anything to do with sinking that little ol' boat. Seven mil. Top offer. It'll buy her a hell of a nice replacement."

"This isn't about a yacht, Conroy, although that little ol' boat was state of the art. Mrs. Suriano lost her husband."

"Hell, you know if you force us into court, we'll work damn hard to prove she's either a liar who made up the story about the lights to cover her own incompetence, or she's so brain-damaged she can't remember anything clearly. And if that doesn't fly, DOHSA's still on our side." The condescension and callousness of the man were stunning. He and Todd Wermling could well have been twins separated at birth.

I fought to keep my voice calm and detached, my tone even. "This case is about more than money."

"Bottom line, Gildea, they're all about money. Trust me, the little lady ain't going to be much of a witness." The briskness had relaxed back into an exaggerated drawl. "It's too bad what happened to her, but not my client's fault. Besides, what more does she want? She wins the case in court, all she gets is money."

I wanted to pace. Work off the anger that was steadily building. "She wants justice."

"Hell's bells, man. Expecting justice is like expecting a steer to impregnate a herd of cows." A harsh laugh punctuated the comment.

I gritted my teeth. "I'll talk to my client."

"Yeah. Do that. We'll be in touch." Conroy made no attempt to hide the sneer in his voice. I was so angry, that had we been in the same room, he would have needed to be wearing a codpiece.

~ ~ ~

"Conroy called again," I told Sophie. "They've upped their offer."

She looked at me, her teacup suspended halfway to her mouth. I'd asked her to come to the office this time.

"No settlement, Max."

"Sophie, I'm not sure you understand. We're required by the court to negotiate. Besides, if we do go to trial, Helice's strategy will be to intimidate and postpone, and if we win, they'll appeal. It could go on for years. It's going to take a toll on you."

"It already has." She set the teacup down with a sharp snap and looked at me.

I shifted, trying to get comfortable. "It's going to get worse. They're going to paint you as an hysterical woman who fell asleep on watch and doesn't want to admit it, so you made up the story about the lights."

"But we still have a chance to show they were culpable. Don't we?"

I hated the way her voice hitched, and I especially hated the look in her eyes. "Only if we win."

She took a deep breath, then looked at me. "We have to win."

Yeah. Right. And even if we won, we might lose.

Chapter Eleven
MAX

I was wrapping up odds and ends at the end of the day, waiting for Rosie to arrive so we could go to the track for a workout.

Cassie walked in and pulled my office door closed before she spoke. "Max, Sophie's here. And I don't like the way she looks."

Feeling uneasy, I waited as Cassie ushered Sophie in without any of the usual tea ceremony. There was also no designer suit today. Sophie wore jeans and a sweat shirt, and her eyes were large and bright, like she was fighting back tears.

I wheeled my chair around the desk to meet her, reaching out a hand to her. She placed her hand between mine, then she stood for a moment, trembling.

"It's okay, Sophie. We'll talk about whatever it is. Come, sit down. Take your time."

"It's this." She fumbled an envelope out of her pocket and passed it to me.

It was addressed to Mrs. Samuel Suriano with a San José postmark but no return address. Inside was a sheet of white paper folded around a photo.

I looked at the photo first. It carried a time-date stamp from two days ago at ten in the morning and was of a girl who looked to be about twenty with the typical features of Down Syndrome. She was standing in front of a building, smiling at the camera.

I looked at the sheet of paper. The simple message was written in block printing.

MOM, HOPE THE CASE IS GOING WELL
LOVE GABRIELLE

I looked up at Sophie. "Gibby?"

"She didn't write that."

I moved as close as possible to her and took both her hands between mine.

"What am I going to do, Max?"

"First, we arrange protection for Gibby. Then you're coming home with me."

"I need to be with her."

"You're upset. And that will upset her."

Sophie stared at me, the terror in her eyes slowly easing into comprehension.

"Rosie can take you to see her tomorrow. And meanwhile, I'll make sure she's safe."

After a moment, Sophie nodded. I had Cassie bring in tea, while I alerted the police in San José and arranged for private security for Gibby. By that time, Rosie had arrived to drive me home. At my urging, Sophie agreed to come with us. I sat in the backt with her. She was calming down, but every once in a while a spasm of shivering shook her whole body. I kept my arm around her without talking as Rosie maneuvered through the rush hour traffic.

When we got to the house, Rosie prepared dinner, while Sophie and I sat in the living room with glasses of wine and watched the sun finish setting over the Pacific.

Sophie turned her wineglass in her fingers, staring at the view, rarely remembering to take a sip. "Talk to me, Max."

"What do you want to talk about?" I shifted my chair so I faced her more directly and set my glass down.

Sophie blinked rapidly, not looking at me. "I don't know." She looked around. "This house?"

"What would you like to know?"

"Who designed it?"

"I decided what I wanted. Then I hired an architect."

"It's a marvelous house. Open. Bright. I love your view."

She looked down at her glass of wine, obviously not paying attention to what she was saying. "Have you ever been afraid, Max?"

"Yeah. Lots of times." Although it wasn't something I enjoyed admitting.

"I didn't think I ever could be that afraid again, until I opened that letter."

"Gibby's going to be okay. She's being looked after."

"Yes. Well..."

Rosie called us to the table. Sophie picked at her food, mostly rearranging it on her plate, and Rosie who, when it comes to food, is worse than any Italian mama, said nothing. After we ate, Sophie and I moved back to the living room.

"I think it would be a good idea if you stayed here tonight," I said.

"I don't want to be any trouble." Her voice was listless.

"Easier for Rosie to make up the guest bed than to drive you home." Not to mention Rosie and I would both sleep better knowing exactly where she was.

~ ~ ~

I was in bed, going over a brief but having a hard time concentrating, when there was a tap on the door.

"Can I come in, Max?" Sophie stood in the doorway, wearing one of my T-shirts and looking all of ten years old.

I couldn't afford to let my relationship with her get any more personal, but it would have been heartless to send her away.

"Of course. Come in."

She walked in, chewing on her lip. I patted the bed. "Here, you can sit next to me."

She sat down, then after a moment, she slipped her legs under the sheet.

I set my work aside. She scooted closer and smoothed the covers. "Do you think they'd hurt her, Max?"

"She's safe now. You don't need to worry."

She was silent for a moment, then she pulled in a deep breath. "I can't go on with the suit. I can't take the chance they might hurt her."

"It's the right decision," I said, although I might have argued the point if it hadn't involved a threat against someone as vulnerable as Gibby.

"I know, but it makes me feel...helpless."

I felt helpless too. *Justice.* The ultimate impossible dream.

A breeze came through the open window and brushed against our faces. I took her hand in mine, and we sat listening to the night sounds.

"Did it take a long time to get over losing your legs?" she asked.

"Yeah. It did." Not that I was over it yet.

"I don't know if there will ever be enough time for me."

"All you can do is take it a step at a time."

"Is that what you did?"

"More or less, except for the step part."

Sophie's mouth twitched with the ghost of a smile.

The breeze faded, the curtains drooped, and the quiet of the night intensified.

"Have you ever wanted to remarry?" she asked.

"Gave up thinking about it." I should have been uncomfortable with this conversation, but I wasn't. Maybe it was the fact the light was dim. Maybe it was the quiet way we were speaking—none of it seeming quite real.

"Because of your legs?"

"What woman wants to be tied to this?" *Easy, Gildea. Don't take it out on her.*

"This. What this?" Sophie said. "No legs? So what. You still have your heart, your mind. You're you. You're alive."

Wrong. At least according to Kelly. And likely my ex-wife would agree with her.

"I'm sorry," Sophie said. "It isn't right. Picking at your wounds so I can forget my own for a while. You know, it's a relief being able to talk to you. Not having to pretend or explain. Some of my friends say things like, 'Gee you look great,' and I can hear the rest, even though they don't say it. 'For someone who ought to be dead. Yeah, you look terrific.'"

I knew what she meant. I'd been seeing those unspoken thoughts in other people's eyes for the past thirteen years, so clear sometimes they might as well have been written in oversize bold letters above their heads.

I switched off the lamp, making the room even dimmer, and we were quiet for a time.

"I didn't think much of you when I first met you," Sophie finally said.

"I know."

"I changed my mind."

"When you discovered I didn't have any legs." I didn't know why I was going back to that. I usually avoided the subject.

"The legs matter only to you, Max."

"Isn't it pretty to think so." All that reading in rehab had to be good for something.

"Have you ever considered getting artificial legs?" she said.

"Tried it once. Right after it happened. The legs were heavy and hurt like hell. The best I could manage was a couple of hours a day." I tried to keep the discomfort out of my voice. "Jeff came up with a lightweight wheelchair design, and it just seemed easier."

Sophie was quiet for a time. Then, "You ever been tempted to kill yourself, Max?"

I almost stopped breathing. "No."

A breeze stirred the curtains, and Sophie shivered. I pulled the covers up higher and put my arm around her.

She scooted closer. "Why not?" she asked.

"I don't know. Maybe setting it up was more than I could manage. You know, stockpiling pills or getting my hands on a gun. I've given my family enough sadness, no sense adding to it. What about you?"

"Sometimes, in the middle of the night, I wish I had the courage to take all my pills, so I won't have to wake up ever again."

Okay. Keep her talking, find out if she's serious. "What stops you?"

"Gibby. And the thought someone might find me before I was dead. You have any idea what it's like being treated for a drug overdose?"

She sounded almost dreamy. As if we were talking about our favorite vacation memories, not discussing whether we'd ever considered suicide.

"If you wanted to be dead in the first place, you'll want it twice as bad by the time they finish with you."

Keep her talking. "How do you know that?"

"I was a nurse. Worked in emergency. It's how I met Sam. He was in an accident. When he came back later to thank us for stitching him up, I was going off duty. He offered me a ride home."

"And the rest is history." I was just stringing words together, trying to forget that for me an accident brought the end of love rather than the beginning.

We listened to the quiet night sounds for a time, then I managed to ask Sophie the important question. "You could have let go out there, on the raft."

"I think about that sometimes. Why didn't I? Without Sam, it's like an essential part of me..." She drew in a shaky breath. "I've always been afraid of drowning, but really, I don't know."

"I'm glad you didn't."

"Maybe someday I will be too."

It was several minutes before she spoke again. "What about the case? What do we do now?"

"I'll call Conroy, negotiate a settlement. You can stay here until that's done."

"I don't want the money."

"Give it to your favorite charity."

"And that's it?"

"Looks like it." I moved my hand to Sophie's head, stroked through her short hair, and rubbed a thumb along the narrow column of her neck. "You need to let it go." An echo of Kelly's words to me.

"I know. But it's so hard. It never stops hurting." She took a deep, shaky breath. "This might sound crazy, but I want to go back to New Zealand. There's a family I stayed with after I got out of the hospital. I think going there I'll feel closer to Sam. I know it doesn't make sense, but it's what I want to do."

My throat tightened, making it impossible to speak.

"Every nook and cranny of the house reminds me Sam is gone. I know some people say it helps to be around things you shared with someone you lost. But I bargained it all away. To God. He could have it all, if He'd just bring Sam back." Her voice faltered. "Now I find I don't care about it. It's too much to carry around. I learned what was important on that raft. None of it's—" A sob cut off her words.

I pulled her in tight against my side and waited, as her body shook and her tears dampened my shoulder. She eventually stopped sobbing, and I handed her a tissue, and she wiped her face and blew her nose.

"I'm sorry, Max."

"It's okay." The ache in my chest joined the constriction in my throat. I put a finger under her chin and tipped her face to mine.

Her eyes caught up light from the moon shining through a gap in the curtains and reflected it softly like a pool of water under a cloudy night sky.

She leaned over and kissed me on the cheek. "Can I stay with you tonight, Max?"

"Of course."

"I'm feeling sleepy," she said.

"Me too," I lied.

We slid under the covers, and I turned and tucked Sophie into the curve of my truncated body. I didn't know what to do with my arm until she pulled it around her. We lay curled together, and after a while, I could tell from her breathing she'd fallen asleep.

The touch of that narrow ridge of shoulder overwhelmed me with tenderness. She was all bones, my Sophie, and the pain in her was bone deep. Perhaps she was right. Perhaps she never would find herself again. Look at me. All I lost were legs, but I still hadn't found myself all these years later.

Although I'd given up thinking about the past, Sophie's questions had pulled that door open, and the ache of all the years and all my losses lapped over me.

Lying there in the dark, with Sophie pressed against me, I saw clearly how my choices had played out. Saw, as well, how different it could have been if I'd been courageous. And I understood, finally, what Kelly had been trying to tell me.

Sophie stirred, murmuring in her sleep. One word, with a question at the end of it. *Sam?* An essential part of her.

There was no name for me to murmur in my sleep.

Chapter Twelve
SOPHIE

When Sam announced he was taking time off to go sailing, his parents blamed me. But really, it was Sam's idea. He said he was tired.

I'd worked hard to be the perfect wife and daughter-in-law, and I was tired too. Spending a year sailing on an ever-changing sea, without the constant input from Sam's mother as she tried to mold me into someone I couldn't quite manage to be...it sounded like bliss.

It took me two weeks and Sam nearly a month to relax. As the tightness around his eyes smoothed out, I no longer awakened to find him sitting in the dark unable to sleep, and when we made love, it was the way it used to be. Slowly, with wonder. And we talked, like we hadn't for a long time, about our dreams and our hopes for the future. And it was as if we'd made it all the way back to the beginning, when Sam's pet name for me had been Sylph.

I asked him one afternoon as we lay in each other's arms after making love, why we never talked at home. He was silent for so long I thought he wasn't going to answer. When he finally did, he spoke quietly, his fingers smoothing through my hair.

"The money kept piling up...all that money." He sounded almost surprised. "I ordered myself to be happy, only I wasn't, and I didn't know what to do. I was lost, but I didn't dare admit it. To Dad or Mom. To you. Now here we are thousands of miles from anywhere familiar, and I feel at home."

"Will we be able to remember this feeling?" I asked.

"We could forget again. If we go back. Maybe we shouldn't go back. God, Sophie, I don't want to ever again stop loving you."

"Did you stop?" I discovered I was crying although I felt more happy than sad.

"Didn't you know?"

"I suppose I did. I may have stopped loving you, too."

When he started to speak again, I put my fingers to his lips. "No more confessions, my love. What matters is what was lost has been found. It's enough."

Not long after that, we arrived in Tonga. After Tonga, we had to keep watch at night because we were near shipping lanes.

Then we were hit.

I've asked myself, was it better to rediscover my love for Sam and then lose him? Or would it have been better to have lost him while we were separated by indifference and busyness?

Of course, the second choice would have been so much easier. Still, I choose the first. I wouldn't trade those happy days on the *Sylph*, not even for the blessed relief of indifference. They are all I have left that I care about. That time. Falling in love all over again. Laughing at flying fish, the rainbows in the spray—our love encircling us as we moved, a small speck across that vast blue and white plain.

After I was rescued and had the surgery on my hip, I awoke to feel a tingle from my leg. So simple, so basic. But when I opened my eyes, my world was shades of gray. My doctor said he didn't know why I could no longer see color. He said some people are born that way. Perhaps it's easier for them, since they have no idea what they're missing.

After a lengthy examination, an ophthalmologist said there was nothing wrong with my eyes. The trouble, it seemed, was in my brain. He tried to explain, but all I could visualize were loose wires flopping about inside my skull. It was really quite funny. After he left I found myself laughing until my stomach ached.

After that, I sometimes awakened, shaking, from dreams I didn't want to remember. Black and white dreams of towering waves, huge ships, and a sliver of cold moon. But sometimes when I awakened it was with a memory of color— Gibby dressed in her favorite pink dress, Sam in the gold and black San Francisco Giants shirt he slept in or wearing his favorite green shirt. Golden hair, ocean blue eyes. So beautiful, so lost.

After a while, I decided it really didn't matter that I couldn't see color when my eyes were open. The doctor still cared though. He stopped by my room frequently to tap, probe, and shine bright lights in my eyes. He told me that seeing color was a matter of allowing the circuitry in my brain to reconnect. I didn't tell him it would be a relief to unhook more of my brain, not reconnect what was already free.

~ ~ ~

It's come down to this. Give up the case, or continue to seek justice for Sam and risk losing Gibby. But of course, that's no choice at all, and it makes me feel so powerless. As powerless as I felt on the raft, moving at the whim of wind and ocean currents.

Why did I survive if it wasn't to hold them accountable?

Chapter Thirteen
MAX

"How're you going, mate?"

Even if Cassie hadn't told me, I would have known immediately who was calling. Gerald Cameron, the New Zealand solicitor who'd put us in contact with Alex Wu.

"How's the case?" he asked.

"We're working on a settlement." Rain rattled against the window, a counterpoint to my filthy mood. "They threatened Sophie's daughter."

"Bloody, bleeding bastards."

"Yeah. Is that why you called?"

"Nope. Wanted to tell you Wu heard through some of his contacts that Helice's had a spot of trouble last cargo they took on. Container fell off the crane. Smashed a hold cover, broke a crewman's leg. Took a week to get the hatch fixed. Things like that count up. Soon the bottom line isn't so rosy."

Maybe a nice shade of bright red. Couldn't happen to more deserving people.

"Wu also said he had a useful voyage, but you asked him to keep what he learned under wraps."

"Yeah. He verified they run without lights on a regular basis, and they knew they hit the yacht."

"Guess it doesn't much matter now."

"No. It doesn't."

~ ~ ~

"Conroy? Gildea here." This was the kind of phone call the

experts tell you is best conducted standing. As a substitute, I sat up straighter.

"Gildea. The little lady ready to settle?" Conroy said.

I had no doubt that despite the occasional grammatical slip the man was smart, but he shouldn't have been so quick to give me an opening. "Yeah. But not for a paltry seven million."

"Paltry, my ass," he said, his tone losing its heartiness.

"We take this to trial, Conroy, and even with DOHSA you're looking at a potential for a very large settlement based on Sam Suriano's projected earnings. He was already making two million a year as CEO of Golden Gate Bank, and he was in line for raises and bonuses for forty more years."

"Hell he was. That would make him eighty."

"Right. And then we get to the yacht and Mrs. Suriano's injuries."

"That's assuming you win," he said.

"Not a bad assumption. When we show a panel of ordinary American citizens the pictures of Mr. and Mrs. Suriano before the accident and then they meet Mrs. Suriano and hear what she has to say about being capsized and abandoned in the middle of the ocean, we think they'll want to make the ship responsible for that pay as much as possible. And that's before they learn she was threatened when she brought legal action."

"What the hell are you talking about?"

Too bad we weren't in the same room, so I could see if his body language matched the outrage in his tone.

"Helice didn't share with you? They've opened their own negotiations."

"Don't know what you're talking about." The outrage was thinning out.

"Oh, it's been subtle. As a sledgehammer. Likely it's going to make those jurors even more determined to see that big, bad ship and its owners pay."

"Okay, Gildea, spit it out." He sounded almost weary. Made me wonder if they'd jerked him around before.

"Mrs. Suriano has been followed, and she's received a note threatening her daughter."

"The Surianos are public figures. Expect they get followed and threatened all the time." There was a tone that sounded like relief underlying his words.

Interesting.

"Unless you got something to tie that to Helice, no judge in his right mind will allow it in."

"I think the note does that, since it specifically mentions the case."

"I think you're bluffing." Relief had been replaced with bluster.

"Do you? Of course that's your prerogative." I let the silence stretch for a time before administering the coup. "We can easily document that fifty million is a reasonable settlement."

"Fifty mil!" He was spluttering so much I would have needed a towel if he'd been sitting anywhere nearby. "That's a helluva lot for us to pay to get rid of a nuisance suit when there's no proof *Nereus* was even involved."

I wondered if he really believed he could make the paint matching and satellite data placing the freighter at the scene go away by denying them. I waited a beat before adding, "And we want an apology."

"That's a non-starter." It sounded like his teeth were clenched. "Don't even think about it."

"It'll take something to get me to stop thinking about it. Say another ten million."

"You haven't got a case, Gildea, and you damn well know it." More denial. The man was backing up, and the edge of the cliff was right behind him.

"Maybe, maybe not. But I figure when this heats up, the press is going to find this trial mighty interesting." I had one more card, Wu's report. I was hoping I wouldn't have to use it. I tried more silence. It often works well, particularly on the phone.

After some heavy breathing Conroy said, "I'll get back to you."

I hoped the defeat in his tone was more than a figment of my imagination.

~ ~ ~

"Gildea. Ten mil. Final offer."

Conroy had his confidence back, but I knew he could be rattled. "Fifty with an apology. Sixty without. Or we let a jury decide." I waited. The man didn't seem to deal particularly well with silence.

"No apology." The grinding of his teeth was palpable.

"Sixty million then."

"Thirty."

I waited.

"Forty," he said.

Got him. "Fifty-five. And save your breath. That's as low as I'm going." I shut up and waited. I didn't care if it took the rest of the day. I was beginning to think like Sophie. Without an apology, the money didn't mean a damn thing.

"You're a hard man, Gildea."

I waited some more.

"Okay, let's get the paperwork started."

He didn't sound happy. But then neither was I. On an ordinary day, this outcome would have made me feel ebullient. It was a good settlement. Hell, given DOHSA it was a fantastic settlement. Sophie's favorite charity was going to be ecstatic. But it was hard to feel anything but flat since Sophie had called to say she was leaving for New Zealand in two weeks.

Only later did it occur to me to wonder why Conroy met our price with only token resistance. In those first moments, all I could think was that without an acknowledgement of responsibility, all the money was good for was keeping score, something that no longer had a point as far as Sophie and this case were concerned.

I sure couldn't hold it in my arms in the dark of night and feel any comfort.

~ ~ ~

I'd always viewed myself as a pragmatic person. Clear-eyed. Level-headed. Cynical, even. Taking on Sophie's case changed all that, at least for a time.

But what did I end up with?

Even if Kelly was right about my having only half a life, it had been a pleasant and comfortable one back before I took on the Suriano case, and it was high time I got back to that life and the kinds of cases that supported it—cases that didn't demand emotional involvement. So what if most of them weren't about anything that mattered.

All this recent exercise had accomplished was to remind me of how I used to feel, waking up to suffocating pain. It took me a long time to get over that. I had no intention of going back.

Ignore Kelly.

Forget Sophie.

Screw change.

Chapter Fourteen
MAX

I rarely take vacations. The last time Cassie brought the issue up, I had, according to her, over a year accrued. I'm happiest—no, that's not the right word.

Content?

No.

Comfortable?

Yes, that's it. Comfortable. I'm most comfortable when I'm busy. *Keep moving, avoid thinking.* Short and sweet. The Gildea philosophy of life.

After I lost my legs and my wife, that meant seventy-hour workweeks. This time, work wasn't working. But taking a vacation, hell, doing what, going where? Probably what I needed were long walks along deserted beaches—preferably somewhere cold.

Hard to do without legs.

Kelly and Sophie insisted legs didn't matter. Easy enough to say if you have two. Prosthetics. Who needs them? I've gotten along fine without them.

Like I've gotten along handling uninspiring cases that provided the easy income?

I tapped my finger on the desk in irritation. The computer screen blinked. *Oh, what the hell.* I stopped tapping, typed in *double amputation*, and hit the Search key. I scrolled through what came up, checking for entries that mentioned legs, and clicked on one of them.

An hour later, I pushed away from the computer and wheeled over to the window, picked up the binoculars, and watched a couple of tugs herd a container ship up the channel. All the while, I let the possibility simmer. I wasn't sure prosthetics were an answer, but I was even less sure what the questions were.

Then I thought about the people I'd just met through the Internet—a teenager from Russia who spoke no English when he came to the U.S. to be fitted with his legs; the young man who, nine months after an accident severed his legs, returned to active duty in the Army; the young woman who skied competitively on her prosthetic leg and was planning her wedding.

It made me feel ashamed. Worse, I saw my behavior for what it was. Not admirable, as in, *You damn well have to admire Gildea. He accomplishes more from a wheelchair than most men with two legs,* but cowardly.

Losing my legs had turned me into someone neither I nor Susan could stand to be around. Susan simply did what I would have done if I'd been able to: She walked away.

And now? As long as I continued to sit in a wheelchair, I had a built-in excuse for whatever went wrong in my life, not to mention it meant nobody, including me, expected me to take risks.

Convenient. Neat. Except it wasn't any longer. Convenient or neat.

So, Gildea. You going to sit here feeling sorry for yourself, or are you going to do something? Hell. Try the legs, man. At the least, it will be a distraction. At the most...well, who the hell knows, but it can't be any worse than doing nothing.

Right!

~ ~ ~

Over the next two weeks, I got in touch with the prosthetist suggested by my physician and made an appointment to start the process of being fitted for legs.

The legs would weigh only seven to eight pounds apiece, less than half what a flesh and blood leg weighs, and much less than the prosthetics I'd previously tried. The design had been improved in other ways as well with built-in vacuum pumps that would automatically adjust the fit of the liner as my residual limbs shrank or swelled over the course of the day, and the liner was gel-filled to reduce pressure points that could cause tissue injury.

With all the improvements, learning to walk should be a piece of cake.

I finally got the legs six weeks after I started the process. That was when the real fun began. As I stood upright for the first time in thirteen years, I felt a pure rush of excitement.

I hesitated for a moment holding onto the parallel bars, just savoring it. But when I tried to take a step, excitement quickly gave way to dismay as I discovered it wasn't going to be as easy to balance and ambulate on fourteen pounds of titanium and carbon fiber, as I'd supposed.

My choices were clear—focus on the walking and be able to manage it in three or four months, or fit learning to walk into my regular schedule and maybe learn in three or four years...if ever.

Sophie had left for New Zealand, and her case was cleared away, with checks sent to all the charities she designated, the largest, in Gibby's name, to an institute that did genetic research. Another of my cases was in pre-discovery, and everything else was perking along under the watchful eyes of junior associates.

There was no reason it couldn't all keep going with only minimal attention from me, making this the best opportunity I'd had in years to take time off. But I wouldn't be going on vacation. I'd be doing the hardest work I'd done in my life.

If I decided to go ahead. Because, really, why bother? I'd managed with the chair this long. There was no good reason to change.

A spurt of anger scorched through me. Kelly was right. I wasn't half a man because I didn't have legs. I was half a man because I'd let that loss define my life.

I turned back to my schedule and blocked out November through February, the first two months completely and the following two with a light schedule. Then I called Cassie in. There would be no turning back once she knew.

When I told her, she sat back with a solemn look. "'Bout time you did it," she said.

"It's only been thirteen years."

Her solemn look was replaced with a wide grin. "You're going to do great." And still grinning, she stood and walked out, something I planned to be able to do someday soon myself.

~ ~ ~

When I started learning to walk, I was thankful I'd stayed in good physical shape. Still, the first day was miserable. Every muscle in my back and what was left of my legs ached and burned, and I went to bed debating whether to continue. Sure, walking had its advantages, but it was also going to slow me down. No more swooping down the wide hallways at the courthouse in a fraction of the time it took an able body. But then, no more sitting at the bottom of a series of steps that for me might as well be Mount Everest.

My walking lessons were scheduled at the same time as those of Darnell and Pammie, ten and twelve years old respectively, both recent double amputees. Our therapist was Carol. After the first two days, if she'd told me she learned her techniques from Nurse Ratched, I would have believed it.

By the third morning, I could see Pammie and Darnell were hurting as much as I was.

"Hey, guys, how about we make a pact," I said.

"What kind of pact?" Pammie asked, looking wary.

"That we stick with learning to walk, no matter what. And anybody who whines won't get a special prize at the end." It was more a reminder for me than for them, actually.

"What's the special prize?" Pammie asked. She had braids and freckles and looked like she'd be the kid sister from hell if she were in top form.

I shrugged. "What would you consider special?"

Her face screwed up in thought. "If I don't whine and I stick with it, I want a makeover."

It was my turn to frown. "A makeover?"

"Yeah, you know. Hair, nails, make-up."

I was appalled, she was only twelve, after all.

She saw my reaction, and her face fell. "Yeah. I know. Stupid idea. They have to have something to work with in the first place, don't they." She turned away and pretended to be adjusting the fit of one of her legs. But she couldn't hide the way her lips were trembling. She firmed them and glared at me. "I guess you'll just have to put up with my whining."

"I accept your terms," I said. "One makeover it is. What about you, Darnell? What reward do you choose?" As I turned to Darnell, I saw Pammie straightening and looking brighter.

"I sure don't want no makeover," he said, putting his hands on his hips. Then he chewed his lip in thought. "Maybe a bicycle. Yeah. That's what I want. A bike."

"Your folks won't let you," Pammie said, her voice authoritative.

"Sure they will." But Darnell's tone had a wobble to it.

Pammie pointed at Darnell's prostheses. "You think after that, they'll ever let you near a bike?"

And I could have kicked myself for setting the poor kid up. I spoke quickly. "Tell you what, when the time comes, I'll put in a good word on the bike. If the answer is no, we'll figure out another prize."

Darnell turned huge eyes on me. I could see he was trying not to cry and also perhaps attempting to judge my trustworthiness. Then he ducked his head.

"What do you get?" Pammie asked, turning that razor intelligence on me.

"I get the two of you to keep me from giving up."

Pammie looked disappointed. "That's all?"

"How about a new car? Would that qualify?"

"Will you be able to drive?"

"Sure." Since I'd been told I'd be able to manage foot controls with the prosthetics I'd chosen, the idea of a car, something sleek and fun to drive, had nudged at me. Pammie's question solidified the nudge into determination. I was going to buy a new car, one that didn't need to have space for a wheelchair.

~ ~ ~

Over the next weeks, Pammie, Darnell, and I worked hard, and there was no whining. The pact was working. I gritted my teeth and kept going, in part, because if I let a couple of kids show me up, Rosie would never let me hear the end of it. And neither would my family, after I showed up for Thanksgiving dinner wearing the legs.

"More good changes, Max," Kelly said, giving me a hug.

78

"But your news is the best," I said. "In remission."

"Sometimes, I still feel like it's too good to be true," she said, taking a deep breath.

"Remember your advice to me. Just live."

"It was good advice, wasn't it."

"On a scale of one to ten...at least a fifteen." We smiled at each other.

Despite the pact, some mornings giving up would have been easy. Often it was only the thought of what Kelly had endured without complaint that forced me out of bed and back to the institute for another session. My progress was so slow, it was only by looking back and remembering what I could do the previous week that I was able to see I was making any. Mostly, I felt as if I were becalmed in the middle of the ocean. But in reality, every day I moved closer and closer to an invisible shore.

As our last week of daily therapy approached, I contacted both Pammie and Darnell's folks. Pammie's mother immediately approved the makeover deal, but when I told Darnell's dad about our pact and that Darnell had earned a bicycle, his response was, "Over my dead body."

I waited a beat before speaking. "You've got a real brave kid there. Impressed the hell out of me. Took me over thirteen years to deal with my disability with the grace he's achieved in a few months." I debated whether to say more, then decided to let what I'd already said simmer.

After a long silence, Darnell's dad spoke, his tone thoughtful. "I'm going to need to think about it."

He called me two days later to tell me I could go ahead and buy the bike. He still didn't sound happy, but he sounded resigned.

~ ~ ~

The first morning I walked into the office, a couple of the secretaries pulled out tissues and blew their noses. I was using forearm crutches for balance, but I found it was an incredible rush viewing my familiar world from a height of six rather than three feet. Gone was the sense of everyone looking down at me. It reminded me of how good I'd felt as a kid playing with stilts.

By the time I reached Cassie's desk, I was beginning to feel the familiar fatigue. Walking was a hell of a lot more labor-intensive than rolling along in a wheelchair. Her face was solemn as she watched me approach. I stopped in front of her, and we looked at each other.

"So, does this mean you get the coffee for the next ten years, Max?"

We both started laughing. Then she walked around her desk and hugged me, and that felt better than anything had since Sophie left for New Zealand.

~ ~ ~

The legs brought other changes. I could now wait for regular boarding at the airport instead of being wheeled on board ahead of time and then having to wait at the end of the flight until everyone else deplaned. I stood to greet clients as they entered my office, and I no longer saw that look of pity mixed with avid curiosity on the faces of those I was encountering for the first time.

I met new people, people who had no idea that instead of flesh and blood legs, I ambulated on two marvels of modern technology. I even began to date, but that soon ended after I encountered one too many divorcées who seemed brittle and needy in ways Sophie, who had lost so much, was not. I missed Sophie, but I was getting used to her absence. Or at least I tried to convince myself I was.

My new car arrived. A Porsche. After I got the hang of driving it, I spent weekends traveling. Sometimes I decided whether to go north or south by flipping a coin. Other times I went as far as the airport and caught a weekend flight to somewhere I'd not been before.

I was rediscovering the freedom of movement I took for granted my first twenty-eight years. It didn't make up for the emptiness Sophie left behind, but it beat sitting around.

Keep busy. Keep moving. Don't think. It always worked...eventually.

~ ~ ~

Now that I could walk, my needs were changing.

Rosie brought the subject up first. "Max, you're getting on good. I'm thinking you don't need old Rosie anymore."

Although it was true, I'd avoided thinking about it. Not having Rosie around, sharing meals and workouts, was going to change my life as profoundly as the legs had. And not in a positive direction. I'd never want to admit it to anyone, least of all to Rosie, but the mere fact of his presence had banished many of my demons over the years.

"You have a job as long as you want it."

He looked away, his throat working as if he were trying to swallow a stone. "I need to be doing some good. Okay with you, I look around?"

"Of course. Let me know if I can help." It was the least I could do—not lay a guilt trip on him.

A couple of months later, Rosie told me that what he'd decided to do was set up a gourmet cooking school for men and women down on their luck, like he was when he came to work for me. He couldn't afford downtown San Francisco, but he'd located a building in San Germano, a quick subway ride away.

One evening, after dinner, he showed me his roughed-out business plan. I sat at the kitchen table, reading it, while he puttered around cleaning up. He'd done a reasonable job figuring out what the renovations and start-up would cost. The biggest problem would be assuring his funding stream, and with the current plan, it was likely he'd be broke before he established one.

"You just telling me this, Rosie, or you asking for advice?"

"Always listen to advice, Max. You know that." He dried his hands, came over to the table, and sat down.

"Plain truth?" I said.

"Sure. Lay it on me. I can take it."

I wasn't so sure about that. Rosie had the look I last saw right before I took a bite of one of his culinary experiments in the days when there was only a fifty-fifty chance it would be edible.

"Your plan to charge students after they have a job is admirable, but it makes your cash flow problematic. Means you need more start-up funds to get this thing going. Without that, you could easily go broke. Lose everything."

He rubbed his hands, looking worried. "I hear it in your voice. You've got a suggestion for me."

"More of an offer."

"You, Max?"

"Why not?"

"What you get out of it?"

"Satisfaction. Worked right, a nice tax deduction."

The worried look was replaced with a question. "We be partners then?"

"No. It's your show, Rosie. I'll place the money in a trust fund to provide you a steady income. A project like this...you ought to be eligible for a slew of grants. I can find someone to advise you on that, but I'll be happy to give you free advice, anytime."

He sat back and looked at me, his face splitting into a wide grin. Then, he swiped a huge hand across his eyes. "Best thing ever happened to me, meeting you, Max."

"You more than returned the favor, Rosie."

Chapter Fifteen
MAX

Cassie brought in morning coffee along with my schedule for the day. "Mr. Micelli's secretary called," she said. "He wants you to join him for lunch today. I've already cleared it."

Anthony Micelli was the firm's most senior partner.

"Any mention of an agenda?"

"Nope. But he's thinking about retirement. You know what that means."

"It means he's thinking about retirement."

"Come on, Max. That's not it. Word is he's planning to designate a successor."

"And you think this is my shot. Hell, Cass, if he doesn't know whether he wants to name me by now, my eating lunch with him isn't going to amount to a hill of beans."

Cassie chuckled. "Now you know it'll be more elegant than beans, Max."

~ ~ ~

Over the years, I've had a number of lunches in the private dining room adjacent to Anthony Micelli's office. Sometimes it's just the two of us, and sometimes other partners are included. This time the table was set for only two.

"Max, good you could join me on such short notice," Anthony said. "The caterer tells me he got in some lobsters from Maine this morning. Thought you and I could check them out. Make sure they're fit to eat."

Usually, I could gauge the gravity of the upcoming discussion by what was on the menu. It didn't get much weightier than lobster.

"You know," Anthony said. "It's done my heart good to see you walking around these last few weeks. Makes me wonder why you didn't get prosthetics sooner."

"Sheer pigheadedness."

He grinned. "Knew you were stubborn, moment I met you. Useful trait for an attorney to have." He led the way to the table, and we sat down. "This has been an interesting year. Watching you handle the Suriano case. Nice job on the settlement, incidentally."

He paused to unfold his napkin before continuing. "As you know, the firm has had an excellent run the past five years. And you've been a big part of that. The crane case in Seattle, the sinking in Alaska."

The waiter set our plates down. "Now doesn't that look nice," Anthony said, surveying the food before forking a bite of lobster from the mound in front of him. "Umm. Good," he said.

I took a small bite and waited while he chewed and swallowed.

"I've just reviewed our quarterly report. You and Todd Wermling are in a dead heat as usual as our top income producers. And yet, I never see you so much as say hello to each other."

Of course he didn't, because we didn't. And Anthony couldn't fool me into thinking he didn't know the reason for it. I concentrated on the lobster, which was really quite good.

"I made a mistake, Max. And you know that's not easy for me to admit. I've let the two of you carry on your grudge year after year and done nothing about it. Granted, the firm has benefited from the competition between the two of you, but there's been a downside as well."

I took a sip of iced tea. When I looked up, Anthony was examining me with a thoughtful look that had a question in it. I knew it would be a tactical error to engage, but then this was Anthony, and he had served lobster.

"And that downside is?"

There was a quick glint of satisfaction.

"Everyone in the firm, from the juniors on up, knows you and Todd hate each other's guts. It takes time and energy better spent on billable hours for everyone to maneuver around you two."

I thought that assessment was unfair.

"I've always made it a point not to let my feelings about Todd poison my other relationships in the firm or affect my work."

Anthony held up an imperious fork. "I know you think that, but while you may believe you're doing a good job of separating feelings from performance, that bad blood is always there. And I want it to end."

It was the closest to a command Anthony had issued since I made partner. But it wasn't a command I intended to do much about. It was definitely time to change the subject, but before I could, Anthony spoke again. "I have a case I'd like you to join. That tanker collision with the bridge in San Diego."

"I heard that was Todd's baby."

"It's mine, and I've decided I want both you and Todd on the team. Time you two buried the hatchet. Learned to work together. You know I'm not going to be around forever to act as referee."

I chewed slowly, thinking about telling Anthony what an asshole Todd was and then maybe telling him I no longer gave a damn about the kinds of dull cases we usually handled. The San Diego case was a good example. An oil tanker misjudged the current and hit a support on the bridge to Coronado. The city was suing the tanker's owners and their insurance company for damages. We'd be defending the tanker's insurer, trying to prove the captain was negligent in order to limit the hit they were definitely going to take. The only thing the case was about was money.

"I prefer to pass."

"No, Max. I'm going to insist on this one. I want to see you and Todd cooperating before I decide which one of you I'm backing to run the firm when I retire."

So, Cassie was correct, as usual. Anthony was contemplating a successor, and he'd just held out the gold ring I'd been aiming at my entire career. So, why did the whole idea make me feel tired?

"Could I have until tomorrow to give you an answer about the case?"

Anthony stopped eating and frowned. "Sorry to hear there's anything to think about, Max." He paused and sat back. "You know, I believe it's time you told me why you and Todd don't like each other. He's a damn fine attorney. And I don't want to leave a war behind when I retire."

I wondered why Anthony was asking for details. His assistant was nearly Cassie's equal at ferreting out and interpreting office undercurrents.

"He's a bigot." A relief to have finally said it.

"Ah. Yes. Of course. That incident when you hired Cassie. Perhaps it might interest you to know that Todd is being forced to change with the times. His daughter is engaged to a man whose mother is African-American."

I didn't know what to say to that, so I remained silent. Anthony examined me for a time before finally giving his head a slight shake. "Tomorrow by noon, then."

I could tell by his tone, not to mention his body language, he was disappointed.

I'd do a lot for Anthony, and not just because he's been a fine mentor. He's also a friend. But what he was asking...I just didn't know if I could stomach it.

~ ~ ~

Shortly after I returned from lunch, Cassie buzzed me to say Kelly was there to see me. Kelly had never come to my office before, and my mind began to spin with the possibility she'd come to tell me the cancer had recurred.

She walked in looking hardier than she had the last time I saw her and gave me a hug. "Max, sorry to show up like this, but this couldn't wait."

She stepped back from the hug, and that was when I noticed two young people hovering in the doorway behind her.

"This is Amy and Neil Bracken and they desperately need your help." She motioned to the two to enter and sit, then she addressed the girl, who looked to be about sixteen. "Amy, maybe you could explain?"

The girl leaned forward, wringing her hands. "Our parents were due back from Australia this morning, but they weren't on the plane. We talked to the airline, but they couldn't tell us anything. Then we tried calling the hotel where our folks were supposed to spend their last night in Australia. They said Mom and Dad never checked in. After that, we called the hotel from the day before, and they said we had to talk to the manager, only he wasn't there. And every time we've called back, he still wasn't there." The rush of words stopped, and she took a deep, shaky breath. Neil, who looked younger than Amy, shifted in his seat, frowning.

"We didn't know what to do, so we asked Kelly."

"We're Neil and Amy's back-up, while their folks are away," Kelly said.

Amy sat back, and some of the stiffness in her posture eased, as if in telling me her story, the burden of what to do next had shifted from her shoulders to mine.

I spoke as gently as possible. "It sounds like what you need is an investigator. I can put you in touch with a good one. He'll contact someone in Australia to work with you."

As I spoke, Amy leaned forward, shaking her head. "No. Please. We need help now. And if we have to go to someone else...Mom and Dad. Something's happened. They need us." Tears were tipping out of her eyes.

In a moment she'd be sobbing, and there isn't a man I know who has an effective antidote to feminine tears. Besides, with Kelly sitting there, I had no choice but to offer my help, and Amy did have a point. If I got the full story now, I'd know better where to refer them.

I picked up a pen and turned over a fresh sheet of paper. "When did your parents go to Australia?"

They both spoke at the same time: "Twelve days ago." "April fourth."

"Have they been in touch?"

"They call every few days," Neil said.

"When was the last time they called?"

"I think it was three days ago?" Amy looked at Neil, who shrugged.

"Did you worry when they didn't call?"

"Not really. With the time difference it was hard for them to reach us when we weren't in school or asleep."

"Was the trip business or a vacation?"

"Dad had a meeting in Sydney, but he and Mom planned to visit the Great Barrier Reef before they came home."

"They're divers," Neil added. "We are too. Boy, the Great Barrier Reef, it doesn't get any better than that. Dad didn't even want to learn to dive at first. But once he tried it, he loved it, just like the rest of us. And he was real excited when they got a chance to take this trip."

They both lost their anxious looks as they talked about the diving. And Amy's tears stopped.

"You have their itinerary?"

Amy pulled a folded paper from a backpack and handed it to me.

I glanced through it. "You called the Marriott in Sydney and the Emerald Isle in Cairns to check on them. Is that right?"

Amy nodded.

"And you haven't called anyone else yet, say the Sydney or the Cairns police?"

They both shook their heads. "Would you do it for us?" Amy dabbed at fresh tears and gave me an apprehensive look. "Please."

"If it's your fee you're worrying about, Amy and I have a couple thousand, and you can have it. Mom and Dad...well, they have to be in some kind of trouble, otherwise they would have come home," Neil said.

Hell. What could I say to that? Especially with Kelly sitting there. "Don't worry about my fee. I'll do some preliminary checking from this end. Then we'll decide what to do next." It was the same strategy I'd employed with Sophie.

You'd think I'd learn.

The three left with my promise I would begin checking immediately. Since it was roughly eight in the morning in Cairns, I made that call first, asking to speak to the Emerald Isles' manager, one Maurice Chalmers.

"Mr. Chalmers, my name is Max Gildea. I'm an attorney representing Neil and Amy Bracken. I understand they tried to get in touch with you."

"No, can't say those names are familiar." His voice sounded more plummy English than casual Australian.

"Do the names Ray and Alexandra Bracken ring a bell?"

"No, can't say they do."

"Mr. and Mrs. Bracken had a reservation at the Emerald Isle. They were supposed to check in on the eleventh and leave on the fourteenth," I said, reading from the itinerary Amy gave me.

"That may well be. Mr....?"

"Gildea."

"Yes. Mr. Gildea. We have a hundred rooms here." His tone was disinterested and pompous. "I certainly can't tell you off the top of my head whether a specific person is staying, or has stayed, in any one of them."

"But you can check your records." I kept my tone pleasant, although the pomposity in Chalmers' voice was getting on my nerves.

"It is our policy not to give out information about our guests to unknown persons."

Time for some pomposity of my own. "Mr. Chalmers, you can either give the information to me or to the police, because I assure you that will be my next call."

"Ah, just a moment." The disinterest had faded. *Good.*

I waited on hold for two minutes before Chalmers returned. "I have it right here. Mr. and Mrs. Raymond Bracken, San Francisco, U.S.A. They checked in on the eleventh and out on the fourteenth."

I tried to decide if Chalmers seemed nervous, or was he merely annoyed he'd been asked to do something as mundane as check a guest's record. Hard to tell.

"You're sure of that?"

"Certainly. I'm looking at their record now."

"Are there any other charges on their bill? Dinners, sightseeing trips, that sort of thing."

"Yes. All right. There's a dinner, two local phone calls, and day trips with OceanQuest and Rainforest Adventures."

"What were the dates of those charges?"

"They're all on the eleventh."

"What kind of a trip is OceanQuest?"

"Snorkel and dive trips. From the price they paid, they must have booked an all-day dive trip."

"What about Rainforest Adventures?"

"That's a jeep safari, into the Daintree Rainforest. Pleasant trip, that one."

"Can you give me the numbers for OceanQuest and Rainforest Adventures?"

"I'm not directory assistance, Mr...."

"Gildea. I'd appreciate the help. I'm calling from San Francisco." I spoke courteously despite the fact I considered Chalmers an arrogant asshole.

With a huff of irritation, he recited the two numbers.

"Thanks, Mr. Chalmers. You've been most helpful." I maintained the courteous tone even though it was an effort.

You get more bees with honey than with vinegar—one of Mom's favorite sayings—and I'd discovered it was true even in those instances when I wanted to cram the whole damn honey pot down a particular bee's throat.

I called the number for Rainforest Adventures next. The young woman who answered was a marked contrast to Chalmers, both in accent and manner.

When asked about the Brackens, she didn't hesitate. "Odd that. That's the couple that didn't show. They were booked, let me see, on the thirteenth, it was. And they never contacted us to reschedule or to ask for a refund."

"That happen often? Someone pays, then doesn't show?"

"Occasionally. Someone oversleeps or something. They've always called to ask for a refund or a reschedule though."

"I appreciate the information. Thanks."

"No worries."

It would be nice to be able to accept her cheerful assurances, but one thing her information didn't do was leave me with no worries.

Next I called OceanQuest. As soon as I stated my business, I was passed off to someone who identified himself as Rob McIntyre. He and Mr. Chalmers had similar styles.

"Sorry, Golden is it?"

"Gildea."

"I don't have that information handy. Besides, our policy is not to give out that kind of info on the phone. You stop by the office, we'll see what we can do."

"Mr. McIntyre, I thought I made that clear. I'm calling from San Francisco."

"Oh yeah. Sorry I can't help you then, mate." On that note, he hung up.

I made one last call—to the American Consulate in Sydney—and asked to speak to Daniel Meredith, a senior aide to the Consul General. He was also the son of an acquaintance. When Daniel came on the line, I explained who I was. I'd never met him, but I was reassured by his calm, competent manner. I outlined what I'd learned about the Brackens' activities in Australia, and Meredith said he'd contact the appropriate Australian authorities.

I hung up and sat back, thinking about it all. Then I did something I wasn't able to do while I was working on Sophie's case. I stood and paced. Not for long, of course. I still tired quickly. After several laps around the office, I stopped and looked out across the city toward the bridge, turning over what I'd learned, picking away at it, like a bird looking for nutmeats in a litter of shells. In aggregate, the information made little sense.

The manager of the hotel in Cairns said the Brackens checked in and out on schedule. Then why did they miss the rainforest tour the day before they checked out? The dive trip with OceanQuest—that had to have been on the twelfth. But that was something Rob McIntyre refused to confirm, not to mention he'd practically hung up on me. Simple rudeness? Or something else?

A picture was forming in my mind, and it wasn't pretty.

I turned to the computer and did a search to locate the Cairns newspaper. The website contained little useful information and no links to archived articles. After more false starts, I stumbled on a site that provided a search engine for the archives of *The Australian,* which appeared to be Australia's equivalent of *USA Today.*

I typed *Bracken* in the search field and entered an appropriate date frame. Nothing came up. Next I typed *Diving Great Barrier Reef* and extended the date frame to include the previous six months.

That pulled up headlines and the first few words of a wide variety of articles. I read through at least a hundred headlines, not really certain what I was looking for, until I found it.

I registered and downloaded the article that caught my attention. It was about an incident that happened on a dive trip in the Cairns area. One of a group of divers on a Silver Seas cruise was caught by a strong current and swept away from the dive boat. The crew's procedures clued them in to the fact he was missing almost immediately, and that enabled them to recover him quickly.

The article describing the incident, had writing that was much more colorful than it tended to be in U.S. papers. I noted down the names of the reporter and the owner of Silver Seas—Jake Rutherford and Gavin Aylliard, respectively—and put Cassie to work obtaining phone numbers for the two.

Not yet knowing where the case was going, I decided to have an investigator call Silver Seas. Likely Aylliard would be willing to talk before the Brackens' case hit the press, something I no longer had any doubt it was going to do.

Chapter Sixteen
MAX

When Cassie checked with me before going home, I expected her to ask if she'd been correct about the agenda during my lunch with Micelli. Instead, her focus was the Brackens.

"I just talked to Amy. She's called every hour. Is there any news?" Cassie doesn't tolerate pushy clients. And she doesn't take a personal interest in them, at least not until Sophie came along.

I shook my head. "I put Tommy on it. We should get a preliminary report soon."

Tommy called at five thirty to say he'd reached Aylliard the first time he dialed his number. "He likes to talk, old Gavin does. Told him I was writing a novel, a mystery. Said I planned to have a couple disappear while scuba diving on the Great Barrier Reef, and I was calling to ask how the tour boats made sure they didn't leave someone behind."

A mystery writer. Leave it to Tommy to come up with something good.

"That started him off," Tommy continued. "Went on and on about head counts, shoe counts, sign-in sheets, sign-out sheets, and what have you. Bottom line, he's a real stickler. There's no way a plot like that'll work if the couple took a Silver Seas cruise." Tommy paused, and I heard the rustle of pages as he checked his notes.

"Makes his captains get guests' signatures when they leave the boat on a dive. When they return, clients sign back in. Crew's responsible for checking the lists, and Aylliard double-checks. I sure wouldn't want to be the one to turn in an incomplete list."

"Is he saying your idea is unworkable? Nice touch, by the way."

"Oh no. He thinks it's all too possible. Said some operators are so slapdash it's a wonder it hasn't happened already. Said he's been preaching safety for years, and if I write a credible book, he'll buy a couple hundred copies himself. Make sure everybody having anything to do with diving in the Cairns area gets one."

"It may be too late for a book."

"Damn, I was thinking of going ahead with it."

"He willing to name names?"

"You mean operators who don't check carefully enough? I did ask who was in the choir with him."

"And?"

"There's nobody else he'd trust his Aunt Sally or his Cousin Jane to, was the way he put it."

"That leaves it open."

"Yep, that's what I said. He said, 'Too right, mate.'"

The next assignment I gave the intrepid author was to call OceanQuest. I wanted to know what size boats they took out, the maximum number of divers they handled, and any other details Tommy thought to ask them.

Tommy called back right before six thirty with his report. "I ditched the author persona," he said. "Told the gentleman who answered the phone I was planning my trip and was interested in pre-booking for a group of six. I figured that would make the old dollar signs light up in his eyes. They take both snorkelers and divers out daily. Use a number of reef locations, with the captain deciding on the specific one they'll use each day based on the tides and weather." He paused, and I heard pages flipping.

"Capacity is fifty passengers, but they take only twenty divers. No resort divers, only fully certified open water divers. Two dive masters go in the water with the customers. They stay in for the first part of the dive, then come back to the boat while the customers finish off their tanks. I asked whether a more intimate cruise was possible. He said all they have is a big boat."

"Did you book a cruise?"

"Hey, if I'd realized expenses stretched to that, I'd have been tempted. But I did better than that. I asked what safety procedures they followed. Said I had a scare down in Cancun once, and I like to know up front I'm not going to get left behind."

"And?"

"Got real huffy. Told me if I had any concerns about OceanQuest meeting my standards, I could take my business elsewhere. Practically hung up on me. All my alarms were going off. Didn't compute."

But it did—if the man talking to Tommy suspected as I did that two OceanQuest customers had recently been left behind.

At seven, Daniel Meredith called from the consulate in Sydney. "Max, I spoke to the Cairns authorities. They went over to the Emerald Isle. The Brackens checked in, but they never checked out. The maid reported on the fourteenth that their stuff was still in the room. Since they were listed as a checkout, it was moved to storage that afternoon."

"Why didn't the hotel report them missing?"

"Figured they were out somewhere, had car trouble or something of the sort. Then, the way they tell it, they forgot about it."

"The manager told me they checked out." I found I was tapping my pen on the desk. I laid it down and clenched and unclenched my free hand.

"Emerald Isle's policy is to bill out whether the person stops at the desk or not."

"The police look at the luggage?"

"Yeah. Clothes, books, cosmetics, that sort of thing."

"Any diving gear?"

"Nope, no mention of that."

"I have an idea. I'd like your take on it. I think the Brackens went out on a dive trip with OceanQuest on the twelfth and got left behind."

"Scheissa..."

"Any chance they could still be alive?"

"Four days? Not much."

I'd known the answer before I asked it. Still the quick reply was like taking a punch in the gut.

I ended the call from Daniel Meredith and dialed the Brackens. Amy answered halfway through the first ring. I told her only that an official from the American Embassy was in contact with the police, that they were checking on her parents, and that there should be additional information in the morning.

Amy sounded resigned. She didn't ask any questions, which was a relief, because I didn't want to lie to her, but I also didn't want to tell her what I thought had happened until I had more definitive information. Even so, she and Neil probably wouldn't sleep much. For that matter, I didn't think I would either.

Next I called Kelly, who said she'd insisted Amy and Neil come stay until there was more information. They were packing overnight bags and would be there soon. I told her what I suspected.

"Oh no. Alexandra and Ray are wonderful people. I pray you're wrong."

"Don't say anything to the kids yet. The police are still checking."

"Thank you for helping with this. I couldn't think what else to do when they showed up."

"I'm happy to help."

But my involvement would soon end with the news I expected to receive by tomorrow morning. If the Brackens had been left behind, it would be up to the Australian authorities to handle the situation.

That would leave me free to attend to that rapprochement with Todd that Anthony had requested.

~ ~ ~

When Daniel Meredith called the next day, I did a quick calculation. It was five in the morning in Sydney.

"Max, you were right about the Brackens and OceanQuest."

My stomach tightened. It was one thing to pace back and forth in my office coming up with wild-assed guesses; it was a whole other animal to have it confirmed.

"The police talked to Rob McIntyre at OceanQuest last evening. At first, he claimed no way was it possible anyone could be missing, but the police made him pull his records.

The Brackens signed off the boat, but not back on after the last dive on the twelfth."

"Unbelievable." I took a sip of coffee to moisten my throat. It didn't help.

"Yeah. Not to mention criminally incompetent." Daniel's tone was angry.

"What are the police doing about it?"

"A search will start at daybreak. The coast is pretty deserted where the Brackens might be expected to come in. If they did make it to shore, they'd likely have a long walk before they came across someone with a phone."

"Is there a chance they made it to shore, then?"

"Possible, but improbable. Reef's thirty nautical miles out. Current comes on shore, but it's a long swim. On the way in, they'd be facing sharks. In closer to shore, saltwater crocs. All the police expect to find is their gear."

I fought off a wave of nausea. "How did it happen?"

"Like I said. Incompetence. Nobody looked at the sign-out sheets. One of the crew also remembered there were two pairs of shoes on the dock after everyone left the boat. He picked them up, threw them back on board. Figured they belonged to a crew member."

I'd been rubbing my head so hard it hurt. I stopped, refocusing on what Daniel was saying.

"The shoes were still there the next day, along with an unclaimed duffel. The employee mentioned it to McIntyre, who told him no worries, that people leave gear behind all the time. McIntyre also told the police he was out at Castle Rock Reef by himself on the fourteenth. He wasn't looking for the Brackens, of course, since he didn't realize they were missing. But he saw no sign of anything amiss."

"Any publicity on this yet?"

"No. But there will be. Minute the chopper takes off, you can bet the *Courier* will be checking."

~ ~ ~

I called Kelly.

"You've discovered what happened?" she said.

"Yes. They were left behind by the dive boat."

There was silence, then the sound of Kelly taking a breath. "Any chance they could be okay?"

"I'm sorry. Probably not. How do you suggest we handle this? Do you want to tell them?" Coward that I was, I hoped she'd say yes.

"I think it's best if we tell them together. That way you can explain how you found out, as well as what's being done."

"Can you bring them in? I don't have the car with me today."

"Of course. We'll be there in an hour and a half if that's okay?"

"I'll have Cassie make sure my schedule is cleared."

~ ~ ~

I'd never done anything remotely like this before, and I had no idea how best to do it. Luckily Kelly took the lead. After she broke the news that their parents had been left behind on the dive trip, I explained what the authorities were doing.

Amy and Neil were silent after I finished speaking. Then I noticed tears running down Amy's face. Kelly was crying as well, and Neil was blinking rapidly, his arms wrapped around his body. Amy turned and put her arms around him, and they clutched each other, their bodies shaking with the force of their weeping.

Kelly and I looked at each other, and then I left to get Cassie. She made tea, and when it was ready, we went back in. Amy, Neil, and Kelly were standing together at the window. All three had faces that were red and swollen, but they were now calm.

Cassie served the tea. I don't particularly care for hot tea, but I was willing to concede to Cassie's view that a simple thing, like holding a cup, can be a comfort in times of distress.

"What do we do now?" Amy asked. She took an awkward sip then set the cup down.

"We wait. The Australian authorities have begun an air and sea search." I was glad they had that information to hold onto as I thought about what I wasn't telling them—that the authorities didn't expect to find anything except gear.

"If they don't find them, what then?" Neil asked. He'd also put his cup down, and his hands moved in an unconscious washing movement as he spoke.

"We don't need to decide that now."

"I want to be there." Amy spoke with quiet intensity.

"Me, too," Neil said.

I opened my mouth to talk them out of it, then decided if it were someone I loved who was missing, I would find it impossible to sit on the other side of the world awaiting word.

"We want you to come with us," Neil added.

I moved quickly to sidestep the pit that was opening. "I have no standing as an attorney in Australia. Besides, there won't be anything to do, not until the authorities finish the search."

"We need someone who can talk to them," Amy said. "Everyone brushes kids off."

"I hate to be the one to sound a practical note, but you did say you don't have much money. How will you manage your expenses in Australia?"

"We have credit cards to use in case of an emergency," Neil said. "And if this doesn't qualify, what does?"

"So, will you come?" Amy asked, looking desperate.

I glanced at Kelly. She mouthed a silent "please."

"We'll pay whatever your fee is," Neil said.

"Let's not worry about that right now." I was turning into a certifiable bleeding heart who was going to exsanguinate if I didn't knock it off.

Of course, there was another reason to say yes to this trip. Since Sophie left, I'd needed to be busy. A trip to Australia would, at the very least, stop my daily obsessive check to see if she'd written. Would eliminate as well the burst of disappointment each time I discovered she hadn't.

And I'd be going to the same hemisphere. Maybe I could stop by, see her.

"Can we leave today?" Neil said, bouncing me out of my reverie.

I shook my head. "Let's plan on tomorrow. Do you have passports?" I asked.

"We got them last year, for a trip to Europe."

I bowed to the inevitable. "I'll have Cassie make the arrangements."

It was damned uncomfortable having the two of them and Kelly sit there looking at me as if I were some kind of savior.

Any port in a storm, Mom used to say, and that's all I'd be in this case—and a very precarious one at that.

~ ~ ~

After meeting with Amy and Neil to inform them their parents were lost at sea and most likely dead, I almost forgot the deadline to call Anthony with my decision on working with Todd on the Coronado bridge case. The Brackens' troubles made the whole fuss with Todd seem petty and the decision to work or not to work with him trivial. Still, I owed Anthony my answer. I lifted the telephone and dialed his private line.

"Max, figured it had to be you. It's eleven forty-nine. You're cutting it damn close."

"Got hung up. A new case came in. A couple left behind on a dive trip to the Great Barrier Reef. It's doubtful they survived. I just met with their two kids to tell them. It was rough."

"I'm certain it was."

"The Australian authorities have begun a search. The kids are going to Australia because they can't stand the thought of sitting here waiting." There was no reason to keep on talking about the Brackens. Clearly, Anthony wasn't interested.

"That's a natural thing to do. Likely you and I would do the same thing. Now for that decision you owe me."

"I told Amy and Neil I'd go to Australia with them."

There was a beat of silence. "I'm certain they'll understand when you explain why you can't go."

"But I am going." There was more silence at the other end, and I knew I'd blundered on this. Big time. But maybe the situation wasn't irrevocable. I could reassure Anthony of my basic soundness. Negotiate a delay in my reconciliation with Todd.

Anthony pulled my attention back with the clearing of his throat, and I didn't know if I'd checked out of the conversation ten seconds or ten minutes ago. Whichever it was, I simply couldn't manage to say the words I needed to say.

"I'm sorry, Anthony. Don't know how I could shave if I sent them off by themselves. They're just kids."

There was another silence that I let ride. Anthony finally spoke. "You always have been a stubborn bastard, Max." He paused again. "Come see me when you get back."

"Yes. Of course." I had no idea whether I'd just thrown the gold ring in Anthony's face, and he would now hand it to Todd, or whether I'd strengthened my position by refusing to be bullied.

And the wonderful, glorious relief of it was, I didn't give a damn which it was.

~ ~ ~

The following day, I checked *The Australian*'s website. This time I had a hit on the name "Bracken." The entire story was a short paragraph stating that a search and rescue operation for a missing American couple had been initiated over Castle Rock Reef and the coastline north of Cairns. No other details were given.

It was time to call Jake Rutherford, the reporter who wrote the story about the Silver Seas diver. I placed a call to the number Cassie had obtained and left a message. Minutes later, Cassie buzzed to say Rutherford was on the line. I picked up the phone and was startled to hear a woman's voice—a firm, no-nonsense woman's voice.

"Mr. Gildea, Jake Rutherford here. You said you had information on that missing Yank couple. That right?"

What followed, after I fed her the information I wanted her to have, was as thorough and professional a questioning as any cross-examination I'd ever conducted. The voice pegged her as tough, lacking in feminine wiles, and not a kid. The questions indicated she was also bright as hell.

"Amy, Neil, and I are coming to Cairns. I'd appreciate you not spreading that fact around."

"No worries. Don't want to lose my exclusive, do I? I'd like to talk to you when you get here, meet the kids."

"I want to keep the media away."

"I understand. But they're going to be news. Can't stop that from happening. Of course, we don't gang up on you the way the Yank media does. More civilized in Oz."

"Oz?"

"Australia."

Chapter Seventeen
MAX

We left San Francisco at ten in the evening and made landfall in Australia at dawn, thirteen hours later. Shortly after that, the white sails of Sydney's opera house passed under the wing, and minutes later we were on the ground.

Getting through Customs and Immigration was more tedious than difficult, and afterward, I found a newsstand and bought the latest edition of *The Australian*. The story about the Brackens was on the front page. I scanned quickly, looking for information on the search, but there was nothing new.

By the time our flight to Cairns took off, the fatigue of the long, sleepless night had caught up with me. I intermittently dozed as the east coast of Australia spooled out beneath us, mostly brown but with occasional bits of green, and all of it edged in bright blue with a thin fringing of white.

In Cairns, we walked from the terminal into a bright, hot day. A cab took us to the condominium Cassie had rented for our stay. It was located near the downtown on a wide, clean street lined with palms alternating with melaleuca trees. I'd decided on the condo because it would be more spacious and less impersonal than a hotel, and it would allow me to keep a weather eye on Amy and Neil.

After we dropped off our luggage, the cabbie took us to police headquarters, driving past buildings that were mostly no more than three to four stories in height and painted, for practical reasons, in tropical pastels. I made a mental note to buy sunglasses.

The Cairns police station was adjacent to the courthouse, a block off one of the main downtown streets. When we arrived, we were escorted to the office of the police chief, one Oliver Geoghan. He stood to greet us. "Amy, Neil, Mr. Gildea, I'd say we're glad to welcome you to Australia, but these are not happy circumstances, are they?"

"Have you found anything?" Amy asked.

"You've seen the newspapers this morning?" Geoghan responded.

"I bought a copy in Sydney," and I was pleasantly surprised by the accuracy of Rutherford's account. Having the facts mangled was an occupational hazard for any attorney forced to speak to a reporter. Additional points to Rutherford for getting her hands on a picture of the Brackens wearing shorts and sun hats and standing next to the gangway of a boat.

"The article gave a good overview of how things stand so far," Geoghan said. "We've had divers out at the reef location OceanQuest used on the twelfth. We've also had aircraft flying grids over the ocean between the reef and the shore and a helicopter checking the shoreline where your folks or their equipment might drift in. And we've notified boat operators to keep a lookout."

"You haven't found anything at all?" Neil's voice sounded strained.

"No. I'm very sorry. You need to understand. It's doubtful we're going to find them alive this many days out." Geoghan spoke gently, but no doubt it was more difficult for Amy and Neil to hear it from him than when I'd said the same thing.

"You can't stop searching." Tears thickened Amy's voice. "You can't give up. Not yet."

Neil gripped her hand.

"I said it was unlikely," Geoghan said. "We haven't yet reached the point where we can say it's impossible. We plan to keep the search going until we're certain there's no chance they survived. If we find anything, we'll inform you first."

I provided Geoghan with our local address and phone number, and we walked back out the way we came in. The lobby, which had been mostly deserted when we arrived, now had a number of occupants. One of them caught my eye—a woman with short blondish hair, sitting by the exit. She was leaning forward with an elbow propped on one knee, chewing on a finger while she talked into a phone. A large, scruffy handbag sat on the floor next to her feet.

She looked up, and seeing us, ended the call and shoved the phone into a holder on her waist. She pushed a heavy lock of hair out of her eyes and stood up. "Mr. Gildea? G'day. I'm Jake Rutherford. How're you going?" She held out a narrow hand and waited, while I shuffled my crutch out of the way in order to shake it. While I did, I struggled to readjust my mental image.

After dealing with Rutherford over the phone, I expected her to be a spinster type, drab and businesslike, certainly not...well, not so tall, for one thing. The shorts she was wearing made her legs appear five feet long.

She shook my hand with a firm grip and gave me a quick assessing look before switching her attention to Amy and Neil. "G'day. Jake Rutherford with *The Australian*. I'm real sorry about your folks. It's criminal, what's happened. I understand you're tired, but I'd like to talk to you. I plan to nail OceanQuest's ass to the wall."

Amy and Neil gave me questioning looks before shaking Jake's hand.

I spoke firmly. "You're right. We are tired. You and I can meet, but later."

She lifted her eyebrows, but after a beat said, "Good-oh. How about we do dinner. At the Thai Chai in the lobby of the Natsuku at six?"

I nodded, acceptance mixed with resignation.

"Here, let me give you my cell number. Call anytime. I sleep with it."

I took the card she handed me, shoved it in my pocket, and then the kids and I walked out. Jake came out right behind us. She'd added huge sunglasses and a straw hat to her ensemble. She smiled, waved, and loped past us to a small red mini. The phone was once again attached to her ear, and she was talking in quick bursts.

"So, they do say g'day," Amy said, watching Jake.

"Yeah. I thought it was a joke," Neil said.

"She's weird," Amy said.

Weird wasn't the word I would choose for Jake although it fit. But what I thought in those first moments was that this was someone Cassie would give a two-thumbs-up.

~ ~ ~

I had to cancel dinner with Jake, after Oliver Geoghan called and asked us to come back to the police station. He also suggested we use the back door. I understood why, when we reached the courthouse. There were two news vans with satellite dishes attached to their roofs parked across the street.

The kids groaned. "We don't have to talk to them, do we, Max?" Nerves made Amy's voice uneven. They'd both already told me they wanted nothing to do with reporters.

"We'll try to avoid them. If we can't, just say 'no comment' and let me handle it." Talking to the media wasn't one of my favorite things either, and unfortunately, the crutches would make me instantly recognizable once they found out who I was.

Inside, we were escorted to Geoghan's office, where we took the chairs we'd sat in that morning.

"Afraid we're going to have our telly friends cluttering up our lobby and the street for the foreseeable future." Geoghan shook his head. "Getting beat on the story by a newspaper reporter has them all mad as cut snakes."

I'd never heard that expression before, but I could guess what it meant. Geoghan sat forward and scanned each of our faces before speaking again. "This afternoon, one of our choppers spotted an air tank on a beach north of Port Douglas. They landed and retrieved it. A few minutes ago, Rob McIntyre identified it as one of OceanQuest's tanks."

"Does that mean our parents made it to shore?" Amy's voice was eager.

It was painful to watch her grab at this tiny ray of hope. She and Neil seemed to be great kids...bright, friendly, and genuinely fond of each other and their parents. Under different circumstances, it would be a pleasure knowing them.

Geoghan shuffled some papers and spoke with obvious reluctance. "It's more likely your folks jettisoned their tanks, and the current carried this one to shore. It has given us an approximate fix on where they might have come in, though. We've sent a boat out to check along that stretch of coast. We're also doing a ground search in the same area."

"If the tank made it, why wouldn't our folks?" Amy said.

Geoghan glanced at me. "We hope they did. That's why we're upping the search in that area." Geoghan's voice was gentle, but his eyes looked tired.

"What are you doing about the media?" I asked.

"I'll be briefing them on a daily basis until we find something definitive, or we close down the search. Do you want to be present for that?"

"We'd prefer to keep a low profile."

"Well, they don't know you're here yet, and if that's what you want, we'll try to keep it that way."

We left by the back door, returning to where the cabbie was waiting for us, while Geoghan went to give the press their briefing. Jake was leaning against the wall by the exit.

"Not nice to cancel on a lady, Max."

My first reaction to seeing her—pleasure—was quickly overlaid with annoyance that she had once again located us so easily. "Aren't you supposed to be at the briefing?"

"I'm off the story. Fair cheesed off our senior guy, Mulroney that I got the contact. I'm supposed to stick to obits and local color."

"Why are you still here then?"

"I'm on holiday. And someone owes me a dinner."

"Sorry." I prepared to walk past her.

"Max, it's okay," Amy said. "We can get back to the condo. You go ahead."

I looked from Jake to the kids. They seemed okay, for the moment, and Jake's article had helped to light a fire under the authorities. It meant I was in her debt. A quick dinner ought to take care of that. "I guess you're driving," I told her.

Given the early hour, the dining room at the Thai Chai was mostly deserted. We were seated at a table in the corner, and we ordered glasses of white wine.

"So, what's the briefing about?" Jake asked.

"An air tank's been found. Geoghan thinks it was one used by the Brackens."

"Where was it found?"

"North of Port Douglas."

"They were going to call off the search yesterday, you know. The only reason they didn't was the publicity after my article."

It was good to have confirmation my strategy had worked, and humility was obviously not one of Jake's failings.

"So, what did Oliver make of finding the tank?" she asked.

"He said the Brackens likely jettisoned it, and it floated in on the current."

A waitress set down our drinks. "Are you ready to order?"

I glanced at the menu. "Chicken basil, medium hot for me."

"Same for me," Jake said, without picking up her menu.

The young woman walked away, and Jake looked across at me. "You a diver, Max?"

I shook my head.

"Okay, stop me if you already know this. When the Brackens surfaced and found the boat gone, they would have been wearing wet suits, weight belts, buoyancy control devices called BCDs, and air tanks. The BCDs would keep them afloat, and the wet suits would keep them warm." She watched to see if I was following.

"Their biggest problem is if they panic. They're relatively safe if they stay right where they are, in the shallows near the reef. Best way to do that is to attach themselves to the anchor buoy used by OceanQuest. Then hang out until they're rescued."

"Why not try to swim ashore?"

"As soon as they start swimming, they up the area to be searched by hundreds of square kilometers. It would take incredible luck to spot two heads bobbing in a lot of empty ocean."

"It sounds like you have some experience with that."

She glanced at me, cocking an eyebrow. "I've been through military survival training. And I was the dive master at Silver Seas for five years."

The dive master part didn't surprise me, but the military part did. Or, come to think of it, it didn't, given her confident demeanor and no-nonsense approach.

"I would think most people would head for shore right away."

She shrugged. "I suppose that might work."

"You think there's a chance they made it in?"

She didn't answer.

"Someone told me if the sharks didn't get them the crocs would."

She looked up, her face tight with contained emotion. "Too right. The kids know that?"

"No."

"Then I'd keep the newspapers away from them, and don't let them watch the news on the telly. Soon as that lot finishes chewing over the air tank, you can bet they'll start speculating. And it won't be pretty. I've got to stay in the background, since I'm not official. But I think I've a shot at a bloody good exclusive when this plays out. That is, if I convince you to only talk to me."

"Why would I do that?" I leaned back and studied her.

Dark blue eyes meet mine. A jaunty spray of freckles on her nose contrasted with the tough, direct expression in those eyes.

"Two reasons. I'll handle your material honestly, and I'll keep speculation to a minimum. Besides, I'm better looking than the guys." She grinned, and I realized why she was so appealing. She had the same irrepressible, brash quality that is Cassie's most attractive as well as her most irritating characteristic.

The food arrived, and Jake took a bite then set her chopsticks down. "The guys working the dailies and the telly, they're hot for angles. The story's interesting only when something's happening. The search turns up more gear...they'll salivate over that for a while. But sooner or later they'll start delving into everything about the Brackens from what kind of marriage they had to...well, you name it."

I continued to eat without commenting. This was beginning to sound like a sales pitch.

"I'm interested in the same thing I think you are, and that's finding out what happened and why. We work together, we have a chance to accomplish that. If we do find out what happened, we can help make sure it doesn't happen again."

No doubt about it, she was good. Of course, there was a slim chance she was sincere, which meant continuing to cooperate with her could be a win-win situation. I took a bite and chewed slowly, thinking through what I wanted to accomplish here. It wouldn't hurt to have an ally, especially one familiar with the local terrain, although the reporter-news source relationship was always tricky.

"You don't think the Brackens are still alive?"

"No. Sorry, Max, I don't."

It had been seven days and counting. I remembered the description of Sophie after three days. Of course, she'd been injured, and the conditions had been worse, but she'd also had a raft.

"What's your plan?" I asked.

"You in?" She pushed her hair back, giving me an eager look.

"How do I know I can trust you?"

"Bloody hell." One of her hands came up in a quick, choppy gesture. "You said you'd been in contact with Daniel Meredith. Wasn't he the one who suggested you call me?"

I shook my head. "I saw your story about Silver Seas losing and then recovering a diver. Excellent piece of writing, by the way."

She blushed, which was a surprise given how hard she'd been working to appear unflappable.

"You know Daniel then?"

"You could say that."

"And if I asked Daniel for a recommendation, what would he say?"

"He'll tell you I'm a good reporter. Honest. Hardworking." She was having trouble meeting my eyes.

"Exactly how well do you know him?"

"We lived together for a year." She stared at her plate, chasing a piece of chicken with furious concentration.

And I was thinking, *damn*. Although why it should make a bit of difference to me what this woman's domestic arrangements were was a mystery I had no intention of exploring.

110

I doubted she'd lie about Daniel giving her a good recommendation. Too easy to check. Unless she was counting on me not checking.

I decided to call her bluff. "Tell you what. I'll give Daniel a call in the morning. If everything you've said checks out, I'll consider working with you."

"Look, we don't have much time. We've already lost a week. Let me get Daniel on the phone right now."

"Want to tell me what you're planning first?"

"I prefer you talk to Daniel first."

I stopped eating and looked at her. She met my eyes for a time without blinking. Definitely another Cassie, which meant she wasn't going to budge. I sighed. "Okay."

"Good-oh. I'll just pop into the loo, give you two a chance to chat." She pulled the phone out, punched in a number and then handed it to me. "Just push the SEND button and it'll ring. Back in five."

She slid out of her chair, collected her bag, and strode across the room. She was out of sight before the phone clicked through. Daniel answered on the second ring.

"Jake?"

"Sorry, it's Max Gildea. Jake suggested I call."

"Huh? How did you two meet?"

"I saw a story she wrote about a missing diver and called her. She's here in Cairns. I need to ask you about her. She said you'd provide a reference."

"Why does she need a reference?"

"She's proposing we work together on the Brackens' disappearance."

"Umm. Okay. A reference. Well, Jake won't lie to you. She's a heck of a fine reporter. Accurate, opinionated, bright, and tough. Stubborn as a piece of old mutton. Will that do?"

"Yes. Thanks."

"How is she?"

I thought I'd detected a strain in Daniel's voice. With this last tentative question, I was sure of it.

"She's fine. Angry about the Brackens."

"Yeah, well, she would be. Give her my best, will you?"

"Sure." I clicked off and set the phone back at Jake's place. Not hard to figure out who ended that relationship.

A couple of minutes later, Jake returned and raised an eyebrow in question. She'd combed her hair and freshened her lipstick. Still, despite the improvements to her appearance, something was missing. For the first time since we met, her confidence had slipped. It was clear she wasn't sure how it had gone with Daniel.

"Daniel says hello." I took a bite of my meal.

She moved her chopsticks around in her rice.

I let her hang a moment longer before letting her off the hook. "He said you're honest and a good reporter."

The self-assurance came back, but when she reached for her wine, I noticed bitten fingernails, a sign the woman might not be as confident inside as the image she attempted to project on the outside.

"Does that mean we're a team?" she asked.

I nodded.

"Good-oh." She put her wine down and leaned her elbows on the table, giving me a direct look.

Sales 101: Step 1. Look the prospect in the eye.

"Here's the deal," she said, her tone earnest. "Everyone else is going to be chasing this story from the search and recovery angle, at least for the next few days. So, who's watching the store? I mean, who's figuring out how it happened.

"I've been nosing around a bit, and I've heard that Rob McIntyre told the police he wouldn't be a bit surprised to learn the Brackens used his cruise to carry out a suicide pact."

"You've got to be kidding me."

"Nope. McIntyre's going to pull out all the stops. If the suicide angle doesn't work, it will be some financial plot."

"There isn't a shred of evidence any of that's true." At least, I hoped there wasn't, for Amy and Neil's sake.

"Doesn't matter as long as it deflects attention from OceanQuest's incompetence. My theory. Most reporters are frustrated novelists. Speculating in cases like this is our only outlet. If Rob McIntyre feeds us the lines, the others will run with them, no worries."

"I thought you said the press here was more civilized."

"Did I?"

"Yes. You did."

"Didn't want to scare you off, did I." She concentrated on her chicken basil for a moment, but then she looked up and grinned. "Deprecation is an Aussie sport, love. You better get used to it if you're going to stick around."

"What is it you want to do?"

Her expression sobered. "Go out to Castle Rock Reef. See if we can locate the weight belts."

"I thought divers already checked there."

"They were looking for big stuff. Bodies, tanks. Besides, they didn't really expect to find anything. Self-fulfilling prophecies and all that."

"So, what good will it do? Finding the weights."

"They'd need to get rid of the weights right away, so they could swim more easily. Finding them would mean they didn't intend to commit suicide. It might also help pinpoint where they surfaced. That will help us figure out if they got disoriented, or if a current pulled them away from the boat. Not much current around Castle Rock, but we still need to consider it."

As I listened to the confident, knowledgeable way she made her points, my doubts about her overall sincerity started to wane. "Sounds like you're familiar with that area."

"Silver Seas also uses it as one of their primary dive spots."

"Maybe you can explain something for me. Is it reasonable that the Brackens would finish the dive so much later than the rest of the group?"

She shrugged. "The length of time a tank lasts depends on several things. How deep the dive is, the fitness of the diver, and the amount of current the diver has to work against. If the Brackens were competent divers, they could have stretched their tanks for considerably longer times than less experienced divers."

"How do we get to the reef?"

"Gavin Aylliard at Silver Seas has agreed to help."

"So, why ask me to come along? Sounds like you and Gavin can handle it."

The waitress showed up to clear our plates. I looked at Jake, and she studied the wall behind me until the waitress finished and walked away. "Gavin's willing to do the run whether you come or not, but I'm hoping you'll be willing to pay for the petrol. We'll be using Gavin's small cat, so it won't be much, but I spent myself into a hole with the ticket to come here. If I get a good story out of it, likely I'll be able to shame my editor into paying part of that, but at the moment..." She shrugged. "You can keep an eye on the boat, while we dive. Keep expenses down."

"I don't know squat about boats."

"But your cases..." She lapsed into silence, looking so much like a kid who'd just been caught doing something she shouldn't, it made me laugh.

"You checked on me," I said, once I'd caught my breath.

"Of course, I did." She sounded irritated. "My editor isn't going to print a story from a completely unknown source. Running a check is standard procedure."

"Look, I've got an idea. Why don't we take Amy and Neil with us. They're both certified divers. It'll give them something to do. I'll even pay for a crew member to run the boat." She perked up at that.

After I paid our dinner bill, we walked out to her car where I stopped her before I climbed in. "Just one more thing. Where we're staying. That's off the record."

"Sure. Tropic Breezes condo, right?"

"How do you know that?"

"I never reveal a confidential source." Her expression was solemn, but I could see she enjoyed getting the best of me.

Chapter Eighteen
MAX

This morning at seven, the kids and I met Jake at the entrance to the marina, and she led us to Aylliard's catamaran. Gavin Aylliard was a man about sixty, thin and fit, with curly gray hair and sun-roughened skin. He'd brought along his son, Randall, a younger version of himself, to help with the boat. Jake performed the introductions.

"Welcome aboard. Shoes off, of course." Gavin spoke briskly.

"Oh." Amy's hand came up to cover her mouth as she looked at me with obvious chagrin.

"It's okay." I smiled to reassure her and then turned to Gavin. "I'm afraid I can't manage without the shoes. Artificial legs." I glanced over at Jake.

She was handing gear to Randall, but there was a quick flash of surprise on her face and a slight hitch in her movement as she picked up another air tank.

"That's okay, mate," Gavin said. "No worries." He spoke easily, without hesitation, as if he dealt with this sort of thing all the time.

After loading the gear, Randall and Gavin helped me board the boat. Without their help, the step from unmoving dock to gently bobbing boat could have been disastrous. Once aboard, I moved to a spot under the awning and sat.

Amy and Neil showed Gavin the diving certifications they'd had faxed to the condo the night before, and he sorted through a pile of wet suits to find their sizes. Jake came aboard and disappeared below decks as I sat watching Amy and Neil get outfitted. Then Jake popped back on deck, carrying a cup. "Coffee, Max?"

"Thanks. I'd better not." No way would I be able to negotiate the stairs to the head.

"Both legs artificial?" she asked, sitting next to me.

"Yep."

"It must have been tough, learning to walk."

The direction of her questions made me uncomfortable, but I could shut her down by not answering. "It was. I've had the legs only six months. Probably be a year before I'll be able to graduate from these crutches to a cane." So, why was I answering?

She cocked her head. "Accident?"

"Drunk driver."

She'd been facing me. Now she turned and sat back and looked out at the water. "Do you swim?" She glanced at me, and I nodded, relieved at the change of subject.

"You should take a look when we get to the reef."

"I'm not wearing a swimsuit." And even if I were, no way was I taking my legs off in front of this woman. She'd probably watch the whole process and then ask another slew of questions.

~ ~ ~

I hadn't totally bought into Jake's assertion that the Brackens' best shot at surviving was to stay near the reef until I saw the miles of heaving water that separated that reef from the mainland of Australia.

The catamaran was equipped with two powerful outboards that pushed us along at a rapid clip, but it still took over an hour for us to reach the place where the Brackens had presumably been left.

It would have been a very long swim.

As we approached the reef, Jake and the kids donned wet suits and checked their equipment, and less than fifteen minutes after Randall hooked the anchor buoy, the four divers were in the water. Gavin and Neil paired up to search one area, and Jake paired with Amy to search another.

With the divers away, Randall sat on the bow to keep watch. Since it was hazardous for me to move around the

116

boat, I stayed put, looking out over water that shaded from blue, where we were anchored, to pale turquoise, over the reef a hundred feet or so away. If I were here on vacation, *and Jake wasn't around*, I'd definitely be ready to doff the legs and take a look.

I was dozing, when the bump of gear against the diving platform jarred me awake. Randall moved to the stern and helped Neil remove his tank.

Neil came into the well of the boat. "It was totally awesome, Max. Hard to believe there can be so many different kinds of fish and corals. And the colors are way cool."

"But no weights."

Neil stopped rubbing his hair dry with the towel and looked up, his face stricken. "You must think I'm a jerk, going on about how beautiful it is when Mom and Dad were left out here."

"Not at all. Better to focus on something positive."

"I guess. Anyway, thanks for letting us come along today. Sitting around the condo was getting to us."

"Hey, Neil, is it?" Randall said, from his spot on the bow.

"Yeah."

"Before you take that wet suit off, why don't you give snorkeling a go. Over there, where the water's light green. I'll blow a toot on the horn when you need to come back to the boat."

"Gee, thanks." Neil picked up his mask, a snorkel, and fins and climbed down to the dive platform. He dived in and began swimming strongly toward the area Randall had pointed out.

"Thanks. He needs to keep busy."

"Too right."

In the next twenty minutes, first Amy, and then Jake and Gavin, arrived back at the dive platform. Randall helped remove tanks and gear. I could tell from their faces they hadn't found anything.

"Where's Neil?" Amy asked.

"Over there." I pointed to the reef where Neil was swimming back and forth in a grid pattern.

Just then, Neil stopped swimming and began yelling and waving his arms. We couldn't hear what he was saying, but clearly he was excited. Gavin moved quickly, jumping back into the water towing a life ring. With a lurch of panic, I realized Neil might be in trouble. We all watched silently until Gavin reached Neil. Once he did, he turned and made an arm signal to Randall.

"Boy's fine," Randall said. "Maybe he found something."

Jake and Amy stood together in the stern, craning to see what was going on. Gavin and Neil disappeared underwater, and when they bobbed up, they draped something over the life ring Gavin had towed out. Then they turned and swam back to the boat.

As the two approached, I felt frustrated at not being able to join the rest of the group in the stern. Jake was chewing on a finger with a look of deep concentration, and Amy had her hands up to her face. Gavin and Neil reached the back of the boat and handed up what they'd found to Randall.

I waited impatiently for Neil and Gavin to climb aboard and for someone to tell me what they'd discovered. Then Amy moved, and I saw it was a white square.

I finally caught Jake's attention. "What is it?"

"A diver's slate attached to a weight belt. And there's writing on it."

Gavin detached the slate from the weight belt and handed it to Jake who carried it to where I was sitting. The kids came and sat next to me, while Randall stowed gear and Gavin changed clothes. The message on the slate was from the Brackens, who'd conserved space by using a shorthand like that on vanity license plates back in the States. The top of the slate was labeled 1 of 2. As we deciphered it, Jake wrote down our conclusions.

We were so engrossed, we jumped when Randall spoke quietly from the bow, where he was once again sitting. "Company's coming. We're going to have to move along."

Although the other boat was still a speck on the horizon, Randall unhooked us from the buoy, and Gavin started the engines, while the rest of us continued to work on the slate. When we finished, Jake read the message aloud.

Alexandra/Ray Bracken, San Francisco, USA. Tel: 333-444-5555. OceanQuest Pt Douglas 4/12/96. Last dive, surface 15:06. Boat gone. Stay at OQ buoy. Use straps/weight belts to anchor.

4/13 Boat on horizon. Small plane, noon.

4/14 Weak, hungry, thirsty, but okay. Will place slate #1 on reef, keep 2 with us. No chance swim now. 10:00 a.m.

Amy, Neil, call Grandpa. We love you. Be happy. Mom & Dad

"But why aren't they here, then?" Amy said, her voice breaking. "They must have tried to swim, right? They've got to be okay, don't they? We're going to find them, right?" Her voice skittered into a high, thin note full of panic and awareness. "Please. They're okay, aren't they?"

I put an arm around her, and she collapsed against me in a storm of weeping. I looked at Jake, hoping for some word of optimism, but her expression was somber.

Neil looked at Jake as well, tears running down his face. "You think they're dead, don't you."

Jake's head moved in a quick nod. Just as quickly, she moved next to Neil and put her arm around him.

Jake held Neil, and I held Amy, while the two cried out their pain at the loss they were only beginning to acknowledge.

Meanwhile, Gavin steered along the inside of the reef away from the oncoming boat. After we were a distance from the buoy, he throttled back.

As I comforted Amy, I also thought about her question. Why weren't the Brackens, plus another slate, found attached to the buoy when the rescue boat went to check, or...more to the point, why didn't Rob McIntyre find them when he went out on the fourteenth?

"Here's what's on the slate." Jake handed Gavin her notebook.

When he finished reading, he nodded and handed the notebook back. "We better get this to Oliver."

"Did you check around the buoy?" I asked. We hadn't yet figured out the message when Randall spotted the other boat.

"Yeah. I took a look when we first went in the water." Gavin cleared his throat. "Nothing hanging off it and no weights on the bottom anywhere near it. But they may have been covered with sand."

Amy and Neil continued to huddle together with Jake and me anchoring them. Their bout of weeping had eased, but now Amy was white-faced and shivery, and Neil looked strained. I kept forgetting how young they were. Sitting there, still wet from their dive, beginning to accept the fact their parents were dead, they looked even younger.

After a while, first Neil, and then Amy, went below to change into dry clothes. Jake changed as well. We knew that after we docked, we'd be going straight to the police station. Jake surprised me by not pulling out her phone and calling her paper as soon as we came in range of the coast. It was a sensational story, and she'd earned it.

~ ~ ~

The policeman who let us in the back door told us only two reporters were left staking out the lobby. We waited in Oliver's office, not talking, until he arrived wearing a Saturday uniform of shorts and a T-shirt.

He listened intently as Gavin and Jake reported what we'd found. Then he asked the question I wanted answered. "So, what do you figure? They give up on the buoy?"

"I doubt it," Gavin said. He pointed at the slate. "That tells me they were smart. They didn't panic. They worked through the possibilities, and they understood the buoy was their best shot. Besides, by the third day, they would have been too weak to try to swim. They knew leaving the buoy then meant certain death. They as good as tell us that."

"If they didn't leave the buoy, you should have found—"

"We didn't." Jake spoke, cutting Oliver off.

He looked over at me and the kids for the first time since Gavin and Jake began their report. "Okay. Gavin, I need you to stay, pinpoint for me where you found the slate. Jake, I'd appreciate a hold on any calls to your paper."

"You banishing me back to the ranks, Oliver?" Her voice sounded strained.

"I'll give you at least a half-hour heads-up before we break this, but I want a chance to talk to Rob McIntyre before he hears about the slate."

"You thinking what I am?" she said.

"Wouldn't doubt it."

"Okay. I'll keep the lid on. Nail the bastard."

"Too right," Oliver said.

Amy and Neil followed the last exchange the way one would a tennis match, their heads snapping back and forth between Oliver and Jake.

"You think Rob McIntyre killed our parents," Neil said.

Oliver cocked an eyebrow at Jake, who answered Neil. "There may be another explanation. But it's a strong possibility." Her tone was gentle, her eyes troubled.

The room was silent until Oliver pushed his chair back. With a sigh, he said he'd better get to work locating McIntyre.

Jake held out her card. "Your word, Oliver."

"You have it, Jake. No worries."

We left the way we came, avoiding the front lobby, and I invited Jake to join us at the condo for lunch. Afterward, the kids went to the pool, while Jake and I continued to sit at the table.

"Thanks for holding the story."

"Yeah. Well, it's going to get bigger." The brashness was back, but it no longer fooled me. I'd seen the way she reacted to the discovery of the slate and how gentle she'd been with Amy and Neil.

"What do you think happened?" I asked.

"I think when that employee went to Rob with talk of leftover shoes and dive bags, he didn't believe it at first. But then, I expect he checked the sign-out sheets. And that made him wonder enough he took a trip to the reef to check. His mistake was telling the police he was back there the morning of the fourteenth. The slate tells us they were alive at ten. So, yeah, I think he killed them." Jake pushed her empty plate away and pressed patterns into the placemat with her spoon.

"But why? Why not rescue them?"

"Who knows?" She shrugged. "Perhaps he panicked. When a person panics he may do things he'd never do under ordinary circumstances. But I don't really know."

"What I don't understand is why they weren't rescued sooner."

"The day after they were left, OceanQuest used other sites, and no other operators went to Castle Rock either." She gave up on the spoon and sat with her elbows on the table, head propped on her hands, speaking in a detached tone.

"Daniel Meredith was right."

She raised her eyebrows in question.

"You are a good reporter."

"I don't feel very good right now."

"Means you're human."

"Yeah." She stood and started stacking the dishes without looking at me. "You know, you're not what I expected."

"What did you expect?"

"A tall poppy."

I frowned. "Tall poppy?"

"You know. Heavy gold watch, big belly, loud talk about who you know and how we'd all better watch out."

Max the ass. I preferred tall poppy.

"I realize you Yanks aren't all like that, but..." She let the statement dangle, while she carried the plates over to the dishwasher.

"You can leave that, Jake. We'll get it later."

She ignored me, making another trip to pick up glasses.

"You aren't what I expected either," I said.

"What did you expect?"

"For starters, a man."

"Actually, my name is Joanna Katherine." She wrinkled her nose in apparent distaste. "My father started calling me JK. That morphed into Jake."

"Joanna Kate." I liked it. The name fit the woman I'd seen comforting Neil, a softer, gentler woman than the one named Jake. "I'm not that crazy about my name either. Franklin Delano."

"The perfect name for a tall poppy." She gave me a crooked smile. "So, where did the Max come from?"

"Childhood nickname." I finished drinking my water and handed her the glass, remembering the last person who had asked me that. Sophie. I let that memory slide away. "Were you a tomboy?"

"I was," she said.

No surprise. She didn't appear to be the kind of girl who would stand on the sidelines, simpering. Easier to picture her all long legs and skinny arms shimmying up a tree on a dare.

She finished clearing the table, came back, and sat down. "You feel like walking, Max? I'm tired of being cooped up."

"I don't walk very fast. You'd be better on your own."

"I'd like the company."

We stopped by the pool to tell the kids what we were doing, and then we climbed into Jake's mini for the short run over to the esplanade by the inner harbor. The day was another hot, bright one. The partially shaded walkway was broad and smooth, easy going for me, although Jake had to shorten her stride to match my pace.

"I'm curious, Max. How did you happen to get involved in this case?"

"Why do you ask?"

"It just doesn't seem like the kind of case the person who defended the *Alejandro* would take on."

Damn. No wonder she expected me to be an ass. The *Alejandro* established my reputation as someone good at limiting the liability of a tanker company after an oil spill. It was a reputation I no longer wanted to claim. "The Brackens are friends and neighbors of my brother and sister-in-law."

"So, why did you choose maritime law?"

"This is beginning to sound like an interview."

"Sorry. Bad habit. I always want to know what makes people tick. Most people like to talk about themselves." She shrugged. "You can tell me to take a flying gander if you don't want to answer."

"I thought it would be more interesting than estates and divorces."

"You married?"

"No." The woman was nothing if not direct. Because she was a reporter? Or perhaps she was a reporter because she had a talent for directness. Chicken and egg. Always an interesting conundrum.

"Divorced?"

"Yes."

"Because of your legs?"

Okay. Enough. She'd had her fun. Now it was my turn. "How about you. You married?"

"No."

"Divorced?"

"No."

"What did you do in the military?" As long as I asked the questions, I didn't have to answer them.

"I was in counterintelligence."

I felt a quick spurt of admiration for the Australian military for recognizing it was where Jake belonged. "How does someone go from military intelligence to reporting?"

I glanced at her just in time to catch a look that she quickly suppressed. "I got my start when I wrote an article for the Cairns paper about a couple of my friends who work on the Captain Cook cruise ship. One was a former missile defense specialist who now chops vegetables. The other, a gunnery instructor, is a cabin steward."

That fleeting expression, not to mention the detailed answer, clued me that this was a sensitive area, one worth exploring further. "Don't buy it," I said.

She gave me a sharp look. Then she looked away, and I felt that small frisson of excitement that comes when a query hits its mark.

"Okay. I thought...this may sound arrogant. I thought I might be able to make a difference."

Yep. Hit a nerve. She'd even forgotten to walk at my pace. "Joanna Kate."

She stopped and turned to face me.

"You're walking too fast."

"Sorry." She stood waiting for me.

I'd been pushing to keep up with Jake, and my muscles were sending out warning twinges. "Can we sit a minute?"

She nodded, and we made our way to a nearby bench in the shade of a large ficus tree. A cool breeze came off the water.

I shifted, stretching out my back and thigh muscles. "Made that difference yet?" I asked.

She looked down at her hands. "This story. Finding out what really happened..." She lifted her gaze to the water. "This morning, when we found the slate, I felt...useful. Now all I can think is how difficult it is for Amy and Neil. And if I use this..." She stopped, and I waited. "How can I use a dead person to get ahead?"

The silence stretched as I thought about Jake's question. There was no good answer, but she was missing a key point. "What you did, Jake, you helped Amy and Neil get answers. And if McIntyre did kill the Brackens, very likely he'll pay. It's a good thing you did."

She sighed. "Funny, isn't it. We think we know ourselves, and then something happens, and we find we had no idea..."

Yeah. Real funny. A relief when her phone rang before I had to come up with a response.

"Rutherford. Yeah, he's right here." She handed me the phone. "It's Oliver. He wants to talk to you first."

"Max, we've just finished with McIntyre. His story is he went back out after that employee alerted him to the possibility the Brackens were left behind. He arrived about noon, claims he found them hooked to the buoy, already dead. He panicked. Took the bodies out to sea and dumped them."

"What are you charging him with?" I wondered if Oliver had as much difficulty buying the fact the Brackens were alive and able to place the slate on the reef at ten and be dead by twelve as I did.

"Murder," he said.

"Good."

"Let me talk to Jake."

I handed the phone to her, and she stood and paced while she and Oliver talked. That call ended, and she immediately dialed another number. All I caught was, "I need at least eight hundred words on the front page," as she turned away.

She paced and talked for over five minutes, ending the conversation twenty feet away. She slipped the phone into its holder and came back. "Do you mind, Max? I need to take you back. I have to get this story in."

Joanna Kate the philosopher had reverted to Jake the journalist, and I was left trying to decide whether that was a relief or a disappointment.

Chapter Nineteen
MAX

Jake's exclusive appeared on the front page of *The Australian*, and the story was the lead on all the Australian networks as well as CNN International. I kept the paper away from the kids and only turned on the television after they went out to the pool.

They were having a tough time. They both kept swiping at their eyes, and their voices, even when they were talking about something like what to have for breakfast, were hoarse with tears.

Late in the afternoon, Jake showed up on our doorstep. "I'm here to ask you something," she said, declining an invitation to come inside. "Gavin's suggested we go back to the dive site tomorrow. For a memorial service. He sent me to ask if Amy and Neil want to go."

"I do," Amy said, from behind me. "Now that we know what happened."

"Me too," Neil added.

"Good-oh. I'll tell Gavin. Oh, and what kind of minister do you want?"

If a lump wasn't blocking my throat, I might have smiled and said we preferred chocolate, since Jake had made it sound as if ministers came in flavors.

"We're Episcopalian," Amy answered.

"I'll get Gavin to see about arranging for a priest then. I'll give you a call later to finalize."

I was pretty sure Jake was the one who'd thought of the memorial service. I was glad she had.

I called Kelly that evening with an update, and she said she'd contact Amy and Neil's grandfather to be there to meet them when they returned from Australia.

~ ~ ~

For the memorial service, we met at the Cairns marina and boarded Gavin's catamaran for the second time. Having learned that Neil and Amy were in Cairns, members of the media were staking out the entrance to the marina, and I had to give the crutches and my elbows a bit of extra swing to clear a path.

Gavin and an elderly priest were already aboard the cat, and Jake arrived right after we did. Gavin cast off, and we headed out. I could tell the kids felt battered after their run-in with the press.

The priest invited them to sit beside him to plan the service. Amy sat and wrapped her arms around herself. The priest gave her shoulder a squeeze, and she relaxed slightly. Neil, on the priest's other side, had a bleak look on his face.

Jake came to sit next to me. "I talked to Rainforest Adventures. If the kids want to take the tour, there'll be no charge. And they're refunding the Brackens' money."

We cleared the harbor, and the low rumble of the engines shifted to a roar. Jake moved closer, so we could continue to talk. "Oliver found out why McIntyre panicked. Said he was afraid since the Brackens were Americans they'd sue him, take everything. Go figure. He's going to lose a lot more than they could have taken away with a suit."

"Your basic unintended consequence. Did Oliver find out about the second slate?"

"Yeah. Rob says he glanced at it, didn't bother to try to decipher it. Sank it with the rest of the gear and the bodies."

"So, what happens next?"

"Police divers will try to recover the bodies. But even if they don't, with the talking Rob's doing, the only possible defense he has left is insanity. I expect he'll plead guilty. After that..." She shrugged. "Everything will go back to normal. Except, operators going out to the reef will bloody well pay more attention to their head counts and sign-in sheets."

I looked toward Amy and Neil, who were bent over the bible the priest was holding, Amy scrubbing her eyes with her hands.

"You know, a story about the memorial service with a picture would make an even stronger impression," Jake said.

"I didn't realize there were strings attached to this. Besides, I thought you had difficulty using a dead person to get ahead?" *Cheap shot, Gildea.* But she'd surprised me. Disappointed me, as well. Not that it was any excuse for my reaction.

She flushed and looked away. When she turned back, her voice was rough with anger. "I don't enjoy exploiting this any more than you do. But sometimes the only way to change something..." She stopped. Took a breath. "Sorry. Bad idea. Forget it."

"Finish it."

"Finish what?"

"Sometimes, the only way to change something...?"

There was a long pause, with only the roar of the engines and the rushing of the wind to fill it. When she finally spoke, her tone was flat, her voice almost too soft to hear. "Sometimes, the only way to change something is to make the world care that it happened."

"Isn't the statement you're looking for 'the ends justify the means?'" Why was I attacking her? She didn't deserve it. I'd used her as much as she'd used me, after all. Besides, she could take a picture and write a story without my permission.

"Do you always use what people say against them?" Her words were full of anguish.

"I'm sorry. That was inexcusable."

She stared at me a moment before nodding, then she looked away.

I touched her hand, and she looked back at me.

"Go ahead. Take your picture."

When we reached the buoy, Gavin shut down the engines, and the others moved to the stern. I watched, trying to quell a swirl of emotion.

The service was simple. The priest said a prayer, then Amy did a short reading, her voice filled with tears. Neil also read a short passage, barely making it through. Then the priest said a closing prayer, and Amy and Neil each tossed the flowers into the sea they'd taken half an hour to pick out. The flowers drifted away from the boat, and Amy and Neil watched them go. When they'd drifted so far we could barely see them, the priest said a final blessing, and then Gavin restarted the engines. I didn't even notice if Jake took her picture.

On the way back to Cairns, Jake and I sat without talking or looking at each other, letting the roar of the engine fill our ears and the wind dry our tears.

~ ~ ~

At dinner, I told the kids about the offer from Rainforest Adventures.

Neil frowned. "It seems disrespectful somehow."

"Remember the message from your folks."

"Yeah, be happy." Amy's voice shook with desolation. "How can we do that, after what happened?"

"You think about the good times. You remember your folks loved you. You keep busy."

"It seems so pointless," Amy said.

"It will for a while, that's why it helps to keep busy."

"Like going on a rainforest tour," Neil said.

"Exactly."

"Okay. We'll go." He spoke firmly, and after a moment, Amy nodded in agreement.

~ ~ ~

With the kids away, I spent the day with Jake. She'd called after we got back from the memorial service with an offer to arrange a private snorkel trip. Not to Castle Rock Reef, but to a different spot Gavin said was even better. Knowing I might not get another chance to see the reef or Jake, I accepted. When I climbed aboard Gavin's catamaran this time, I was wearing a swimsuit under my slacks, and I was as nervous as a damn debutante.

We arrived at the reef, and I took off my slacks then moved with Randall and Gavin's help to the stern before I removed the legs. I refused to acknowledge what Jake might be thinking as she watched. And she was watching. She was the one who stepped forward and took the legs to stow.

I got through it by not looking at her. With the legs off, I placed my arms around Gavin and Randall's shoulders, and they eased me into a sitting position on the edge of the diving platform. All I had to do then was lean forward and fall into the water, which I did as expeditiously as possible.

I enjoy swimming, and I'm pretty good at it, in spite of having little to kick with. Of course, I'd always be at a disadvantage speed-wise against someone wearing fins. Like Jake. Then I noticed Jake wasn't wearing fins. She swam up to me and pushed her snorkel aside. "Race you to the reef, Gildea."

"You're on, Rutherford."

With the mask and snorkel in place, I kept my face in the water, and that made my stroke more efficient than usual. When I saw the edge of the reef below me, I stopped swimming and looked for Jake. She was behind me.

"Damn, Max. Expected to beat you good."

"Should have worn your flippers then."

She shook her head and grinned, and I knew she'd forgiven me for being Max the Ass the day before.

We swam slowly after that, side by side, hovering over the reef for an hour and a half. It was like swimming in a huge aquarium and also a bit like being in church, not that I'd done that in years. Periodically, Jake touched my hand to get my attention, so she could point something out.

Peace flowed through me as we floated over the reef, pushing aside the ugliness of the Brackens' deaths. I was glad Amy and Neil had also seen the reef. Perhaps, someday their memories of its beauty would help lessen the pain of their loss.

When we returned to the boat, I pulled myself out of the water, then Gavin and Randall lifted me back onto the bench.

Jake's presence made me more acutely aware of my mutant status than usual. I toweled off and put the legs back on, quickly working the stumps into the sockets without checking what she was doing. When I finished, I looked up to find her sitting on the edge of the platform with her legs dangling in the water, watching me.

"I'm surprised how light they are. The legs," she said.

"They need to be. It's a lot harder to move an inanimate object with your thigh muscles than a real leg."

"Do they make them the same length as your actual legs?"

I was toweling my hair to stop the rivulets of saltwater from dripping down my neck. "Depends. Mine are about two inches longer in order to accommodate the knee joints." I emerged from the towel. "Means I started out a bit shorter than you."

Hell, who was I kidding. I was three feet, or two legs, take your pick, shorter than she was.

"How do you keep them on?"

"The socket is formfitting, and it has a liner that acts like a suction cup."

As we talked, my discomfort and self-consciousness slowly dissipated. Maybe it was her matter-of-fact approach and calm interest that did it. And it helped that she was able to look at me minus my usual camouflage without a shudder of distaste.

After a while, she stood and went below. When she came back, she had changed into shorts. Too bad. She'd looked good in that bathing suit. Turquoise. The same color as the water near the reef. One-piece, but to my eyes sexier than those tiny patches of cloth that leave nothing to the imagination.

Gavin stuck his head over the stern and asked if I planned to sit there all the way back to Cairns. When I said no, he and Randall came to help me back to my usual seat. As Randall cast off from the buoy, Jake came and sat next to me, her knees pulled up under her chin, eyes invisible behind sunglasses. I couldn't tell what she was thinking, but what I was thinking was that it felt good to sit next to her, close enough that my arm brushed against hers whenever a wave shifted under the boat.

~ ~ ~

That evening, our last in Cairns, Jake joined us for dinner at a Chinese restaurant. I listened as she drew Amy and Neil out. First they talked about the trip to the rainforest and about when and where they learned to dive. Then they talked about their parents.

131

Listening to the easy give and take between Jake and the kids, I realized I felt comfortable with her as well, although it was unusual for me to relax with someone I barely knew, especially when that someone also happened to be a reporter.

Okay, okay. And a damned attractive woman.

After dinner, we said our good-byes out on the sidewalk. Jake hugged Amy and Neil, and then she turned and gave me a long look before leaning in and kissing me on the lips.

She stepped away before I had a chance to respond, the brash reporter's mask resettling on her face. "Right-oh. Have a good flight home."

"Good-bye, Joanna Kate."

She met my eyes for an instant then shifted the tote on her shoulder, turned, and with long strides, crossed the street, moving quickly without looking back.

I thought about how I might have handled that kiss if Amy and Neil hadn't been there.

What I would have liked to do was catch her hand and pull her back into my arms. Check out if her lips felt as good as I thought they did from that brief contact. Of course, it would have been awkward with the crutches. If I let go of them, I might easily have ended up in a heap on the ground looking like a puppet whose strings had snapped.

This was better. I'd kept my dignity.

It really is too bad, though, that San Francisco and Sydney are so far apart.

Chapter Twenty
JAKE

Never let sentiment or personal feelings interfere with a story: one of the first things I learned in journo 101. And I never had any trouble with it. Before Max. A damn good thing he left Australia when he did. Before I made a right drongo of myself.

I've never been one to volunteer for the hanky stories, trying to be the first on the scene to get bereaved survivors' reactions. Personally, if someone had held a mic in my face and asked how I felt when Terry went missing, I'd have shoved the mic up their nearest orifice.

In my view, a person who pulls it together to do an interview at a time like that couldn't be all that grief-stricken. Although I'll concede that sometimes using a survivor is the only way to make the damn pollies, or the public for that matter, pay attention.

A fine line though. Teetering on the edge of exploitation. Especially after Max acted like a cut snake about me taking a photo of the kids. I like to think it worked out, and I didn't do too badly by Amy and Neil.

There was still enough emotional fall-out for everyone to be chockers, though. And that was before I figured out I was seeing Max as more than a news source.

I knew from the get-go, when Max first called, it was the break I was waiting for, but when I wrote the story up and gave it to Peter, he'd patted me on the shoulder and said next time refer that kind of call to Mulroney.

Man had a kangaroo loose in the upper paddock, if he thought I'd consider handing off a source to the Roon. Before the words were even out of Peter's mouth, I knew he wasn't going to send me to Cairns to do the follow-up.

I went back to my desk, filled out the paperwork for a holiday, and booked a flight to Cairns for that evening. No way was Mulroney getting anywhere near Max Gildea, not if I had anything to do with it.

I planned to watch for Max and the kids at the airport, but then I figured I'd have better luck spotting them at the police station. Amy was the one who tipped me this was the group I was waiting for. She looks just like the picture of her mum. I would have looked right past Max, though, if he'd been on his own. I was expecting middle-aged, flabby, and flashy. The only part of that I'd gotten correct was his age.

The first things I noticed about him were the forearm crutches and his odd gait. The next thing was that he appeared to be a whole lot fitter than I expected someone who needed crutches to look.

I'd checked him out, of course. One of the top maritime solicitors in San Francisco—handled a lot of oil spill cases. Frankly, I expected to thoroughly dislike the man.

As soon as I approached the three of them, I could see he was in charge. The two Brackens practically scooted behind him, when I spoke to them. Obviously some media phobia there and another stereotype shot down. I thought most Yanks were just waiting for their chance at the spotlight, and it could make my job more difficult if these three weren't, although I do prefer people who are content to stay behind the scenes. They tend to be more credible than those seeking out the front and center position.

Still, I figured when the telly gals showed up, batting their eyes and jiggling selected body parts, Max would revert to type. I was reluctantly impressed when he didn't. I was already more attracted to him than was wise for a whole raft of reasons.

I try not to think about it, but sometimes, when I'm real tired or sick or just sick at heart, I can't stop the memories of the last time I let my guard down with a man.

Terrence O'Bannion.

Terry and I were in military service together. I'd signed up in order to pass the time until I figured out what I wanted to be. He planned to make it a career. I didn't find being in the military that different from boarding school or going home for hols and having chores. And survival training was no more challenging than spending a week mustering sheep from the far paddocks.

After basic, I was assigned to counterintelligence, the Cairns unit, because I had some familiarity with Mandarin and Cantonese, thanks to the Chinese cook we'd had for as long as I could remember. I think Lam Shun Fa taught me to speak Cantonese and to recognize Mandarin characters in order not to forget. I certainly had no idea there was anything extraordinary about it until the military got all excited.

The intelligence job was interesting, and I was good at it. Trying to make sense out of the bits and pieces they gave us was like working crosswords, acrostics, and word jumbles at the same time.

I met Terry shortly after I arrived in Cairns. He came up to me one day and said he'd heard I posted the highest score ever recorded in survival training. Said he wanted to know how I'd done it. I told him if he got us both a week's leave, I'd show him. Didn't figure I'd ever see him again, but he reappeared a month later with leave papers, and we drove out to Koorboora, left the car, and started walking.

When we set out, I let Terry bring only the clothes he was wearing. I expected an argument, but he just raised an eyebrow and told me to lead on.

I didn't make it easy, might have even made it harder than it needed to be—just to see if he could take it. He didn't whinge once. Impressed me, and I'm not easily impressed.

By the time we'd made the hundred-kilometer circle back to the car, we'd both lost half a stone, and nobody would have found it pleasant being downwind of us.

When we got back to Cairns, he took me to dinner, and I looked across the table at his freshly shaved face in the candlelight and realized that nothing up to then had prepared me for what I felt looking at him—a dreamy, melting feeling that even made me forget how hungry I was. The miracle was, it turned out he felt the same way about me.

That was the beginning of the happiest year of my life.

It's been twelve years since he disappeared during a training exercise off Possession Island, and I've yet to come good. The military sealed the files on what happened, claiming national security.

Early on I'd learned that death leaves a thing as still as a stone and that grieving over something dead is a waste of time. But that didn't help with Terry. Maybe it was the not knowing for sure. A person can keep hoping beyond any sensible limit when there's no proof.

The puzzles lost their appeal after that. When my enlistment was up, I used the money I'd been saving for the wedding to travel. I went to Canada and stayed with my sister for a while. From there, I just wandered, eventually ending up with my other sister in the UK.

Whenever I ran out of money, I found a job for a week, a month, or whatever amount of time I needed to make enough to go on to the next place, until I ran out of places. That's when I came back to Cairns and took the dive master job with Gavin while I went to journo school.

Now I've let it happen again. Let myself begin to care about a man I'll never have.

Why did I let it get started?

Chapter Twenty-One
MAX

Amy, Neil, and I parted at the Sydney airport. They were flying back to San Francisco, where their grandfather and Kelly would be waiting for them, while I was going to New Zealand to see Sophie. She was staying with a family on a sheep farm outside of Whangarei.

When I arrived at the farm, Tess Wulsin greeted me and led me to a comfortable living room, and then she went to get Sophie. While I waited, I walked over to the window. It framed a serene view of white sheep in green pastures edged by deep woods, and seeing it, I understood why Sophie had chosen to return here.

At the sound of a gasp, I turned to find Sophie standing in the doorway, hands covering her mouth. I walked carefully over to her, leaned the crutches on a chair, and pulled her into my arms.

She returned my hug then stepped back, and holding my hands, smiled at me. "Max, what an incredibly wonderful surprise."

"You're the one who gave me the push, you know."

"I'm so glad. After all you did for me."

"How are you?"

"Fine. Good."

It appeared the correct answer was anything but fine or good, although she wasn't as thin and she no longer needed her cane.

"You've arrived at the perfect time," she said. "Dinner will be in an hour."

"I planned to take you out."

"I already told Tess we'd be having dinner here. They all want to meet you."

~ ~ ~

When I returned to the living room before dinner, I found Sophie chatting with two men: William, Tess's husband, and Philip, Tess and William's nephew. Both men had humorous demeanors and hands that were blunt and rough from hard work.

During dinner, the Wulsins asked me the usual get-acquainted questions. I told them I'd been in Australia in connection with the Bracken case, and that led to additional discussion. When I finally ceased to be the center of attention, I ate and listened while the others interacted. In particular, I found myself watching Philip and Sophie. She was very much at ease with him, but then she'd spent a lot of time with the Wulsins—long enough to explain the casual intimacy.

After dinner, Sophie and I went for a walk. Being able to do that was a miracle I was not yet taking for granted.

"It feels strange and quite wonderful walking with you," Sophie said.

"I'm kicking myself for not doing it sooner."

"Look at it this way, at least now you can kick yourself."

"That *is* nice."

We smiled at each other, and she looked more herself.

"Tell me about the Wulsins," I said, although the one I was most interested in was Philip.

He taught history at Queens College in Whangarei, Sophie said, and he spent his breaks and weekends helping William with the sheep. I wondered if he'd developed his extracurricular interest in sheep before or after Sophie arrived.

"How are you, really?" I asked her.

She sighed. "It's been two years. But every time I think I've let it go, I dream about it again and wake up feeling so angry and...so helpless. Helice paid such a small price." She'd stopped walking, and her voice shook. "Blood money. I didn't survive in order to... Money! There has to be more to it

138

than that. I owe it to Sam to do something. I failed, Max. I might as well have died too. I didn't want money. I wanted...I want justice."

She sounded as if she were on the verge of tears. I struggled to set aside the crutches, finally just dropping them, and put my arms around her. I rested my chin against the top of her head and spoke calmly, hoping to forestall the onslaught of grief that lay just beneath the surface of her words. "How do you define that, Sophie? Justice?"

She spoke with a quiet intensity. "I want an acknowledgement that *Nereus* ran us down and left us to die and an apology for doing it."

"Even if you got that, it wouldn't be enough, you know."

She pulled out of my arms, and in the pale wash of moonlight, her face was smooth as marble, the look in her eyes as cold. I stared at her, thinking how hopeless my loving her was. She would never live fully until she let go of the past, and two years was no time at all.

As I well knew.

~ ~ ~

I spent the first part of the night awake, trying to think of a way to free Sophie from feeling her survival had no meaning. Finally, exhausted, I organized the problem into the form of a question to my subconscious and then concentrated on my breathing, blanking out any further thoughts. After a time, it worked, and I fell asleep.

I came awake shortly before dawn to the crowing of a rooster and the memory of Jake's words echoing in my head. *Sometimes the only way to change something is to make the world care that it happened.*

If Sophie's case had gone to trial, there would have been publicity. Lots of it. It would have been one of my strategies, and it wouldn't have been difficult to get the media's attention. It was, after all, the kind of story they love. Tragedy, survival against enormous odds, evil ship owners, the possibility that justice might be thwarted...

But what about now? Would anyone even be willing to write a feature about it at this late date, and if someone did, what could be gained? Although, perhaps knowing she had a choice, to speak or to remain silent, would be enough to ease

Sophie's helplessness. And if she no longer felt helpless, maybe she could find a way to put it behind her and begin to live.

~ ~ ~

I'd already had breakfast when Sophie came downstairs the next morning. I poured myself another cup of coffee and kept her company while she ate. Philip had eaten even earlier. I'd met him walking out of the kitchen as I arrived. He said he was off to do something to the sheep, using a word I didn't recognize. I said that didn't sound like much fun, and he grinned and said I had that right.

"What do you want to do today?" Sophie asked, pulling my thoughts away from Philip. She looked better this morning, her usual calm replacing the fierce look she'd had last night.

"Why don't we take a walk," I said. "There's something I want to talk to you about."

She led me to a smooth, well-trod path across a pasture full of sheep. Beyond the pasture, the path continued a short distance into the woods, until it reached an open glade beside a small stream. I sat on a boulder, and Sophie sat on a fallen tree trunk.

"I can see why you wanted to come back here," I said.

She leaned over and picked up a pebble that she proceeded to roll around in the palm of her hand. "I may be ready to come home soon," she said. "When I do, I'm going to sell the San Francisco house and buy a place away from the city. One with a view, like you have."

I wanted to tell her she didn't need to buy a place like mine. That mine was at her disposal. But I was uncertain exactly what I would be offering. A temporary place to stay or something more permanent? I equivocated and told her it was wonderful news she was coming home.

"You said you had something to tell me?" she said.

"You know part of it. It has to do with the Brackens. Do you want to hear more, or would you rather not?" When I'd talked about the Brackens at dinner last night, Sophie had stopped eating, and she'd had a strained look on her face.

"No, that's fine. You can tell me."

140

I gave her the details I'd skimmed over the night before. As I talked, I watched her carefully to make sure she was okay. She sat bent over, rolling the pebble, apparently concentrating on that and on the water splashing over the stones.

When I stopped speaking, she sighed. "Amy and Neil are lucky you took their case."

"It wasn't exactly a case, and I didn't do that much. If it hadn't been for Jake, we'd still be guessing what happened, and McIntyre would probably have gotten off scot-free."

"Too bad Jake wasn't around when we were fighting with Helice."

As birdsong and the small sounds of insects replaced Sophie's listless words, I thought about whether to tell her the rest of it. *But why not?* It was, after all, what I'd been leading up to.

"What if Jake were to write an article about what happened to you?"

Sophie bent her head, staring at the stream. "What good is it, to have someone write a story now?"

"At the least, it will shine a light on it." Besides, it was the only option she had left.

"Do you believe it could be helpful?"

"Yes." Odd. I didn't realize I believed it, not until this moment when it seemed a perfectly reasonable assumption.

"Do you think I should do it?" Sophie sat up straighter and gave me an intent look.

"You need to do what will help you."

"I don't..." Her head moved from side to side. "No. I don't think I can do it."

I tried to decide if that was a relief, or not.

Sophie set the pebble back amongst its fellows on the edge of the stream, and we returned to the house.

After dinner that evening, she asked me to arrange for Jake to come for the interview.

~ ~ ~

I felt a quick jolt of pleasure when I spotted Jake at the airport, dressed more formally than she had been in Cairns.

141

Sophie, dark-haired and slight, appeared delicate standing next to Jake with her sun-streaked hair and golden skin. I'd told Sophie Jake was tall, but it was obvious she hadn't managed to quite picture the reality.

Sophie drove back to the farm, pointing out the sights to Jake. In between, she asked Jake questions about herself. Listening from the backseat, I learned a lot about Jake's background. That she grew up on a sheep station one hundred kilometers of rough track from the nearest town. That she went to boarding school and after school entered the military. That after the military, she bounced around the world for several years before returning to Cairns and beginning her journalism studies. Degree in hand, she'd moved to Sydney and her current job at *The Australian.*

I thought about the attraction I felt for Jake. It hadn't a chance of going anywhere. And it wasn't just a question of time zones. She didn't even live in the same hemisphere. Kelly would likely tell me I was doing it on purpose—choosing to care about women with whom a deeper relationship was either impractical or impossible, and perhaps she'd be right.

At the farm, we gathered in the living room for the interview. Sophie and Jake sat across from each other at a small table, while I sat in an easy chair off to the side.

Jake spent the first thirty minutes asking background questions about the Suriano family and the sailing trip. Sophie answered Jake's questions easily, but without animation, while Jake listened with an absorbed expression, moving a pen slowly back and forth through her fingers. She was recording Sophie, so she didn't need the pen for anything except to give her fingers something to do.

Finally, she asked the questions she'd been building up to.

Chapter Twenty-Two
SOPHIE

I felt like I was standing next to giants as Max introduced the reporter. Jake Rutherford is her name. She gave me a direct, calm look, and I had the fanciful thought that if she were a teacher, she would be one of those the students could never fool, but would love anyway.

When Max looked at her, his face changed, the hard, firm angles softening, making him appear younger. For her part, Jake worked at not looking at Max.

When we sat down for the interview, she began by asking questions that I could answer with minimal discomfort. I could see those other questions though, perched like vultures on her shoulders. Waiting.

When she finally asked about the accident, it felt as if cold water was closing over me, shutting off my breath and all the light. I wanted to sink into that darkness, let it fold around me, the way the sea folded around Sam.

~ ~ ~

We were hit on the leg from Tonga to New Zealand. That's a 2,000-kilometer run. We'd had clear weather the first two days out. On the third day we started encountering line squalls that continued the next several days, although sailing conditions were good.

Close to New Zealand and the shipping lanes, Sam and I took turns on night watch. The night it happened, we had scattered clouds, a quarter moon, and five-foot swells. Visibility was excellent. Sam helped me check the sail trim, and he made certain all our lights were on and everything was as it should be before he went below to sleep.

During my watch, I set my alarm to go off every fifteen minutes to remind me it was time to check for the lights of other ships. Right before midnight, I did my final visual check before going below to note our position in the log and to have a snack before waking Sam. I'd been downstairs no more than seven minutes when there was a series of loud booms followed by cracking, ripping sounds. The next thing I knew, I was lying on the floor looking at the ceiling, and the cabin was filling with seawater.

~ ~ ~

When I awoke in the Whangarei Base Hospital, I had no idea where I was. Then I remembered, or at least I remembered enough to know why I was lying in what appeared to be a hospital bed.

The bed was elevated. From my half-sitting position, I moved my eyes from right to left. Pale gray walls, a window with half-open Venetian blinds throwing a pattern of bars across the white blanket covering me. A gray hospital table sitting off to the side, a black chair at the end of the bed. The quiet clicking of an IV pump.

I tried to move. My arms moved, my legs didn't. My whole lower body felt like a block of cement. When I tried to lift my right hand to my face, a sharp pain made me catch my breath.

In the next moment, a woman leaned over me. Looking at her gray skin, black hair, and dark eyes, I figured I had to be dreaming, although I don't ever remember a dream hurting as much as this one.

"Ah, waking up, are you? How do you feel, lass?"

I ran my tongue over my lips. They seemed to be coated with Vaseline. I tried to speak, but only a cracked whisper emerged.

"That's okay, lass. Don't fash yourself. There's plenty of time. How about a sip of water?"

I attempted a nod, but I couldn't move my head. When I tried to speak instead, the yes came out as *yesh.*

The woman held a bent straw to my lips. I sipped. The water was cool and tasted better than icy champagne.

Abruptly, everything turned dark, and I didn't wake up again for another twenty-four hours.

Or, so I've been told.

The angel of death came for Sam and me, but somehow he missed me.

~ ~ ~

After we were hit, there was no time to think. I pushed away the hair plastered across my face, trying to see. And what I saw. The mast broken, lying over the side in a tangle of sails that was pulling us down. The deck already awash. The lifeboat gone.

Sam pulled the raft loose.

There was no time for anything else. No time to grab supplies, no time to think what we were going to need. No time to get it if we were able to think.

I don't know how long it took the *Sylph* to sink. Two or three minutes? Maybe longer, but not much. And after that all that was left on the surface of the sea were the raft, Sam and me, and the random debris that was once our beautiful yacht.

Thoughts tumbled about my head. What had happened? Something must have hit us. But what?

It had to be big, something huge. A ship. But I'd just finished scanning a few minutes earlier, and I'd seen nothing. Everything had been dark and quiet, except for the wind slapping against the sails and the shushing of the hull against the swell of ocean.

No ship then, how could there be one now?

But there was. Her bulk was visible against the quadrant of sky where a slender moon slipped in and out of clouds. A dark ship. That struck me as strange. I tried to think why, but I couldn't think, not until it moved away from us, and I realized the only lights anywhere on the vessel were in the stern, where they outlined the shapes of the men who stood looking down at us.

Sam yelled and waved his arms. The men stood motionless as the ship drew away. They were leaving us. I couldn't believe it. Sam screamed at the men until the raft pitched in the ship's wake, knocking him over.

We clung to the raft, shivering, watching, until all we could see was the faint shine of light from the ship's stern when we were tossed up on the crest of a swell. Then that too disappeared, and we were alone on a vast, black, heaving expanse.

I wonder if there is anyone who can possibly know how we felt then, left to toss in a six-foot-long rubber raft, its thin skin all that separated us from the icy water. No paddles, no rudder, no way to signal for help.

Sam had a deep cut on his arm. He reached toward my face, and his hand came away dark, and I realized I was bleeding as well. My vision blurred with a pain I hadn't noticed until that moment.

Sam was in nightclothes, and it was so cold. We were wet with seawater and blood. As we tossed on the sharp swells, I took one arm out of my jacket, pulled Sam close, and wrapped the jacket around the two of us. A second pain bloomed in my hip. I shifted my leg and gasped at a stab of agony. After that, I tried not to move, relieved when the pain subsided into a dull throb as the leg went numb.

But if we were to live we needed to keep talking, moving.

Sam's mantra, "No food, no water, no radio, we're going to die," was driving me mad. Then I noticed he was slurring his words.

Hypothermia.

As he murmured nonsense, I pulled him close and told him it was okay, that we'd be rescued in the morning, then I let him sleep for a time. I had no strength left to force him to stay awake. If we could just stay on the raft until the sun came up, we could dry out, warm up.

After Sam fell silent, the raft continued its sickening up-and-down lurch toward New Zealand. My legs felt heavy, and my head hurt. I curled around Sam's body and tried not to cry.

Funny. All that money we had. What good was it? It couldn't buy us a drink of pure water, a dry down comforter, or an end to the ceaseless motion of the raft. In that moment, I would have traded all that we had for the longest line at any welfare office. As long as Sam was with me.

I realized I was thinking nonsense.

I tried to decide if there was any material thing—house, car, pictures, jewelry, clothing, or the money itself—I wouldn't hand freely to God, or to any emissary He cared to send, if He would let us survive. I would willingly land on a beach with nothing, nothing, if Sam and I were together. It was all that mattered. That and Gibby.

Gibby. What would she think—how would they tell her, would the police do it? What would they say? Would she even understand? But I was thinking like Sam.

"We're going to live. We're going to live." I chanted it softly, and Sam pushed against me with a mewling sound like a kitten.

Up and down, up and down, we tossed, one end of the raft rising, and then a moment later we'd slide sideways into the trough. It was like riding a horse that was jumping and twisting, trying to dislodge us.

Everything ached from the effort of adjusting to the movement of the raft, to avoid being flipped into the water. All except my legs. They were numb and heavy, two stones anchoring me firmly.

We were only thirty kilometers from New Zealand when we were hit. Eighteen miles. I knew the ocean currents would move us toward land. I knew if we stayed in the raft, it was only a matter of time before we drifted ashore or were seen by someone on a boat. I knew we would survive. And then we were going to find the ship that hit us and make them pay.

Sam was muttering again. I wondered how long it had been. A few minutes before midnight when we were hit. It felt like we'd been tossing for days, but the sun hadn't yet come up. I tried to remember the taste and smell of things. The sugar cookies I was eating before waking Sam up, the warmth of the hot chocolate sliding down my throat.

Now I was learning what the phrase "cold to the bone" meant. It was a cold that was nothing like the icy freshness of snow brushing against a cheek, or the feel of a single breath of crisp winter air. It was a cold so heavy and dense, it made me feel like I weighed a thousand pounds. I sent a message to my hand to tuck the jacket around Sam. After a time my hand moved feebly. It was hard work, pulling a breath in and pushing it out again.

The sun was overhead before I noticed it. I pulled at Sam's arm. After a time he opened his eyes. Twelve hours since it happened.

~ ~ ~

I remember only snatches of my fifty-six hours on that raft. It was an incomprehensible amount of time. In the first fifteen hours, we drifted close enough to see a smudge of coastline and an occasional boat. In the second dark period, the seas were calmer, and we lay close together in the center of the raft and slept. The next morning, we woke to rough seas. It took all our strength to stay in the raft. Then the raft lurched, and I felt Sam's arm slide through my grasp. He was gone, over the side. I reached for him, but a wave pushed him away.

"Stay with the raft, Sophie."

Those were Sam's last words to me. The gap between us widened. I closed my eyes at the awful pain, and when I opened them, he was gone.

I don't remember the rest of it. I don't know why I struggled to stay in the raft. Why I didn't simply let go, join Sam. How could I have let him go on without me?

Sam was right.

I was right.

He died.

I survived.

Now I sit in Tess and William's living room telling Jake my story. I wonder, have I told her all of it, or did the memories surge through me like heavy waves against rocks, with only some of my words slipping in between?

But it really doesn't matter. This is the last time I'll do this. And if it doesn't work to purge the pain...well, perhaps I'll do what I should have done when Sam drowned.

Let go.

Chapter Twenty-Three
MAX

When Sophie stopped speaking, there was no sound except the quiet hum of the tape recorder. After a moment, Jake leaned forward and snapped it off. At the click, Sophie flinched, but her eyes lost their remote look, and she spoke in a more normal tone. "Is there anything else you need?" The words were polite but flat.

"I may have questions once I start writing, but this should do for now. You need to know I'll do my best to make them pay for what they did." Jake spoke softly, but her tone was fierce.

"I want to lie down for a while." Sophie sounded listless and looked exhausted. I walked her to the stairs, pulled her into my arms, and smoothed a hand along her back. She rested her head on my chest and put her arms around me, but there was no strength in them. After a moment, she stepped away and headed up the stairs. I fumbled with the crutches, and feeling heavy and stiff, returned to the living room.

Jake had her head bent, leaning on the mantel. When she turned, I tried to read her expression. It appeared to be a mix of sadness and anger. "I suppose everybody wonders what their life is about at times. Then something like this comes along, and it seems...perfectly clear." She paused, and I wondered what she was seeing. Hoping she'd share it.

"Stopping people like Rob McIntyre and the crew of the *Nereus* from hurting anyone else. If I manage to do that, I won't feel I've wasted my time on the planet." She walked over to the table and fiddled with the recorder, and then she spoke without looking up. "I need a walk, Max. You want to come?"

"Sure."

I led the way across the pasture toward the woods, following the path Sophie showed me the day before.

As we moved through the sheep, Jake spoke in a thoughtful tone. "It's a good thing sheep have no desire for world domination. With a little effort they could take over New Zealand, and they'd have a bloody good shot at Oz."

"I wonder if they'd do a better job than humans."

She shrugged. "Couldn't do any worse. They don't have missiles."

When we reached the glade, Jake sat on the same tree trunk where Sophie had sat two days before. I watched the play of dappled shadows on her face and hair.

"Rob McIntyre was offered a deal," she said. "He pled guilty to two counts of manslaughter. It happened this morning. Oliver called me at the airport to tell me."

"So, what happens next?"

"He'll be sentenced, and then everything will get back to normal, but with a few changes. Gavin tells me other operators have asked his advice on updating their safety procedures. We managed to make a real difference, Max."

"You did."

She shook her head sharply and looked away. "It feels good, but the price was too high. Still, being able to help..." She picked a long strand of grass and curled it around a finger.

I noticed the bitten fingernails had been transformed into short pink ovals. "Jake, you need to be careful what you write about Sophie."

"What do you mean?"

"This is off the record." I waited until she nodded her agreement.

"When we were suing Helice, Sophie was stalked, and her daughter was threatened."

She gave me a sharp look. "You think Helice was behind that?"

"I do."

"Did you report it?"

"Of course. But there was no way to prove they were

150

involved. We also put an investigator aboard the ship, and he heard the crew talking about the yacht. They knew they'd hit it. He also discovered the *Nereus* routinely ran without lights."

She was silent for a moment, concentrating on the circlet of grass.

"So, why didn't the crew of the *Nereus* try to save the Surianos? Since they were inbound to New Zealand it would have been very little trouble."

"Either they panicked or they thought they'd get away with it."

"Maybe."

"You have another thought?" I said.

"Nope. Never underestimate the power of panic, nor of denial."

"You will be careful, Jake? Sophie may think she needs this, but don't light too big a fire under Helice. These are not nice people."

"Bloody hell, as if I don't know that already. Anyone who'd slice into a yacht then sail off leaving people to fend for themselves is by definition not nice." The anger in her voice overrode the peace in the glade. A bird that had been singing stopped abruptly. Jake looked away from me.

"It's unlikely the captain or the crew members of the *Nereus* were involved in making the threats against Sophie," I said. "But someone connected to Helice had to be involved. I don't want that someone pushed into coming after her again."

"Then why give me access at all?" The anger was gone, and she sounded tired.

"Sophie thinks the reason she survived was to prevent it from happening to anyone else."

"And you want that for her."

"Yes. But I also want her to be safe."

Jake was silent. Carefully, she added another strand of grass to the circlet she'd already formed, working with deep concentration, twisting the strands together. "That's a tough lady you have there, Max."

"She's tough, but she's also fragile." And I didn't exactly have her.

Jake slipped the circlet onto a finger, and then she looked at me. "She's more than a client, isn't she?"

I spoke without hesitation. "Yes."

Jake was silent for a time, slipping the circlet on and off her finger, then she tossed it into the water and watched it dance downstream out of sight.

I was left wondering why I'd answered her question about Sophie the way I had. It was the truth—I did consider Sophie more than a client. It just wasn't the whole truth. But now it would be awkward if I attempted to expand on my answer. Not that I understood what that expansion might include.

What was Sophie to me? Did I even know?

Some things I did know. I knew I felt a deep affection for her, and that I'd do anything, perhaps even give my life, to protect her. And that night, after Gibby was threatened? If Sophie had wanted more than simple comfort...but she hadn't. And it was clear she still wasn't ready to put her past behind her. As I finally had? Was Kelly right? Had I changed?

I didn't know the answer to that either, except that for the first time since my accident, I was looking at a woman, or was it two women? and thinking about possibilities. Joanna Kate Rutherford and Sophie Suriano. They both disturbed my inner landscape in a fundamental way.

I knew Sophie better. We'd gone through a tough time together. But the feeling I got whenever I saw Jake—a lightness.

It could, of course, be pure and simple lust.

Only I suspected it was neither pure, nor was it simple.

Jake stood and faced me. "You ever thought there may be another angle to this?"

"What do you mean?" I stood as well.

"The threats they made. Why would they do that? And then cave on the settlement so soon afterward?"

She was fishing, and I wasn't having it. "You can't print any of that."

Her chin came up, and she looked steadily at me. The discomfort I'd been feeling about Sophie talking to Jake came to a roaring head. Reporters. Ultimately, like pet mambas, you could never trust them.

"I'll need the name of the investigator you put aboard," she said.

"One condition."

She shook her head.

"Yes. If you're going after a bigger story, I want Sophie out of it. No direct quotes. No indication you talked to her."

"I can't promise that. Not until I see how it plays out."

"You go too far, you may endanger the very person you've set out to help."

"I guess you'll have to accept my word that I won't do anything that will put Sophie in danger." She looked away from me, her bottom lip caught between her teeth. "Sometimes..."

"What?"

"There's risk in almost everything we do. Sometimes we risk more by doing nothing."

"The risk in this case lies in stirring it up too much."

"Then I'll ask you again, Max. Why did you invite me here?"

She stood there so straight, tall, and strong, and I felt diminished somehow. Because I feared the consequences that could arise from our actions here today? I wouldn't suffer those consequences, at least not directly. Sophie was the one taking the biggest risk, but that was, after all, her decision, one I had no right to contravene.

"You go after Helice, you need to take care, Joanna Kate."

She returned my look without speaking.

"Three days notice before the article appears," I said.

"You have my word."

"Then the name you need is Alex Wu."

After Jake and I parted, I called Alex to tell him what I'd done.

"If she ask, I glad to help. No more under covers, eh?"

~ ~ ~

That evening, my last in New Zealand, Sophie went directly to her room after dinner, while Philip and I went to the living room. He lit a fire, and when it was crackling, sat down and filled a pipe. "I've noticed Sophie's been distressed these last two days," he said, tamping down the tobacco.

He seemed to be picking his words carefully. I focused on the fire and left him to it.

"I think she's more than a client to you," he continued.

His statement was an echo of Jake's. "Yes. She's a dear friend."

"I'm not trying to butt in where I don't belong, mate, but Sophie's my friend too. I'm concerned about her. She's suffered a great deal. She seemed to be getting over it, until you arrived."

"I think she only appeared to be getting over it."

We both stared into the fire for a time, Philip drawing slowly on his pipe.

"You planning to be around a while longer?" I asked.

"School's back in session Monday. But I'm always here weekends and holidays."

"I need your help with something. The woman who was here yesterday, Jake Rutherford, she's writing a story about what happened to the Surianos. When the article comes out, Sophie may be in danger. Don't leave her alone in the house, don't let her go walking alone. Go with her into town."

"You're serious," he said, looking startled. "Why would you let Sophie do such a thing?"

"She needs to feel her survival has meaning."

He nodded slowly. "I'll talk to Tess and William. We'll start putting precautions in place. When will the article appear?"

"I don't know exactly. Jake's going to give me three days' notice."

"Sophie will be safe here. Strangers stand out, and we'll do whatever it takes to protect her."

"Appreciate it."

"Glad to do it. For Sophie." He leaned toward the fire and knocked out his pipe. His face was hidden, but I could tell from his voice that Sophie was important to him.

It would be difficult to leave her with this man, but I didn't doubt Philip would do whatever it took to keep her safe.

~ ~ ~

Shortly after my return to San Francisco, I met with Anthony Micelli. He said nothing more about either my working with Todd or his own retirement plans, but then I didn't expect him to. I'd had my chance. Oddly enough, I didn't seem to be feeling any particular distress over missing out. I wondered if my indifference was temporary or the new state of affairs.

A couple of weeks later, I picked up a case involving an oil spill off Tampa. I was as enthusiastic about it as a kid being told to eat his vegetables. Still, I'd taken a lot of time off, and now it was time to refocus and get back to work.

The only bright spot in my life during this period was Rosie's cooking school. I stopped by at least once a week to see the progress on the renovations of the old house he'd purchased in San Germano. The first two floors would house kitchens, classrooms, and offices. Rosie planned to live on the third floor, which meant I'd soon be on my own. As that realization sank in, there were times I began to wish I hadn't started this particular ball rolling.

In the meantime, Rosie was still living with me, spending his days riding herd on his contractors. In the evening, we met at either the track or the health club to work out. According to him, I came back from Australia and New Zealand in sorry shape.

I did feel better after a tough workout. Less restless, less irritable.

~ ~ ~

Jake finally called three months after the interview to say the Helice story would appear in next Sunday's *Australian.* "The editor's planning to start mentioning the story in tomorrow's edition. Page one, above the fold, banner headline. My byline. We think it'll go worldwide."

"But why would it? It's an old story," I said.

"I was right about there being a reason the *Nereus* didn't rescue the Surianos."

"Care to share what it was?"

There was silence at the other end.

"Jake, you still there?"

155

"Yeah. Look, Max, I'll tell you, but you can't breathe a word to anybody, not until the story comes out. If my editor knew..."

"I give you my solemn word, Joanna Kate."

"The *Nereus* was smuggling. Illegal immigrants."

I sucked in a breath.

"Max?"

"Yeah. Sorry. I was thinking. How did you figure it out?"

"Alex Wu. I met with him and went over everything he heard during the time he was aboard the *Nereus*. I was looking for more quotes from the crew about sinking the yacht. But then he mentioned that one of the cook's helpers told him he had it easy doing the leg back to China. That they worked their asses off in the other direction. When Alex asked why, guy got cagey. I didn't know if it was anything other than testosterone, but I decided it was worth checking.

"Anyway, the last time the *Nereus* docked in New Zealand, Alex spent an evening entertaining a couple of the crew, including the cagey guy. They ran off at the mouth real good once he got them topped up."

I wondered what I would have made of the comment if Wu had included it in his report to me. Likely, not as much as Jake had.

The woman was amazing...relentless. Terrifying. Pity the poor devil who fell in love with her.

Chapter Twenty-Four
MAX

Shortly after I arrived in the office on Monday, Cassie rushed in and snapped on the television. "Just wait. They'll repeat it in a minute." She stood staring at the screen.

"What?"

"Helice Shipping. On CNN."

It had to mean Jake was correct about the story going worldwide.

The coverage, which focused on the smuggling aspect, continued the rest of the day. Eventually, immigration authorities were interviewed and provided sound bites about how extensive such smuggling was. Thousands of illegals, paying up to $50,000 each, were smuggled from China, North Africa, and the Middle East every year. Most were then indentured after their arrival. The dream of freedom they'd been following, turned into the nightmare of slavery, and the *Nereus* was only the tip of an extensive iceberg.

That evening, the story was reported by all three network news programs. NBC showed footage of a Helice ship docking in Seattle, and they reported that Helice ships called regularly at other west coast ports.

By Wednesday, rehashes of Jake's story had appeared in the *Los Angeles Times* and *San Francisco Chronicle*, and there was a call in the California legislature for a measure to ban Helice ships from California ports.

I called Jake to congratulate her. "Outstanding piece of work, Joanna Kate. I hope you celebrated."

"Daniel came by with champagne."

I was sorry I'd asked. I cleared my throat, tried again. "They transfer you from obits and local color yet?"

"Next opening is mine. Want to thank you, by the way. For putting me onto the story. Is Sophie doing okay?"

"The Wulsins have mobilized the neighborhood." Although I doubted it was necessary, since the story was only peripherally about the Suriano sinking. "You need to be careful as well."

"Sure. Oops, someone's on the other line. Thanks for your call, Max. Nice talking to you."

Yeah. Right. Real nice. So why did she cut the conversation short?

Chalk another one up to the Gildea charm?

I hung up, and it was a moment before I could blank out the picture of a tall woman in a turquoise swimsuit and get back to depositions discussing oil viscosity and beach cleanup.

I realized, as my mind refused to focus on the lines of print, that since I'd returned from Australia, life had been dull...flat, insipid.

Talking to Jake had done nothing to lighten my mood. She sounded so alive, engaged. I envied her her passion.

Somewhere along the way I seemed to have lost mine.

I thought about what Jake had accomplished and regretted the fact we'd lost the ease we had with each other in Cairns, although it was unlikely we'd ever see each other again.

We were just two people who, given more advantageous geography and the right timing, might have...okay, it wouldn't kill me to admit it...might have cared for each other.

Of course, we might just as easily have ended up adversaries, given Jake's strong views. Still, it would have been interesting scrapping with her. A lot more interesting than sorting out oil spills.

~ ~ ~

After a brief flurry of attention to the smuggling story, the media moved on, although I knew there was a *Sixty Minutes* piece potentially in the works after I was called for a comment.

I still talked to Tess or William regularly to encourage them to remain watchful, although I was reasonably certain Helice no longer had anything to gain from harming Sophie, except more bad publicity.

Occasionally, I spoke with Sophie herself, but our conversations were brief and never about anything important.

In late August, Sophie returned to the States. When she started clearing out her house in order to sell it, she spent an occasional weekend with me. We shared the cooking, I taught her about bonsai, and we spent time on the terrace overlooking the ocean—Sophie reading while I worked on my pending cases.

I enjoyed having Sophie around. I knew she wasn't yet ready for more than friendship, but I was willing to wait.

~ ~ ~

Sophie and I watched the *Sixty Minutes* piece together on a Sunday evening a month after her return. It started with a short segment crediting Jake with breaking the story and showing her at work in the newsroom of *The Australian.* The unexpected sight of Jake made my heart pick up its pace for a minute or two. Ridiculous, of course.

The rest of the story consisted of interviews with American immigration officials and crew members from two of the ships in the Helice fleet that called at U.S. ports. The faces of the crew members were blanked and their voices altered as they confirmed Helice ships smuggled illegals into the U.S. as well as into New Zealand and Australia. The attorneys general for the states of Washington and California, where Helice ships docked, were quoted as saying they intended to conduct full investigations.

As the segment ended, it was clear Jake's story was a snowball that had started an avalanche, and Helice was shortly going to be in a world of hurt.

"She did it, didn't she," Sophie said.

I muted the commercial and looked at her. "Convicted in the court of world opinion, you mean?"

"And more. She stopped them. Not just from running without lights and possibly sinking another boat, but worse.

Slavery. If they hadn't hit us, and Jake hadn't written the story...those poor people. Giving up everything they have for a chance and then paying with the rest of their lives. She stopped that, Max. I think..."

I waited, watching Sophie. Something had changed. She was sitting straighter, perhaps. Or maybe it was the look on her face, a lightness in her expression.

"It isn't what I wanted," she said. "What I wanted was justice for Sam. But this...it's so much more. It's hopeful." There were tears in Sophie's eyes, but she didn't sound sad. "Do you believe good can come from evil, Max?"

For the first time I could see the woman who'd stood next to Sam that long-ago day, smiling into the camera, looking young and strong.

"It's what Jake has done," she said.

~ ~ ~

I spent the week after the *Sixty Minutes* piece in Tampa at a hearing, and I returned to San Francisco to a transformed Sophie. While I was away, she'd convinced Rosie to give her a free hand with the paint selections for his building, something I considered a major feat on his part until I realized he might have no idea she was colorblind.

She insisted on showing me how it had turned out. As we drove up, she made me close my eyes while her driver parked the car. Commanding me to continue to keep my eyes closed, she helped me out of the car, and then turned me to face the building, a large Victorian that had been perched at the edge of the business district when it was first built.

Two weeks ago it had been a dull, peeling beige. Today, its layered trim was painted an alternating green, blue, and brown, while the building itself had been painted cream.

"What do you think?" she asked.

"It certainly stands out."

"That doesn't sound like a compliment."

I was teasing, but she looked disappointed.

"It's very handsome," I said, smiling at her.

"Thank goodness." She let out a breath when she saw my expression. Then her excitement and pride came bubbling out in a rush of words. "Rosie said he liked it, but I really wanted your opinion. Sam's mother helped me pick the colors...navy blue, cinnamon, and hunter green. I'm going to use the same colors as accents inside. I'm so glad you like it." The whole time she was talking, her hands were moving in excited arcs, and she looked at the building with shining eyes.

~ ~ ~

More surprises were in store.

Sophie was at my place for the weekend, and we were sitting on the terrace sipping wine and watching the sun set when she announced she was going back to college to work on a degree in design.

"Why design?" I asked.

"I discovered I loved it when I was working with your bonsai, and that was confirmed when I worked on Rosie's place."

"But won't it be difficult, not being able to see color?"

"Design is more than color. It might seem like a strange choice, though."

"Rather like a deaf person wanting to be a musician," I said.

"There are deaf musicians."

She said it so decisively, I didn't challenge her, although it seemed an unlikely proposition.

"Without color to distract me, I see the world differently than I used to," she said.

I watched the sky color deepen from blue to rose as the orange sun slowly descended through narrow bands of clouds floating near the horizon. I tried to imagine what it looked like to Sophie in her Ansel Adams world.

"You know, working on Rosie's place, I felt...content, I guess. I didn't think I'd ever feel that way again."

"I thought you were content being here," *with me*. Luckily I'd managed to stop those last two words from coming out.

Sophie reached out a hand and laid it over mine. "You saved my life, Max. But I have to stop leaning on you so hard. It's not fair to you."

"I love having you lean on me."

Sophie shook her head, giving me a rueful smile that made my throat close up.

"So, when do you start school?" I said, trying for safer ground, where I could get my emotions under control.

"I've applied to the Design Institute of Chicago, for the winter term."

It took me a moment to catch my breath. "I'll miss you," I said.

She looked away from the sunset and into my eyes. "I'll miss you too, Max. You're a wonderful friend."

It was a major effort to string together the words to let her know I was glad she'd found something to care about. After that I concentrated on the sunset and on the glass of wine in my hand, until they were both finished. We went to the kitchen then and worked on dinner together.

But something had irreversibly shifted between us.

~ ~ ~

When I arrived at work the next morning, Cassie followed me into my office, sat down, and proceeded to fidget—a sure sign something was going on.

"What's up?" I asked, glancing at her.

"I promised not to tell you, but I promised before I realized what I was promising, so that means I've got to follow my own judgment, right?" She was wringing her hands and looking worried.

I stopped pulling papers out of my briefcase and stared at her. "A promise is a promise, Cass."

"Yeah. You're right. You been by Rosie's school lately, Max?"

It seemed a strange segue. "Sophie and I went over last week."

"It'd be a good idea for you to stop by again, real soon, and that's all I'm saying."

"Okay, Cassie. Got it. Do I need to go now, or can it wait until this afternoon?"

"You can take Rosie out for lunch," she said. It was a typical Cassie communication, except the usual good humor was missing, and that lack didn't bode well.

~ ~ ~

I found out immediately what Cassie wasn't supposed to tell me when I got my first look at Rosie's building. The painter had already erased part of the sprayed-on black words, but enough was left for me to get the gist. Rosie was being accused of being a crack head and a drug dealer, with racial epithets thrown in for good measure.

I clenched my fists around the crutch handles in impotent rage, and I had to ease my grip before I could manage to walk across the street and in the front door. Inside, the smell of smoke and charring was strong. I swallowed, fighting off a wave of rage and sadness, and then walked toward the back, where I found Rosie and a carpenter working on a broken window. Next to the window, the back door and part of the floor were blackened. Puddles of water made the floor treacherous going for me.

I waited in the doorway until Rosie looked up.

When he saw me, he frowned, looking tired and suddenly much older. "Max. What you doing here?"

"I was in the neighborhood. Thought I'd stop by, take you to lunch. Just lost my appetite, though."

He stood up. Distress deepened the furrows on his brow and carved out grooves on his cheeks, and I knew why he'd made Cassie promise not to tell me. He was so proud of handling everything himself. But such raw, ugly hate. No one should have to handle that alone.

"Friends stand together when there's something tough facing one of them." I spoke carefully, trying to keep the frustration and outrage at bay for the moment.

"Don't like sharing no ugly stuff, Max."

"I understand that. The police been by?"

He shrugged. "Yeah. Took pictures. Flapped their mouths. Bottom line, ain't nothing they can do."

"This the first sign of a problem?"

He rubbed his forehead, leaving a black streak behind. Then he signaled me to walk out the door with him. More black paint was sprayed in a random pattern on the back of the building.

"I got a couple of notes pushed under the door. Saying they don't want no nigger drug users in San Germano. Signed, concerned citizens. Gave them to the police this morning."

Although Rosie and I were both speaking calmly, as if we were discussing what to have for dinner, I could see the strain in his face. For my part, I felt the same helpless anger brought on by those old newsreels of police with fire hoses and dogs protecting white Southern schools from little black children.

"Okay if I talk to the police?"

"It's a waste of your time, Max. They've already decided. Ain't no evidence."

~ ~ ~

Rosie was correct. If the police had any ideas, they weren't sharing them. When I got back to the office, I called Tommy Dorset and arranged for him to keep an eye on Rosie's place for the next few nights. He came in two days later to give me a report.

"Rosie has someone staying inside the building at night, and I've got someone watching from the street. My guy tells me not much action in downtown San Germano at night."

Cassie handed Tommy a cup of coffee and sat down to listen.

"I've also done some nosing around during the day. Got into conversations in the coffee shop. Even stopped in the beauty salon and tried to sell them a new line of shampoo."

That made Cassie snort.

"And?" I said, moving him along. When Tommy has a good story to tell, he enjoys dragging it out.

"Lots of people uneasy about Rosie's business plan. San Germano is a nice, clean, safe place. They don't want any ex-addicts, ex-cons, or homeless cluttering up their town even if they are there going to school. Of course, what they're really saying is the subway service is there to allow San Germano citizens to get to and from the city. Not for city people to bring any city problems their way." He stopped and took a sip of coffee.

Cassie and I remained silent, waiting for him to finish.

"My guess. A couple of people did the painting and threw the Molotov cocktail, but a lot of people cheered them on from behind closed doors."

Yeah. That's how this sort of thing usually got done. "So, why now? It wasn't a secret, what Rosie was planning." I'd been surprised actually, that Rosie's building permit requests had gone as smoothly as they had.

"Just didn't sink in, I guess. They heard cooking school, sounded good, till they noticed the owner was black and heard the kind of students he hoped to attract."

Outrage threatened once again to sweep over me, and I had to keep reminding myself I'd be more effective if I stayed calm.

"San Germano has a town council form of government," Tommy continued. "The next meeting's in seven days. You and Rosie need to be there. Word is Business Council—that's a two-cent version of a Chamber of Commerce, by the way— is planning to push Rosie out. Plan seems to be to introduce a motion of concern at the next council meeting. That will put pressure on the building inspectors to make Rosie's life hell with additional requirements. As soon as he complies with one request, they'll have another ready to go. They'll just keep at it until Rosie gets tired and throws in the towel. There was also talk Rosie lied on his license application. If they can prove that, likely they won't need the other strategies."

"Rosie didn't lie on his application." I knew it for a fact. At his request, I'd checked it after he filled it out.

"You want my take?" Tommy said. "They may not have legal grounds, but they've all got their moral danders up. Save our town from out-of-town problems and all that shit. It's going to be a real uphill battle. Rosie might be better off finding another place."

"Rosie won't run from a fight," Cassie said. She looked worried and sounded upset.

"Seven days until the meeting?" I said.

"Yeah, the twentieth at eight o'clock in the town hall."

Tommy left, and I asked Cassie to cancel a dinner I had scheduled for the same evening. Then I stood for a time, looking out at the fog beginning to erase the outlines of the Golden Gate Bridge, trying to set aside my anger in order to think through what needed to be done to help Rosie.

Chapter Twenty-Five
MAX

I was still thinking about Rosie's difficulties, when Cassie buzzed me to say Daniel Meredith, my contact in the Sydney consulate and Jake's friend, was on the phone.

"Max, Jake's been shot."

Time slowed as Daniel continued. "Last night...neighbor found her...shot in the back...bullet clipped a lung...major blood loss...coma."

I swallowed and tried to speak. Found I couldn't. Dread pooled in my gut, along with fear for Jake. Daniel kept talking in jerky sentences, or maybe my brain, caught by the image of Jake, unmoving, was refusing to process the words. "Condition critical...doctors not happy."

"How? Who shot her?" As the reality of Jake being shot started to sink in, pictures of her flashed through my mind. Jake, impatiently pushing her hair out of her eyes and then nibbling on her thumbnail as she talked into the phone. Jake with that look she always got when something caught her reporter's attention. Jake at the Brackens' memorial service with tears making silvery tracks down her cheeks. Jake sitting in a forest glade with light dappling her skin.

Slowly the room came back into focus. I wondered what I'd missed, or if my memories had occurred in that instant between one word and the next.

"Look, Max, the reason I called. Her doctor said she doesn't seem to be fighting like he expects. And there's something else. On the way to the hospital she kept asking for Max. As far as I'm aware, you're the only Max she knows. The doctor thinks it might help if you came."

I barely managed to speak calmly. "What good can that do?"

"The doctor thinks it will help." His voice had a dogged tone.

"I barely know Jo...Jake," I said.

"What difference does that make? She asked for you. She could be dying."

Exactly the part I couldn't face.

Cassie buzzed me on the intercom to announce another call, and I realized I'd terminated the conversation with Daniel and hung up the phone with no memory of doing either. I told Cassie to hold my calls and walked over to the window. A fog bank was rolling in, turning the world to mist.

Although Daniel said the police had no leads, I had my suspicions. And if it turned out they were correct and her wounding was tied to the Helice story, then it was my fault.

The fog swirled in until it blanked everything. I turned back to my desk, where the depositions for the Tampa case were stacked. I was supposed to be working out a strategy for the pre-trial negotiations, but I had already been having a tough time concentrating as thoughts about the vandalism at Rosie's place and the San Germano town meeting kept jostling me.

Now this.

Kelly had started it, telling me I wasn't living. Then everything was set into further motion by Sophie's case. If I hadn't taken that on, I wouldn't have her or Jake to worry about, Rosie wouldn't have left to start a cooking school, and I'd still be sitting safe and sound in my wheelchair making a comfortable living.

Slowly dying of boredom.

Where the hell did that come from? I hadn't been dying of boredom when Kelly started interfering in my life. But what about now? What if I tried to undo everything?

Yeah, okay, I admit it. Boring. But I didn't know how to handle this new life. It kept demanding I take risks. Wasn't the old way better? Win, lose, or settle out of court—still get paid. What was wrong with that?

I sighed. My arguments weren't working. I had no idea why Jake had asked for me, but I owed it to her to be with her. I also owed it to Rosie to be at that meeting in San Germano. It was more likely my presence would make a difference in Rosie's case than in Jake's, since I could do something concrete to help Rosie, while I had no idea what I could do for Jake.

But it was Jake I couldn't stop thinking about.

~ ~ ~

I called Anthony Micelli and asked to meet with him as soon as possible. To my relief, he made time available immediately.

"So, what's going on?" he asked.

"Something's come up. I need to take another leave."

"You'd better tell me about it." He sat back, flicking the crease in his trousers.

When I finished telling him about Jake and Rosie, he sighed. "I see why you might think you should go to Australia, but I don't see what you expect to accomplish."

"I don't know that I'll accomplish a damn thing except to stand by a friend."

"This reporter is in a coma. She won't even know you're there. Meanwhile it sounds like Rosie can use all the legal and moral support he can get."

Anthony had encapsulated my dilemma perfectly. How to choose which friend to stand beside when they were separated by six thousand miles and both needed me at the same time.

"I'm going to try to get back for the town meeting. But just in case I don't, I'm organizing legal help for Rosie."

Anthony peered at me. "Interesting. You're an excellent attorney, Max. One of the best I've ever known. You do your homework. Approach your cases with cold logic. Never show any emotion. Always wondered what you'd be like if you felt strongly about a case. Doubted for a long time I'd ever see it."

I didn't know if I was supposed to answer, but it didn't matter. I couldn't, even if someone put a gun to my head and ordered me to.

"What if I told you that if you go to Australia, I'm backing Todd Wermling as my successor?" he asked, leaning forward.

What the hell. I thought he'd already decided that, just hadn't announced it yet. I took a breath and let it out along with the last of my regrets. "You have to do what's best for you, and I have to do what's best for me."

"Ah." He pursed his lips and stared at his folded hands a moment before looking at me. "It might be wise, while you're in Australia, to do some thinking about what you want out of your future."

If Anthony had said something like that to me five years, hell, two years ago, before I met Sophie—and Joanna Kate got shot—my gut would have done a loop. Now it seemed a completely trivial remark.

I realized Anthony was waiting for an answer, although I couldn't exactly recall the question. "You ever been tempted by the road not taken?" I asked him.

"Can't say I have. Plenty to keep me interested here on this road."

"I seem to have made a detour, and I can't guarantee I'll ever make it back, but I do know one thing."

"What's that?"

Anthony's frankness permitted me some frankness of my own. "If you back Todd Wermling as your successor, I'll be leaving the firm."

"That a threat, Max?" He gave me a questioning look.

"No. I'm simply informing you of what I intend to do."

Anthony held my eyes for a moment before he spoke again. "Who are you getting to provide the legal support for Rosie?"

"Thought I'd asked Jim Beamis over at Sheamus and Sealley." I was glad to get off the topic of detours and Todd. And my future, for that matter.

"Why not someone from this firm?"

"It's not exactly our area of expertise."

"I wouldn't mind giving a hand. Believe I can remember enough of the Constitution to stand up to a rabble and not let them trample Rosie's rights. He's a good man. Rosie. Don't want him hurt any more than you do, Max. I'll do my damnedest to help him."

I swallowed the lump that had suddenly formed in my throat. "I appreciate the offer. It'll be easier for me to go to Australia if Rosie has you watching out for him."

"I do have one condition," Anthony said. "Before you go, I want you to talk to Todd."

I looked at Anthony, counted to ten, took a deep breath. "About?"

"Just drop in. Congratulate him on the case he just closed, perhaps. Then go on your fool's errand. I'll see to Rosie. When you get back, we'll talk."

~ ~ ~

While Cassie made my airline reservations, I walked down the hall to speak to Todd with no idea what I was going to say. In spite of his narrow little mind, or perhaps because of it, he's one hell of a litigator. Maybe I could manage to say that without choking.

In the end, I congratulated him on the settlement he'd recently obtained, as well as on the marriage of his daughter, since he had a wedding picture of the happy couple prominently displayed. That was a surprise in itself, given the groom's dark skin. Then I told him I was returning to Australia.

He sat back and stared at me. Picked up a pen and started fiddling with it. "Rumor has it you never billed the last time you went to Australia, Max."

"That's correct. I was on leave. You got a problem with that?" I kept my tone even, although it was a struggle.

"Heard friends of your brother were involved. Guess I would've done the same thing."

I blinked and looked at him more closely. He sounded so unlike himself, I wondered briefly if he could be ill.

"Besides, you go back, you do me a huge favor."

"How's that?"

"Word is Anthony is going to decide on his successor soon. Doubt this will advance your candidacy."

"Frankly, Todd, I don't give a damn." I spoke calmly. Easy to do, because I really didn't give a damn.

"Sorry to hear you feel that way, Max. Good luck in Australia." Once again, Todd had surprised me. Twice in one conversation. A record. Maybe he *was* sick. In the last year he'd lost his paunch. Still, if there was something going on, Cassie would know about it, and whatever Cassie knew, she shared with me.

I turned in the doorway and gave Todd a long look. For once, he met my eyes without squirming or looking away. Then I walked out closing the door quietly behind me.

~ ~ ~

"You need more coffee, Max?"

"I'll get my own coffee, Rosie. Sit down. We need to talk. I have some things to tell you."

Rosie stood up, got the coffeepot, and topped off my cup, anyway. "I'm supposed to meet the plumber at eight," he said.

"This won't take long. I have to be in the office by eight myself."

In the old days, after we finished breakfast, he would have driven me to work. These days he headed for San Germano, while I drove myself to work. With a grunt, Rosie sat down across from me and started eating.

"I've had Tommy keeping an eye on your place," I told him.

"You don't have to do that. I got a brother been staying overnight."

"I know. Tommy's also found out the business community is working on a way to push you out."

Rosie froze, a forkful of scrambled eggs halfway to his mouth, and looked at me. "How they do that, Max? I got my permits fair and square. Been jumping through their damn hoops near nine months." Rosie rubbed at the furrows in his forehead. He looked tired and strained. Had ever since the vandalism.

"You still have to pass your final inspections," I said. "And there's a group working to make sure you don't. Next council meeting, they plan to offer a resolution on the matter. If they're successful, you won't be able to operate a hot dog stand, let alone a cooking school."

"You got any *good* news, Max?"

"We can fight it. Starting with legal representation at the meeting. I'd do that, but unfortunately, something else has happened." As I told Rosie about Jake, he put his fork down and pushed his half-full plate out of the way, looking even more strained.

I couldn't manage another bite myself. Could barely manage to get the words out to tell Rosie I was likely going to be halfway around the world when he needed me to stand by him at the council meeting.

"No, never you mind, Max. That reporter. She helped Sophie. Sophie told me. We all owe her. All us that loves Sophie. You go and stay as long as you got to stay."

"You've been my friend a long time, Rosie. I don't feel good about not being here when you need me."

"I can't do nothing 'bout the way you feel, Max. Know how I feel though. You stay for my meeting and that reporter dies, we both feel guilty. Don't need no more guilt in my life. You go to Australia. I'll manage."

"Micelli's offered to help out. He's a good man in a fight."

Rosie sat back and folded his arms. "Hell, I got Micelli, why I need you?"

"I know you're trying to make me feel better."

"Working, ain't it?"

"More or less."

"You go to Australia. I'll be fine. We lose in San Germano, I'll sell out, find another spot. That reporter, she dies, that's it. No more chances."

~ ~ ~

I called Sophie and asked her to have lunch with me. As we finished up with coffee, I told her about Rosie's troubles.

"Oh, Max. How awful. Is he okay?"

"The physical damage was confined to the building. But Rosie's been hurt all right. And they're not finished with him."

I explained about the town meeting. And then I pulled in a breath and told her about Jake. As the meaning of my words sank in, she put her hands up to cover her mouth and her eyes glittered with tears.

"She asked for me, and I'm going. It means I probably won't make it to Rosie's meeting."

"She's in love with you."

I shook my head. "No. Why would you think such a thing?"

"Call it woman's intuition."

"If your intuition's so good, how come you never realized I'm in love with you?"

We looked at each other, startled into mutual silence. I felt as if the words I'd spoken were separated from me somehow. I no longer seemed to be able to hold in my thoughts, my feelings, as if what happened to Jake had stripped off some protective covering.

"Sorry. That didn't come out exactly right." I had to work to meet her eyes, the coffee I was reaching for abandoned.

Sophie placed her hand on mine. "I did know. At least, I suspected you thought you were. But you're not really, Max."

"How do you know that."

"You didn't try to change my mind when I said I was going away. To New Zealand and now Chicago."

"I want you to be happy. I plan on waiting for you."

"I know." She cocked her head at me. "There are different kinds of love, Max. You and I...well, we've helped each other through some difficult times. I'm so grateful you're part of my life. I consider you my dearest friend."

Dearest friend? I tested it, expecting to feel rejected, but what I felt instead was something like relief. And recognition. It was how I felt about Kelly...and Sophie, as well?

As for the rest of it, I didn't see how she could be correct about Jake. But say she was. Sophie was still missing the boat on how I felt about Jake. I liked her. And yeah, I found her attractive. Watching her climb around a boat in a swimsuit, I'd had an impure thought or two, but then likely so did Gavin Aylliard.

That wasn't love. Besides, look at our last two interactions. They'd been...distant. And to top it off, if that wasn't enough already, she lived in Sydney, while I lived in San Francisco. Impossible as well as improbable.

But if I didn't love her, what did I feel? How to label the sickening surge of emotion when Daniel Meredith told me she'd been shot? Sorrow? Yes, definitely sorrow. But something else, as well. A something that pushed sorrow out of my mind as if it never existed. It wasn't love, though. It was white-hot fury.

When I went to Australia it wouldn't be just to see Jake. It would also be to try to discover if Helice was responsible for hurting her. If they were, I would make them pay, and I wouldn't stop at a few million. I wouldn't stop until Helice was destroyed, and I didn't care if it took the rest of my life to do it.

"Max, are you all right?"

"Yeah. Fine."

"You look so ferocious."

I shook my head and rubbed a hand across my forehead, trying to wipe away whatever it was Sophie had seen.

"Don't worry about Rosie," she said. "I'll go to the meeting, too. You concentrate on Jake."

Chapter Twenty-Six
MAX

I finally met Daniel Meredith in person when he arrived in the late afternoon at my hotel in Sydney to take me to the hospital to visit Jake.

Shaking his hand, I figured so much for Sophie's intuition about Jake being in love with me. Daniel was a tall, handsome man with an athletic build and the same long-limbed stride as Jake. From my previous interactions with him, I knew he was a competent diplomat, and his grooming and tailoring were impeccable. In short, he was precisely the kind of man any woman in her right mind would find irresistible.

Maybe I was wrong in thinking Jake was the one who ended their relationship. Or maybe, given Daniel's presence now, I'd misinterpreted, and the relationship hadn't ended.

On our way to the hospital, Daniel briefed me on the progress the police were making, which wasn't much. "I've arranged for you to meet with the detective in charge of the case tomorrow afternoon," he said.

We walked into the hospital, and Daniel led the way, visibly altering his stride in order not to leave me behind. I felt like a tugboat bobbing in the wake of a sleek yacht. I focused on that discomfort, trying to ignore the hospital sights and sounds that brought back such a clear memory of both my own time in one and Kelly's.

When we arrived on Jake's floor, Daniel stopped at the nursing station. A man with tired eyes wearing a white coat over surgical greens came over to be introduced—one Dr. Hickam, the doctor who thought a visit from me might help Jake.

"Mr. Gildea. Good of you to come all this way."

"How is she?"

"She came through surgery like a champ. We managed to repair the damage."

I felt a lift of relief, but he wasn't finished. "Unfortunately, she's developed pneumonia, so we've had to put her on a ventilator so she doesn't have to work so hard. But her condition has been worsening. That's why I'm grabbing at straws, like asking you to come."

"What do you want me to do?"

"Sit with her. Talk to her. Hold her hand."

"I'm sure you have other things to do, Daniel," I said. "I'll catch a cab back to the hotel."

"That's okay, Max. I'll be in the waiting room over there. No rush."

I followed Dr. Hickam to find a uniformed police officer sitting outside Jake's room. After checking with the officer, we went in, and Hickam took Jake's hand in his. "Jake, it's Dr. Hickam. I've brought someone to see you." He was addressing her exactly as if she were awake. "Your friend, Max Gildea. You asked for him."

If he hadn't identified the woman in the bed as Jake, I never would have known. In the dim light her skin was sallow, her hair dull and lifeless. There were dark smudges under her closed eyes, and a tangle of wires and tubes emerged from under the blanket that covered her. She herself lay motionless.

Hickam gestured for me to come over to the bed. "As you can see, we had to do a tracheotomy after she had an allergic reaction to one of the drugs and her throat and tongue swelled. She's currently sedated, and the monitor there is showing her heart rate, blood pressure, and oxygen saturation." He pointed at the green and yellow lines on the screen at the head of the bed.

"Bullet clipped one lung. She lost a lot of blood. If she hadn't been in such good physical shape, she never would have made it this far. She needs to know we took care of her injuries. She'll be fine if she can just lick this infection."

While he spoke, he continued to hold Jake's hand, while I dealt with a rush of memory—those machines, their quiet clicks, a dim room, and waking up to all that and discovering my legs were gone. I took a breath and refocused on what he was saying.

"I'll be back to check on her at seven thirty. I'll try to talk Daniel into going for dinner." He patted Jake's hand. "You hang in there, Jake." He released her hand and with a nod to me walked out the door.

After he left, I stared at Jake. Her hand lay where Dr. Hickam placed it after releasing it.

I looked down at it and smiled. The elegant pink ovals she'd had in New Zealand were gone, replaced by everyday chewed-on nails.

It felt strange thinking about talking to this woman who didn't resemble anyone I knew. But Dr. Hickam had showed me what to do. I pulled a chair over, sat down, and took her hand in mine. When I curled my fingers around hers, I could feel the slow beat of her pulse. I closed my eyes and tried to bring up a picture of her, sitting across from me at the Thai Chai or walking rapidly down a Cairns street talking into her cell phone.

Then I took a breath and started speaking. "They tell me you aren't fighting hard enough, Joanna Kate. I find that difficult to believe. If it's one thing I thought I knew about you, it's that you're a fighter."

Her hand remained perfectly still in mine.

"I have an apology to make, you know. I never told you how much I admired your courage in going after Helice. You took a hell of a chance. And it's making a difference. Helice will be facing prosecution soon. You stopped them. You made them pay."

I listened for a time to the shushing of the ventilator and the soft clicks of the intravenous pumps. Green, white, and yellow lines marched across the monitor, culminating in large, easy-to-read numbers, but whether the numbers were good or bad was something I couldn't decipher.

When I'd talked to my brother Link before coming, he told me that, along with being spoken to, patients in a coma needed to be touched. I picked up the bottle of lotion from the side table and put some in my hand. Then I massaged Jake's arm from shoulder to wrist. As tall as she was, I could still encircle her wrist with the thumb and first finger of my own hand.

I took her hand in mine and rubbed and pulled on each of her fingers, then I moved to the other side of the bed, and as I smoothed the lotion into her skin, I started talking again, at random, to give her something to listen to besides the equipment noises, if she was able to hear, the way Hickam and Link thought she could.

I told her about my life. About how I lost my legs. About Cassie and the time I defended her against Todd Wermling's prejudice. About Kelly and what finally led me to give the artificial legs another try. And I told her about Rosie and his cooking school. When I finished with her arms, I massaged her feet. I didn't know if she felt anything, but doing something Link said might be useful made me feel not quite as helpless.

At seven thirty, Dr. Hickam came back. "How's our girl?"

"I haven't seen any change."

"We better let her rest now." He picked up her hand. "We're going, Jake, but Max will be back in the morning. You work on getting well." I expected he talked to her that way to keep from being discouraged himself.

We walked out of the dim room into the brightness of the unit. Hickam covered a yawn, looking even more tired than when I arrived. He told me he'd left orders to allow me to see Jake the next day, but to check in with the nursing station first. I left him and made my way back to Daniel, who insisted on taking me to dinner. I was exhausted from the long flight and the visit with Jake, but I was too hungry to turn him down.

"What about Jake's family?" I asked before starting on the lamb stew I'd ordered.

"Her mother was here until yesterday. She had to get back to the station to take care of Jake's grandmother. Jake's sisters live overseas."

"You said she asked for me on the way to the hospital?"

"Apparently she was agitated, until the ambulance guy finally made out what she was saying and told her he understood and they'd call Max right away. After that she calmed down."

This second telling still didn't make sense, unless Jake suspected the shooting was because of the Helice story, and she was trying to get that message to me. It was all so tenuous. Not just Joanna Kate's hold on life, but my coming six thousand miles to be with her because some stranger thought she asked for me.

~ ~ ~

The next afternoon, I took a break from the hospital to keep my appointment with the detective on Jake's case.

George Lewiston was a large, untidy man with a wild bush of white hair and an even wilder set of eyebrows. His office was furnished with a gray metal desk, a couple of wooden chairs, and several dilapidated file cabinets, all covered with piles of thick file folders. My immediate reaction to the chaos was to question his competence, but I discovered as we talked, that unlike his office and person, his mind was tidy and extremely sharp.

He started by wringing every bit of information on the Brackens' case out of my memory, and then he proceeded to ask what I knew about Helice. He told me one thing in return. "We've cleared the boyfriend."

"You mean Daniel Meredith?" I wondered why I bothered asking when I already knew the answer.

He nodded. It meant I was wrong in assuming Jake and Daniel's relationship had ended. It was something I'd already suspected. No reason then to find this confirmation so unsettling.

"Do you think it's possible Jake was shot because of the articles she wrote on Helice?" I asked.

"Yeah. Could be. Hit looked professional. One shot from a high-powered rifle. Only unprofessional thing about it, the victim didn't die."

"What about if I offer a reward?"

"Umm, might help. That honor among thieves stuff is bullshit. Wave enough dosh in front of them, they salivate like bloody dogs. How much you have in mind?"

"Is fifty thousand US enough?"

He looked startled then blew out a breath that became a low whistle. "Let's start with fifteen K Australian. See if we get any nibbles."

~ ~ ~

The hours by Jake's bedside began to take on a bizarre aspect. On one level, I knew how tenuous her hold on life was, but on another, I was busy denying it. I refused to let myself consider any other possibility than that one day she would open her eyes, and I would see the woman I'd known in Cairns.

It was a tricky emotional balancing act—trying to feel neither hopeless nor too hopeful, not thinking at all about what it would mean to me if she died. I watched the nurses and Hickam carefully, trying to read from their expressions some hint of what I was too afraid to put into words.

Early on, I found talking at random difficult, so I began reading to Jake instead. It beat trying to come up with more personal stories or sitting silently watching the numbers on the monitors and worrying about things I had no control over, like whether Jake would recover or how Rosie's situation would be resolved.

In the mornings, I read aloud from *The Australian*, telling her the name of the reporter who wrote each article before starting to read. Bob Mulroney's name was the byline on several prominent stories, and I wondered if he was as "cheesed off" by Jake's Helice story as he'd been about her scoop on the Brackens.

I asked Daniel if he knew what kind of books and music Jake liked, and he said he thought she read mysteries, and she liked classical music, jazz, and classic rock. I took a cab to a bookstore and picked up several books, then I went to an electronics store and bought a small CD player, after which I picked out a mix of music.

I spent the time with Jake alternating between giving her massages, reading out loud, and playing music. One of the nurses told me that when I massaged Jake's feet I should bend them ninety degrees in order to keep her calf muscles from shortening. If the muscles shortened, Jake would have trouble walking when she woke up.

I took those instructions as a hopeful sign that the nurse expected Jake to wake up and need to walk. I felt it was even more hopeful when a physical therapist started coming once a day. She showed me how to move Jake's arms and legs and said if I did it for five to ten minutes every hour it would lessen Jake's time in rehab.

Dr. Hickam usually stopped in to see Jake in the morning and in the evening. He said he was pleased with her progress, and he thought the massage, exercises, reading, and music were all great ideas.

There were times when I sat there just holding Jake's hand, letting the music play. In that room, time seemed to flow like a calm river, and it was peaceful sitting with her, in spite of the battle going on in her body. It was at any rate a quiet battle marked only by the march of numbers and lines on the monitor and punctuated with the soft machine sounds of the intravenous pumps and ventilator.

I noticed Jake's fingernails had begun to grow out. I ran the tip of my finger over each one, feeling the hard ridge of recovering nail. "*She's in love with you,*" Sophie had said.

But then Sophie hadn't met Daniel.

No contest. Not only was Daniel a thoroughly nice man, he was a whole man, one who walked around without the assistance of titanium and carbon fiber. I forced that thought out of my mind. Better to focus on something I could manage, like assuring Jake's long-term safety.

Right now, she was safe. Lewiston was providing a police guard, and he'd asked *The Australian* to tamp down on the publicity side. The last report they printed said Jake was still in critical condition. He figured that would keep whoever had attempted to kill her from trying again in the short run. But if Jake pulled through, whoever shot her might try again, something I intended to prevent no matter what the cost.

Lewiston said there was no indication that any of the other stories Jake had worked on had the potential the Helice story did to upset someone so much they'd want to kill her. Also, there were no ex-lovers who might be stalking her. It meant Helice was the prime suspect.

~ ~ ~

Every evening Daniel showed up at seven. He said it was to give me a ride back to the hotel, but I thought it was mainly to check on Jake. I knew how difficult it was making conversation with a person who was comatose. If someone were standing there listening to me, I'd dry up completely, so I always left the room when he arrived. He usually came out after a half hour or so and drove me back to the hotel. Some nights he came in with me to have a drink.

The better I got to know him, the more I liked Daniel. He was steady, intelligent, and caring. The perfect man for Jake.

Chapter Twenty-Seven
MAX

When I first arrived in Australia, I was hoping to make it back for Rosie's meeting. But that hope faded as the days went by with little change in Jake's condition, or at least any change I could see, in spite of Hickam's increasing optimism.

Each evening, after I'd finished at the hospital for the day, I went back to the hotel and checked on what Cassie had sent me. She'd promised to keep me fully informed of events, but her communications had a stiffness that suggested she wasn't.

One evening, I faxed her a list I'd been working on all day. Afterward, I tossed and turned most of the night, trying to think if I was forgetting anything. In the morning, I woke up with the dull ache of a bad night radiating through my head and neck.

The first thing I noticed when I reached the door to Jake's room that morning was that the soft pulse of the ventilator had been replaced by a steady sound like running water. I stopped in the doorway, my heart pounding, afraid to go any farther.

"Wonderful news. She's off the ventilator." One of the nurses had walked up behind me as I stood there.

I saw that a tube was still delivering air to Jake's neck, but it was now plugged into a wall socket, and the bulky ventilator had been removed.

Hickam was standing beside the bed watching Jake. When he heard the nurse speak to me, he turned and smiled. "Our girl's breathing on her own."

It was the first time I could remember seeing him smile.

"We stopped the sedative last night and decreased the pain meds. I was waiting for you. Thought you'd like to be here when I try to wake her up."

The nurse came in and walked to the opposite side of the bed. I stood off to the side, feeling nervous and thinking Daniel, or Jake's parents, ought to be the ones to welcome her back. I watched as Hickam proceeded to squeeze Jake's hand and speak to her. After a minute, she moved slightly. After another couple of minutes, her eyes fluttered open.

I couldn't remember the last time something gave me more pleasure than Jake growing slowly aware. But then I saw the beginnings of panic as her eyes flickered frantically between Hickam and the nurse.

Hickam spoke, and Jake's eyes switched to him and steadied. "Jake, my name is Dr. Hickam. I've been taking care of you. You're in hospital. You're safe."

Hickam motioned me to step closer and take Jake's other hand. "Talk to her." He nodded, encouraging me.

I took one of her hands in mine. "Joanna Kate." I stopped and cleared my throat before I could go on.

She glanced at me, and her eyes widened in surprise.

"Welcome back."

Her lips moved but without sound.

Dr. Hickam interrupted. "You can't talk yet, Jake, you're breathing through a tracheotomy tube. Keep up the good work, and we'll get that out soon. Meanwhile, I'll try to answer some of those questions you've probably got."

I watched Jake as Hickam told her what had happened to her. In response, her fingers tightened against mine.

"Now, you just keep breathing nice and easy, and we'll get you on room air, so you can start talking. Max is going to stay with you. Okay?"

Jake looked back at me and nodded slightly.

As soon as Hickam and the nurse left, she pulled her hand out of mine. I tried to think what to say to her and finally settled on telling her how gutsy I thought she was. In response, she continued to give me that steady look. Then she looked away, scanning the room. She was aware, but her eyes had none of the sparkle, the sheer life force I associated with Jake.

Abruptly, she fell back asleep. While she slept, I went to the gift shop and bought one of those kids' writing tablets. The kind where you lift the plastic sheet to erase the words. When she woke up an hour later and made a writing motion, I handed her the tablet.

"Up bed," she wrote.

I showed her where the controls were. When she was sitting up she wrote, "Sophie?"

"Sophie's safe. She's back in the States now. She plans to start a design course soon." I stopped abruptly, realizing there was little reason Jake would care about Sophie's plans.

"Y R U here?" she wrote.

"You asked for me."

She frowned.

"On the way to the hospital."

She shook her head and pointed at the question again.

"Dr. Hickam and Daniel thought my being here would help."

She gave me another solemn look. Then she erased the question with a tug on the plastic and wrote, "Tired."

"You want me to leave?"

She glanced at me long enough to nod her head. I had the feeling she was trying to communicate something else, something she didn't have the energy to write on the tablet, but then she closed her eyes, and the moment passed.

It was strange. She was awake. She was going to be okay. It was what we'd all been hoping and praying for, but my excitement that it had finally occurred faded, to be replaced by puzzlement and disappointment at the way she was acting.

When I'd asked Link's opinion about coming to Australia, he'd warned me about that, though. He called it intensive care paranoia, brought on by a lack of natural sleep while a patient was either in a coma or sedated and hooked up to machines. Letting Jake sleep was the best thing I could do for her even if it left me feeling at loose ends.

While Jake slept, I called Daniel to tell him the news. He wanted to come right away, but I told him Jake was sleeping, so he might as well take his time. I went to the cafeteria for lunch. When I got back to Jake's room, Daniel was there, and she was awake. She had more color in her face, and she was smiling at something he was saying. When she saw me walk in, the smile disappeared, replaced by another of those somber looks. The nurse arrived then and said they were moving Jake to a medical floor, and we could see her once she was settled.

~ ~ ~

Jake was recovering, which meant I could start thinking about getting back to San Francisco, although there was no immediate rush since I'd already missed Rosie's meeting. According to Cassie, it went well. I had some suspicions about that, but I doubted she'd actually lie. Still, Cassie rarely used one word when ten would work as well.

With Rosie's problems taken care of, or in hiatus, it meant there was nothing I needed to rush back for except my current cases, all of which were being competently handled by junior associates.

There was also no reason to stay in Australia. Jake no longer needed me to read to her, to hold her hand, to stretch out her calf muscles, or for any other damn thing. I might as well leave. It had been a mistake to come. Best then if I left as soon as possible.

I'd given Kelly's way a fair shot. She was wrong; I was right. Happiness is an illusion.

I'd even given Sophie's intuition some credence. Bullshit as well.

The old way, my way, was better. Much better.

~ ~ ~

I asked Hickam how much longer Jake might be in the hospital.

"Impossible to predict right now. We'll have to wait and see how fast she progresses."

"I need to get back to the States soon, but I don't want to adversely affect her recovery."

"As far as her physical recovery is concerned, you could leave anytime. I hope you'll stay a couple of days longer, however. To make certain her mental condition is also improving."

185

"I think her family and Daniel Meredith can assure that."

"Perhaps. But it wasn't until you arrived, that she started fighting," he said.

Nice try, Doc. I wondered how he could have missed the fact that Jake had not been exactly thrilled to see me since she woke up.

I returned to Jake's room to find her asleep again. Her breathing tube was out, and the room was quiet. I retreated to the corner, put a Bach CD in the player, and picked up the book I'd been reading out loud to her. I read silently, glancing over at her periodically. As far as I could tell, she looked exactly as she had for the past four days except most of the tubes and wires were gone.

It had been stressful worrying about her, and with the pressure released, the weariness I'd been ignoring took over, and I dozed. When I awoke and looked toward the bed, she was lying there watching me.

"How long have you been awake?" I asked, walking over to her.

She put her finger to her throat to close the hole from the tracheotomy and said, "Few minutes." Her voice was whispery and hoarse.

"How are you feeling?"

"Stomped by a ram."

"The police want to talk to you. Think you're up to it?"

"Bloody hell."

She still didn't look like the Jake I'd known in Cairns, but she was beginning to sound like her.

~ ~ ~

That evening, when Daniel and I arrived to visit Jake, she smiled at him, but once again the smile faded when she looked at me. I let Daniel do most of the talking, with Jake interjecting a whispered question or comment here and there.

When Daniel asked about her interview with the police, she frowned. "Couldn't tell them anything. Don't remember." Her head moved restlessly from side to side. The question obviously upset her.

There was a tap on the door, and a woman who was a shorter, rounded version of Jake rushed in. It was several minutes before the woman stopped patting, first Jake's face and then her hand. In between, she wiped her own eyes with a tissue. All the time she was patting, she was telling Jake how worried all of them had been, thinking about her every minute. That when Grandmum took a turn for the worse and she'd had to go home, it had nearly killed her to leave Jake. And when Dr. Hickam called to say she was conscious, Dad insisted she leave immediately to come, that he'd get the neighbor to watch Grandmum.

Then he'd driven her the hundred kilometers to the nearest airstrip, where she caught a ride with Billy in his two-seater as far as Melbourne—and wasn't that lucky Billy was coming this exact day—before catching the train to Sydney.

Listening, I finally understood why the Rutherfords had not been back to see Jake. When the flow of words slowed, Jake introduced her mother to me, and then Daniel stepped in and explained who I was. As soon as I could, I excused myself and took a cab back to the hotel.

In the morning, I arrived at the hospital to find Jake's room vacant. I checked at the nursing station and was told she was in physical therapy. When I entered the physical therapy area, it reminded me of the room at the institute where I learned to walk.

Jake was working the arm bike. Her police guard sat close by, and her mother was standing next to her. When I walked over, Mrs. Rutherford greeted me with a glad cry, while Jake gave me a nod and continued slowly pushing the handles in a circle.

In the time Jake had been awake, we'd exchanged less than two dozen words and not a single smile. After watching her with Daniel and her mother, I knew the way she was reacting to me couldn't be explained away by saying it was the result of her being in intensive care.

Jake, who could only join the conversation by stopping and placing a finger over her tracheotomy hole, kept her hands gripped on the handlebars, turning the handles slowly, first in one direction and then the opposite, while her mother and I chatted. Mrs. Rutherford told me she was leaving to go back to the family station in the afternoon.

After several minutes of conversation, fueled by Mrs. Rutherford's comments, I left Jake to her therapy and went back to the nursing station to ask what her schedule was going to be. When the nurse said she had a series of appointments and wouldn't be back in her room until four, I left the hospital and spent time checking in with Cassie.

In the early afternoon, I met again with George Lewiston. He'd called the day before and asked me to stop by. When I entered his office, he pushed his chair back, put his feet up on the desk, and gave me a big smile, waggling his eyebrows.

"Well, well, Mr. Gildea. Seems I've once again been proven correct about the effect of money on the criminal mind. I hope you're prepared to part with your fifteen K."

"If it helps identify the person who tried to kill Jake, I'd be willing to part with a hell of a lot more than that."

"Fifteen is more than adequate."

"You mind telling me what you're getting for that?"

"Got. Phone number."

"Expensive phone number." I hoped he wasn't going to just leave it there.

"Yeah." He grinned, then swung his feet off the desk and thumped his chair down. "Our lucky contestant said he's got a mate, and mate got a call. Mate's likely a fabrication, mind. Caller wanted a hit in Sydney, but when the mate discovered Jake's a sheila he pulled out. Claimed he'd never offed a woman and didn't plan to start. When he read about the hit, he figured they found someone who didn't have his principles." Lewiston snorted after this last bit and leaned forward.

"Our winner gave us the number of the man requesting the hit. Turns out to belong to an ex-con, name of Roscoe Purdy. We got a judge to let us take a look at old Roscoe's phone records." Lewiston shook his head. "Shouldn't still surprise me how dumb most criminals are, but it does. Seems old Roscoe's been in close contact with someone in Hong Kong, a guy by the name of Xuefu Wong. His private line. You want to guess who Xuefu is?"

"CEO of Helice Shipping."

Lewiston twitched his eyebrows in obvious irritation. I'd stepped on his best line.

"Good guess," he said.

But I wasn't guessing who Xuefu Wong was. I'd known that name from the beginning of Sophie's case, and in the last two days, I'd learned a great deal more about the man. His had been the second name on the list I sent Cassie.

"Xuefu runs Helice shipping but he doesn't own it. His father does," Lewiston continued.

I knew that too. The father, Shaoming Wong, the first name on my list, started out with a couple of tramp steamers after World War II and built the company to its current position, becoming extremely wealthy in the process. Xuefu was raised with all the advantages of that wealth, including a Harvard education.

Tommy had managed to track down Xuefu's roommate from his freshman year at Harvard. That man, now an executive in a large computer firm based in Seattle, said that in college Xuefu had used his expertise in the martial arts to pick fights and beat up people he didn't like.

After Harvard, Tommy reported, Xuefu returned to Hong Kong. He spent three months on one of Helice's freighters before taking a job in the home office. Over the years, he'd moved steadily up the ladder. Along the way, he married the daughter of another wealthy Hong Kong family, and five years ago, when Shaoming became Chairman of the Board, Xuefu was named CEO.

What wasn't clear in the material Tommy had unearthed was whether Xuefu had changed as he'd aged, although it was my experience people who were cruel as teenagers didn't usually turn into gentle, caring adults. Besides, if Xuefu arranged for Jake to be shot for giving Helice a hard time, it was an indication that, if anything, he'd changed for the worse.

"The evidence of Xuefu's involvement in the case is circumstantial," Lewiston continued. "I don't need more convincing, but a prosecutor will. We'll pick Roscoe up, but it's unlikely we'll get anything out of him. Still, that will stir things up. Make both Roscoe and the shooter think twice about giving it another go."

"Jake still isn't safe, then."

"Nope. It'll help some. Word gets around fast. If we hassle enough people, offing her becomes too risky. Not worth the money."

"How long do you plan to guard her?" I asked.

"Can't for much longer, I'm afraid."

"Is it okay if I look into hiring somebody?"

"Good idea. I can suggest some people."

"I'd appreciate it if you wouldn't tell her. Let her think it's a continuation of her current protection." Assuring her safety was the least I could do, now that I knew for certain I was the one who got her shot.

At four, I was back in Jake's room. She arrived with an aide who helped her back into bed. Neither of us spoke until the aide backed out of the room with the wheelchair.

"You've had a busy day," I said.

"They're pushing hard. Dr. Hickam said they need the bed."

"I'm sure he's teasing you."

"He may be teasing, but all the therapists seem to be taking him seriously." She was speaking more easily, although she still needed to cover the tracheotomy hole to do it.

"How *are* you doing?" I asked.

"I'm tired, and I'm tired of being tired. And I hurt. Quite a bit, as a matter of fact."

"You want me to get the nurse to give you a pain pill?"

"No. They make me all muzzy. I'd rather have the pain." She fussed with the bed controls, raising the head then lowering it slightly.

I waited for the whine of the mechanism to stop. "Jake, I need to ask you something."

"That sounds ominous."

"I don't mean it to."

"Okay. Go ahead." She shifted a bit and settled her covers, mostly, I suspected, so she wouldn't have to look at me.

"I'm wondering if you remember why you asked for me?"

It was a moment before she answered. "I don't remember any of it. I don't even remember driving home the night it happened."

I concentrated on her tone, trying to decide if she could really be as indifferent as she sounded.

"My last memory is saying good night to Mulroney and walking out the newsroom door. Then blank, nada, zip." The blanket had been thoroughly settled and the view out the door thoroughly perused. She still wouldn't look at me.

"The reason I'm asking is because of the way you've been acting." I was feeling my way, keeping my tone calm. "You know, when a witness refuses to look me in the eye, I know they're hiding something, but in this case, it escapes me what it could be."

When she didn't answer, I gave up being diplomatic and tried being blunt instead. "You don't seem particularly pleased that I'm here. Dr. Hickam asked me to stay a little longer, but I don't want to unless you want me to."

She frowned. "It's up to you, Max. I appreciate you coming, but I'm sure you're ready to get home." Most of that was addressed to the door, although she gave me a quick glance at the end.

I wanted to shake her...or take her in my arms. I let myself think about that last idea, but only because I had no intention of doing it. I hadn't touched Jake since she pulled her hand out of mine right after she woke up, and that appeared to be just fine with her.

It was no longer fine with me. I missed being close to her, missed the feeling I was helping. Instead, I felt let down, confused. And I didn't like it.

It was definitely time for me to go home and start working to forget the whole episode.

Chapter Twenty-Eight
JAKE

When I woke up in hospital, I thought I was either dead or dreaming. A stranger in a white coat was squeezing my hand, telling me I'd been shot. Perhaps he was an angel, which would indicate I threw a seven. Except I hurt so much, I had to grit my teeth to keep from moaning. I know enough about physiology to know if you're dead, it shouldn't hurt.

Then the man in white finished speaking, and I knew I had to be dreaming because Max was there. I last saw him in New Zealand, where I watched him take Sophie Suriano into his arms. I hadn't been able to see his face when he did it, not until he released her and turned around, but then I was a wake-up. He loved her. It wasn't a surprise, of course. Just the way my luck seems to run.

~ ~ ~

The day after I woke up, I had a bubbly little nurse who almost drove me crackers with her questions and comments about Max. She said wasn't I the lucky one having a good-looking man like that so crazy for me he would sit there day after day, holding my hand while I was unconscious.

She giggled and said if I didn't want him, she'd take him. I was seriously tempted to smack her, although I didn't fully understand why she made me so angry. I guess it was better all around I managed to restrain myself.

After Nurse Bubbles finally left, I had a parade of visitors—doctors, nurses, police. The medical types all asked if I could remember anything since I arrived in hospital. And then they poked and prodded and told me to take deep

192

breaths. The police types asked if I remembered what put me into the hospital. I told them all the same thing. I didn't remember any of it.

But the truth is, I do remember some of it—floating on the edge of dark and light with Max holding my hand, touching my cheek, pushing on my feet. I hadn't liked the foot part, but I couldn't seem to wake up and tell him to stop it. And Max's voice, like strands of titanium and silk, anchoring me. Holding me in this place, even when I floated up and turned to see myself lying there.

Once I woke up, I was too weak and in too much pain to have to cope with having Max around, knowing he loved Sophie. Unbearable to have him so close I could reach out and touch him, but if I did, it would just hurt more once he left.

Who can explain why one person known briefly can be missed down all the long corridors of the lonely years, while another fades from memory the moment they're out of sight?

I don't know why I love Max. It doesn't make any sense. But there you are.

Chapter Twenty-Nine
MAX

I was having dinner in the dining room at my hotel, when Daniel showed up. I was pleasant to him. After all, it isn't his fault Jake likes him better. "I'm going home tomorrow," I told him.

"I know. Jake told me. That's why I'm here."

A waiter came over, and Daniel ordered a glass of red wine.

"I want to apologize for panicking like that and insisting you come to Australia," he said. "But I thought you were the Max she was asking for."

"And now you don't?" No surprise. I'd already decided the same thing. So, why did it upset me to have Daniel say it?

"She said she must have been referring to a dog she had as a kid," he said.

A dog? Was the man joking?

He didn't seem to be. The waiter delivered the wine, and Daniel took a sip.

I thought about it a while. About Jake having a dog named Max she loved enough to ask for when she was more than half dead, and I didn't buy it.

"You and Jake. You getting back together?" I could think about the dog story later.

"What do you mean?"

Are we not speaking English? "You were a couple, right? And something happened." *Or maybe not.*

"Jake tell you that?"

194

Was he smiling?

"She said you lived together."

Not smiling. Laughing.

"What's so funny?" I said.

"That's pure Jake. Yeah, we lived together. In a house with two other people. All of us, I might add, in separate bedrooms. But Jake moved into her own place right before she went up to Cairns to cover the story on the Brackens."

"You two aren't a couple?" The assumption was so strong, I was having a hard time coping with this new information. This terrific new information.

"Nope. Not that I'd be opposed to the idea, but all Jake wants is friendship. Made it perfectly clear from the get-go. Anyway, she finally met someone, while she was working on the Helice story."

The conversation was beginning to feel like a roller coaster ride. After soaring, when Daniel said he and Jake weren't a couple, I'd just hit a sharp, very hard turn.

"Only problem. He was already taken," Daniel continued, oblivious. "Last time I saw Jake that down..." He stopped talking.

I looked up from my careful dissection of a lamb chop, waiting for the rest of that statement. When it didn't come, the look on his face prevented me from pushing the issue.

"I didn't mind coming," I said, ignoring the sinking feeling that had arrived with Daniel's news that Jake had fallen in love.

After the waiter cleared my plate, I ordered a cup of coffee. "I need to talk to you about Jake's safety. I spoke with Lewiston this morning. He'll be pulling the bodyguard soon. I'm hiring someone to keep an eye on her after that. I wasn't planning to tell her I was paying for it, though."

"You got that right. She'd hit the roof. She's already fussing about the police guard. But you can't protect her forever."

"Lewiston has evidence the CEO of Helice Shipping, Xuefu Wong, was behind the attempt to kill Jake."

Daniel sat up, suddenly alert. "I'd forgotten that Xuefu Wong was connected to Helice." He took a sip of wine, looking thoughtful. "Hong Kong was my last posting. Rumor had it Xuefu was a bad person to cross."

"You ever meet the father?" I asked.

He shook his head. "I don't believe so."

"His name is Shaoming Wong. He has an interesting history. Educated at Cambridge. Studied Greek and the classics. Went back to Hong Kong and started Helice Shipping in the forties."

Daniel frowned. "I'm pretty sure I never met him."

"He lives in Vancouver now. I want to set up a meeting with him. Make sure he knows what his son's been up to."

"Let me think." Daniel sat turning his knife in a circle on the tablecloth, looking past my shoulder. I sipped coffee and waited.

"Got it," he said. "I know someone who may know the old man. He's a Brit. Name is Godfrey Paisley. Posted to Hong Kong for years. Now he's on staff in the Washington embassy. Godfrey's a classics buff. If he did run into Shaoming, the two of them should have hit it off."

We discussed Daniel approaching Godfrey Paisley to ask him if he knew Shaoming, and if so, was he willing to provide me with an introduction.

~ ~ ~

This morning, when I arrived at the hospital, Jake was once again in physical therapy, this time moving her legs in slow circles on an exercise bike. Her eyes were brighter, and her hair had been washed and combed.

Since she hadn't yet spotted me, I stood for a time looking at her, remembering my reaction when Sophie said she thought Jake was in love with me. And now that I knew she wasn't, how that made me feel.

It wasn't easy, sorting through my emotions, given I'd made as much of a career out of suppressing them as I had the practice of law. I probed, trying to decide. Was the feeling sadness or disappointment? Or something more fundamental?

I tested it out, watching Jake. Whatever it was, it was still there, and accompanying it was a heavy fatigue that made it difficult for me to move.

It was all absurd, of course. I couldn't be in love with Jake. I barely knew her. Besides, hadn't I decided that loving a woman was an exercise in futility?

Jake lifted her head and saw me. I walked toward her, remembering the conversation with Daniel the night before. "Daniel tells me you cleared something up for him," I said.

She frowned.

"That Max was the name of a dog you had as a kid."

After a moment she put her hand up to her neck, so she could speak. "Yeah. Nice blue heeler he was. Lovely dog." Her whisper seemed strained.

"Blue heeler, huh? I'm certainly glad we cleared that up."

She concentrated on the instrument panel of the bike.

"I'm on the Qantas flight at noon."

"I appreciate you coming," she said.

What was I expecting? That she'd burst into tears and beg me to stay? *Well, yeah. That would be a good start.* "It was my pleasure," I told her.

"Right. First class hols. Come to Australia. Read to a comatose person for a week."

"Then find out you've been mistaken for a dog." It was only by looking closely that I saw the quickly suppressed smile. It triggered a flash of memory—the first time Jake treated me to a grin—the time she'd told me deprecation was an Aussie sport. God, I missed that woman, the one I'd known in Cairns.

She lifted her hand back to her neck. "I'm sorry you went to all the trouble."

"No trouble. I'm delighted you're getting better."

"Yeah, so am I."

"Jake, there's something else I need to say." I wondered what it would take for her to look at me. "What you did, finding out about the smuggling. It was splendid. You were splendid. And it helped Sophie. She no longer feels... You gave her back her life."

She lifted her head, and I could see her eyes were bright with unshed tears. Her legs stopped their slow circling, and in the sudden quiet, we looked at each other.

After a moment, she looked away. Her hand moved to her throat. "You're going to be late," she said.

"You're right. I need to get going." It was hard to form the words, given the size of the lump in my throat. And was this going to be it? These awkward words? Words that had nothing to do with anything that mattered.

You're going to be late?

You're right. I need to get going?

It was better this way, though. Better not to know how Jake and I could be together. Easier to say good-bye before there was something concrete to regret. This vague sense of loss wouldn't last. All I needed was one complex case to keep me busy twelve, fourteen hours a day, and my life could return to what it was before Kelly and Sophie. And Jake.

"Take care of yourself, Joanna Kate."

"No worries."

If it wasn't for the crutches, I would...what? Touch her?

Something.

Instead, I turned and walked away. Half-way across the room, I lost my concentration, and my left leg dragged, making me stumble. The crutches were all that saved me from a fall.

I gritted my teeth and took a breath, refocusing on the careful movements required to put one foot safely in front of the other. By the time I reached the doorway, I was covered in sweat.

I walked on through without looking back.

Chapter Thirty
CASSIE

First thing after he got back from Australia, Max met with Mr. Micelli. Word floating around the office was that Max offered to resign, but Mr. Micelli said absolutely not. I decided maybe Mr. Micelli was smarter than I'd always thought, given he'd kept Todd Wermling around.

Course, I can't keep ragging on Todd after he helped Rosie. Max didn't hardly believe anything I told him about that until he met with Mr. Micelli, who told him the same story. Only time I can remember Max doubting me, although it was pretty unbelievable.

The night of the town council meeting, we all arrived a half hour early. We were lucky we got seats together because we needed practically a whole row. Mr. Micelli, Sophie, her father-in-law, Charles Suriano, and Todd Wermling, along with me and Melvin were all there. Now that was a surprise, seeing Mr. Micelli walk in with Todd after he told Rosie not to come. Oh my. I didn't worry about Max not being there until I saw Todd.

All those bad feelings with Todd go way back to when Max hired me and Todd said something about it. Ever since, those two, they move round each other like a couple of those ballet people—on their tippy toes. Well, Todd on his tippy toes and Max in his chair. Now Max has legs, Todd moves even more careful.

Although lately, there have been a few changes. Todd's lost a lot of weight and some of that attitude. He's even been real pleasant to me. He used to avoid me the same as he avoids Max.

And there's that wedding photo on his credenza. His daughter and a man who's darker than I expect Todd would prefer. But then, I also noticed him mentoring Tyrel Johnson, one of our new juniors.

Course, it could all be window dressing. Todd polishing his diversity image for Micelli, hoping for the top spot. But people can change, and I say, if he's trying to be a better man, more power to him.

Todd Wermling aside, I tell you, when I looked around that room, I felt a whole lot uncomfortable. My Melvin and me, well, we stuck out like a couple of crows in a flock of seagulls. Lordy, that audience was white.

There were a few Asians and Hispanics scattered about, but not many. The council, sitting at their curved table in the front of the room, were all middle-aged white men. Now that amazed me. I didn't expect to see any people of color up there, but I sure expected to see a woman or two.

That first half hour was dead boring. When I noticed Mr. Micelli coming to attention, I listened real close to what was being read. Didn't make any difference. I've been typing up Max's legal stuff for more years than I want to admit, but I had no idea what that motion was saying. If I hadn't heard Rosie's name mentioned, I don't believe I would have realized it was even about him.

"The motion is now open for discussion."

Finally, something I could understand. The mayor looked around the room. I expected Mr. Micelli to get up, but he wasn't the one who jumped up when the mayor reached for his gavel. Todd Wermling did. I shifted in my seat real sharp and nudged at Mr. Micelli. He ignored me.

"Before we discuss this matter, we need to be clear exactly what's involved," Todd said. "Now I for one had a hard time understanding the motion, and that's not easy for me to admit, since I'm supposed to be fluent in legalese. So, Mr. Mayor, if you could clarify the matter for me, I'd sure appreciate it."

I looked at Todd, all surprised. I still didn't expect he was on our side, but what he was asking for, well, I thought it was a good start. The mayor cleared his throat and peered over the top of his glasses at Todd. "As I understand it, the owner of 547 Main Street is rehabbing that building with the idea of turning it into a cooking school. However, when the owner applied for the permits, he was less than forthright.

Based upon that initial *incomplete* information, we approved the permits. Now those issues have become clear, and we have an obligation to all the citizens of San Germano to reassess that approval."

"So, exactly what was the owner not forthright about?" Todd asked, standing up again. "Sorry, folks. Real hard for me to get my mind around innuendo. I'm a just-the-facts kind of guy." He looked around at the audience with a smile, and a few people smiled back. Not many though.

The mayor stared hard at Todd. I was still trying to decide if Todd was doing us a favor or not. Being Todd, I figured the answer had to be 'or not,' even though Mr. Micelli was sitting there all calm and cool as a bowl of whipped cream.

"I don't think we need more detail, Todd," the mayor said. "Everybody here knows the facts."

Now I thought that was mighty interesting that the mayor knew Todd, although he didn't seem to be happy about what Todd was saying. I figured that was good for our side.

"Obviously, not everybody here knows them, or Mr. Wermling wouldn't have asked the question." This time it was Sophie's father-in-law speaking.

Oh my. Now there's a man who knows how to dress. A charcoal suit that had to be cashmere, a white shirt that would be ashamed to wrinkle, and a silk tie in colors rich enough to open their own bank account.

"I have to admit, I don't have all the facts either," Mr. Suriano continued. "I would appreciate it if you would explain, so we'll all be on the same page, so to speak."

"Sir, would you mind identifying yourself? I don't believe we've met." The mayor was peering over his glasses. Made him look real comical, but I didn't think it'd be a good idea to laugh.

"Certainly. I'm Charles Suriano. Perhaps I shouldn't be speaking here tonight since I'm not a resident of San Germano. My bank does, however, hold the mortgages for many of the businesses here, including the one under discussion. When I heard about this meeting, I felt it was in the bank's interest that I attend."

Boy, was the room quiet after that, until Todd spoke again. "I for one am pleased to welcome you here, sir. Now, Mr. Mayor, some facts, for all of us, if you please."

"It's my understanding the business council proposed this motion," the mayor said. "Fred, how about you explain."

Fred was sitting in the front row. He stood up, and we still could barely see him. I swear, man was built like a beach ball and with a squeaky voice to boot.

"I don't see any point to this beating round the bush. The owner lied about his background on his application. I don't hold with lying myself, and neither does anyone else in the San Germano business community."

"Exactly what were these lies?" Mr. Suriano asked.

"He didn't disclose the fact that he got out of prison a year ago. He was up for drug trafficking, and now here he is trying to set up his filthy business in San Germano under the guise of a cooking school."

If that wasn't the most unbelievable thing I'd ever heard in my life. I started to jump up, but then I realized I couldn't. Melvin had hold of my left arm, and Mr. Micelli had hold of my right. Soon as I settled, Mr. Micelli stood up. He moved out of our row right into the center aisle. He's not a real tall man, but he looked mighty impressive standing there, dressed almost as nice as Mr. Suriano.

"My name is Anthony Micelli, and I happen to know a thing or two about Roosevelt Hawkins. I know, for example, that he did not just get out of prison. You see, Mr. Hawkins is the personal assistant of a colleague of mine, Max Gildea. Max is currently at the bedside of a seriously ill friend. Since the friend lives in Australia, that made it impossible for him to be with us tonight. He asked me to be here instead, to make sure Mr. Hawkins' rights aren't violated."

I could tell Mr. Micelli was just getting warmed up. I patted Melvin on the hand, so he knew he didn't have to hold on so tight.

"When Max lost his legs in an accident over ten years ago, he hired Rosie, Mr. Hawkins that is. Since then, Rosie has lived with Max, kept house for him, driven him to and from work, cooked the meals—incidentally, I can certainly vouch for Rosie's skill as a chef. Recently, Max was fitted with artificial legs. It meant he no longer needed as much assistance. That was when Rosie decided he'd give someone else a hand."

Mr. Micelli paused before beginning to speak real slow and distinct. "Not only is Roosevelt Hawkins not a drug dealer, he happens to be one of the finest men I'm acquainted with. If Max were here, he'd tell you he trusts Rosie with everything he owns, and he'd trust him with his life. For my part, I want to tell you that San Germano is damn lucky to have someone like Rosie choosing to do business here."

I slid my eyes sideways at Melvin. He sat there as serene as a man full of Sunday dinner. I gave up and looked back at Mr. Micelli.

"A while back, Mr. Hawkins' property here in San Germano was vandalized. Hate messages were spray-painted on the front of the building, and an attempt was made to burn it down. Perhaps some of you saw the damage before it was repaired. This evening, an attempt is being made to complete that destruction, only this time you've chosen the law as your torch and spray can. You seek through the law to deny this man his property rights and his right to a livelihood." He paused and looked around the room.

People were shifting, so they didn't have to look at him.

"I'm here tonight on Rosie's behalf, along with Todd Wermling, who is a member of this community, and Charles Suriano, a major investor in this community. Our purpose is to assure you that the students at the San Germano Gourmet Academy will be chosen for their commitment to the program and will be closely monitored during their studies. That doesn't mean ex-cons need not apply. It's Rosie's intention to make this school a model for others to follow in helping to rebuild lives."

He stopped for a long beat before continuing. "There's an old saying that applies here. Give a man a fish, you feed him for the day, and tomorrow he'll be hungry again. But teach a man to fish, and you've fed him for life. San Germano has nothing to lose by welcoming Rosie and his school, the aim of which is to teach men and women not only how to fish but how to cook it afterward."

He stopped speaking and turned in a circle to look at everyone in the room. "You, the residents of San Germano, have a choice to make here tonight. Do you want to be a community that cares for its residents and supports diversity or one that embraces the prejudices and narrow-mindedness of the past?"

The room was completely silent as he took his seat. After a moment one person clapped, then two, then a whole bunch. It started in a corner of the room where several Asians were sitting. Next a Hispanic group sitting on the other side joined in, and it built and built until everyone was clapping except Fred and the council members.

The motion was withdrawn.

I have to admit, in spite of Rosie being okay with Max going off to Australia, I still hadn't been sure about it, not until it all worked out. As for Max and Todd, I don't expect they'll ever be best buddies, but since Max heard about the role Todd played in the council meeting, they talk to each other, and when they do, the atmosphere doesn't roil and snap like it used to.

Of course, Melvin, Rosie, and I know the people in San Germano who cheered when Rosie's building was vandalized aren't going to be won over just like that by what Mr. Micelli had to say, no matter how well he said it. Proof of that was the editorial in the next issue of the *San Germano Free Press*. It said care and caution must be exercised to ensure the school didn't become a magnet for undesirables, and that its impact on the community should be re-evaluated after six months.

"Ain't nothing worthwhile that's easy," was Rosie's take on it.

Chapter Thirty-One
MAX

Daniel Meredith called me two days after I returned to the States.

"How's Jake?" I asked.

"According to Hickam, making good progress. Grumpy as hell, though. But she's doing her therapy without too much complaining. She'll be released soon."

"Tell her hello for me," I said, keeping my tone even, my thoughts in neutral.

"Will do. I talked to Godfrey Paisley. He and Shaoming Wong do know each other. In fact, they're friends."

"How are we handling my getting in to see him?"

"Godfrey talked to Shaoming. The two of you have an appointment with him in Vancouver next Thursday at ten o'clock."

"What do you mean, the two of us have an appointment?"

"Best way Godfrey could think to handle it. I expect he'd appreciate it if you'd pay some of his expenses."

Initially I was annoyed that Godfrey had insinuated himself into the meeting, but after I thought about it, I decided if he was as sharp as Daniel said he was, he could be a real asset.

~ ~ ~

It took no psychic leap to recognize Godfrey Paisley when he entered the dining room at the Four Seasons Hotel in

Vancouver. Although he was a stooped crane of a man, he walked briskly, swinging a cane that had a heavy carved brass handle that would make an excellent club. All the man needed to complete the picture of the Hollywood-perfect upper class Englishman was a monocle.

When I stood to greet him, intelligent, pale blue eyes gave me a thorough going over.

"Mr. Gildea, I find I'm rather in your debt." He folded his long body into the chair opposite me. "Chance to see an old friend, don't you know."

"Daniel said he'd briefed you on what I hope to accomplish," I said.

"Yes, indeed. Terrible, that young woman getting shot. Terrible."

"Do you think Shaoming knows about it?"

"Oh, I doubt it, Mr. Gildea. Doubt it very much."

"Do you know the son, Xuefu?"

"No. Never met the lad. Heard a good deal about him. Yes, indeed, a good deal. Not a credit to his father, I'm afraid."

By the time the waiter showed up to deliver menus and take our drink orders, I was beginning to feel bogged down talking to Godfrey. I glanced at him over the top of my menu, remembering Daniel's words. "Don't be fooled, Max. Godfrey has perfected giving the impression he's not very bright, but I've encountered few sharper diplomats in my day."

After we placed our orders, Godfrey picked up his gin and tonic and dropped the heartiness that had begun to make me question Daniel's assessment. "Mr. Gildea, now we've arranged for our food, I'd like to hear what you plan to say tomorrow, if you don't mind. I'm risking a valuable friendship. I'm doing it for that young woman. Daniel tells me she may still be in danger."

"Yes, I believe she is."

"Understand she's a journalist?"

"Yes. She wrote the articles that started the investigation of Helice Shipping. There's evidence Xuefu Wong arranged to have her shot because of it. But I need to begin earlier than that. Are you familiar with the Suriano case?"

206

"The couple whose yacht was hit? Nasty business, that."

"A Helice ship hit them. Afterward, it sailed off, making no attempt to rescue the survivors. That's where this started." I reviewed the story for Godfrey, finishing as our dinners were served. Godfrey savored his meal, showing no inclination to speak further about the situation. Objectively, I knew the food was excellent. Subjectively, waiting for Godfrey's verdict on what I'd told him, I had to make a conscious effort to chew and swallow.

When Godfrey finished eating, he gestured to the waiter and ordered a snifter of brandy. When it came, he sat back warming the glass in his hands. "Here's what I think, Gildea. Talking to Shaoming is a good idea. But you'd better be prepared for him to have little influence on his son."

Although not a surprise, the assessment was still unwelcome.

"The Chinese have a strong belief in the power of names," he continued, swirling the brandy in his glass and taking an appreciative sniff. "They believe their names shape what they become. Shaoming means 'one who introduces brightness, right, or courage.'" He stopped and took a sip before continuing. "Xuefu means 'learn to be a famous poet.' It was Shaoming's wish, expressed in the name he gave his son, that the boy would find the same joy in knowledge and intellectual pursuits as his father."

"Xuefu has learned, all right," I said. "But not to be a famous poet."

"Yes. It does appear from what you've told me, the boy gives his allegiance to a different god than does his father." Godfrey looked troubled.

"I take it you think Xuefu has the upper hand."

"I fear he has. Still, Shaoming was a successful businessman in a difficult part of the world. Such success requires strength, ruthlessness, and clear vision. We'll just have to wait and see what the situation is." He paused and sipped his brandy before setting down the glass and looking across at me. "How familiar are you with the Asian mentality?"

"I only know Asians who have been Americanized," I said.

"Ah, that's unfortunate. Fascinating people, Asians. Very different from Europeans. Short-term thinkers on issues of daily life, long-term thinkers when it comes to major issues. At the most, we consider the past only as far back as our grandparents and the future only as far forward as our grandchildren. The Asian, on the other hand, considers his position as being on a continuum of hundreds of years. He looks back to honor his ancestors, and he plans for a future that is a hundred years or more beyond his lifetime."

He took a long, thoughtful sip of brandy before speaking again. "Although Shaoming was influenced by his experiences in England as a young man, he has a traditional soul. Don't be fooled by any Western trappings we might see. As for tomorrow, it will be best if you say nothing about your purpose until I give you a cue. Then simply tell the story as you told it to me, and we shall see."

~ ~ ~

Shaoming Wong's house was a one-story pale brick structure, perched on one of the many hills overlooking Vancouver and its waterways. A small courtyard at the entrance gave the house an Oriental feel. We'd come in a taxi, and we asked the driver to wait for us.

A Chinese woman ushered the two of us into the house. She bowed and gestured for us to follow her to a large, bright room with a view of downtown Vancouver.

I spared the spectacular view only a glance before focusing on the two people waiting for us. The woman, who could have been anything between thirty and fifty, was wearing traditional Chinese dress. She stood with her hand on the back of the wheelchair in which the man, obviously Shaoming Wong, sat. At first I thought he was sitting in a lotus position. Then I realized he had no legs. For the first time, I understood why so many strangers had looked shocked upon meeting me.

Shaoming was nearly bald, and his face, the color of old newsprint, was finely wrinkled. When he greeted Godfrey, his eyes disappeared completely within the folds of his smile. Cassie would no doubt give a thumbs-up—this was a person I was going to enjoy.

Not what I'd been expecting.

Shaoming invited us to sit. The woman, introduced as his daughter Yimei, left the room then returned with tea and a plate of cakes. After pouring a cup of tea for each of us, she left again, and Shaoming and Godfrey began to visit. Wong's excellent English had a British flavor, but I had no difficulty understanding him after being exposed to Godfrey's conversational rhythms.

I was beginning to fear Godfrey might never mention the reason for my presence, when he finally said, "I have brought Mr. Gildea with me today because he has something he wishes to discuss with you. It is an important matter, or I would not have allowed it to intrude on our friendship. I ask that you hear him."

Shaoming turned to me. "I am listening, Mr. Gildea."

I spoke slowly, feeling my way, watching him closely as I told him about Sophie and then about Jake.

When I finished, Shaoming blinked several times. "It is an intriguing story, Mr. Gildea. Very sad. But it is unclear, why you are telling it to me."

"I understand you are a man of great influence. Sufficient influence, that if I name the person behind these events, you can stop him from again trying to kill the journalist."

"Why should I be concerned about that? This woman is not Chinese."

Why indeed? "You are acquainted with the teachings of our greatest scholars. Have they not all come to the same conclusion? That we are interconnected. No man, or woman for that matter, is an island." I seemed to be falling into Godfrey and Shaoming's formal rhythms of speaking, but it felt like the right approach. "I believe our pains, sorrows, and joys are the same. When we injure each other, it hurts all of us."

"Ah. Well said, Mr. Gildea," Shaoming said. "But do you say this from heart or head?"

"From heart, head, and experience. Tell me, how did you lose your legs?"

Godfrey shifted sharply. He'd warned me it was best to be indirect. This approach was anything but.

"Why do you ask this?" Shaoming said. The gentle, jolly man who'd chatted comfortably with Godfrey had abruptly disappeared. In his place was the man who succeeded in business in, as Godfrey put it, a difficult part of the world.

"Because of an accident," I said, "I was forced to view life from the height of a small child for many years." I waited for Shaoming to process the words.

A frown appeared among the finer mesh of wrinkles on his brow. "What you say makes no sense."

"It makes perfect sense to those who know me well."

"You are saying, you also lost your legs?"

"Precisely. I know, as do you, the emotional and physical pains of such a loss. How it makes us dependent on others for the simplest of activities. Does it matter you are Chinese and I am American? Do we not suffer the same?"

"I do not believe you."

I bent over and slid my trousers up. He leaned down, peering at the rods extending from my shoes, then his eyes met mine. "Who is behind this killing and almost killing, Mr. Gildea?"

"Xuefu Wong." I watched Shaoming closely as I said it, but as far as I could tell, he didn't react.

"My son is young and strong and has both his legs." He turned to Godfrey. "It has been good to see you again, my friend."

Damn him. Sitting there so calmly dismissing us, sentencing Jake to a life of fear because she wasn't Chinese. I wanted to grab him by his skinny shoulders and shake him until his teeth rattled, but then I'd always known this was a very long shot.

Godfrey and I stood and bowed slightly to Shaoming who spoke to Godfrey in what I supposed was Mandarin. Godfrey answered.

The two exchanged several more comments before Shaoming turned to me. He held my gaze for a moment, before tipping his head to me.

The young woman who had showed us in appeared in the doorway, and we followed her to the front door.

Godfrey waited until the taxi pulled out of the driveway before he spoke. "A near thing, old boy, but Shaoming will do what he can."

"Is that what he was saying?"

"He asked if I knew these women, the one who has been shot and the one whose husband drowned. I said I did not. He asked why then was I concerned in these matters. I said I was concerned because I was part of the human family. Then he told me to tell you he is saddened by the shooting of Jake and the loss of Mr. Suriano, although they are not Chinese."

"That's it?"

"It's what you asked for. He's saying he has accepted your argument. He will attempt to stop Xuefu."

"Do you think he can?"

"I don't know, and I doubt he does."

"That means Jake is still in danger." And I was out of ideas.

"It won't be indefinitely. Shaoming will let us know if he's successful."

~ ~ ~

Three weeks after I went to Vancouver, Godfrey Paisley called. "Gildea, old chap. Afraid I have rather rotten news. Shaoming Wong is dead."

My immediate thought was Xuefu. "How did it happen?"

"Died in his sleep. Yimei found him. He'd just told her he'd summoned Xuefu for a visit. Sounds like he planned to confront his son, but time ran out. You'd better assume that young woman is still in danger."

"She can't live with a bodyguard the rest of her life." And I didn't want to live with the possibility that any time the phone rang it could be Daniel calling to tell me Jake was dead.

"Then she may need to change her name and place of residence," Godfrey said.

"She's a journalist and a well-known one, given what's happened. Besides, she's not that easy to disguise. She's six feet tall, for Pete's sake."

"You're saying she's a good-size frog in a small pond. Perhaps what's needed is a change of pond size."

211

"You're suggesting she move to the U.S.?" Of course, if Godfrey was acquainted with Jake he would never have considered that a reasonable idea.

"You must admit, old boy, it's easier to hide in a mob, and you Yanks have a bigger one than the Aussies."

Godfrey's suggestion might be a non-starter, but I wasn't coming up with any alternatives. And I needed to. The last time I talked to Daniel, he reported his neighbors across the street had returned from a weekend away to discover evidence of a break-in. Nothing seemed to be missing, but they found a gum wrapper on the floor by the front window, a window that overlooked Daniel's house, which was where Jake was staying as she continued to convalesce.

That news ratcheted up my feelings of helpless frustration. I thought about Godfrey's advice and wondered if there was any chance I could get Jake to move to a bigger pond, even temporarily.

Decided it was not bloody likely.

Chapter Thirty-Two
CASSIE

These days, when I take in Max's coffee or his mail, I often find him standing, looking out the window. I figured he was thinking about Sophie, who up and moved to Chicago. But when I mentioned Sophie to him, he looked startled.

Of course, Max never has been one to share his feelings. Like most men, you ask him how he feels, he says, fine. Doesn't matter he has a sore heart and no legs. He's still just fine. But it surely is clear to me he needs to find another lady to love, now he's remembered how to do it.

Shortly after he got back from Australia, Max went to a meeting with the president of PacTran, the company that insures Helice ships. He took an envelope with him that he didn't have when he got back. My guess? He showed the president the evidence that Helice Shipping intimidated Sophie and ordered that reporter shot.

According to Max, it wasn't strong enough for a legal case, and he would surely know that. "But combined with the stories of the smuggling, it may be strong enough for what's needed," he'd said.

I expect Helice is going to find it mighty difficult to get insurance from now on.

Shortly after that, Max arranged a trip to Vancouver to see an old Chinese man. Turns out, this Chinese man might not know what his son has been up to. I figured Max planned to not leave him in ignorance on that issue, something he says to me all the time when I'm trying to keep him up to date on the important gossip. "I doubt you're going to leave me in ignorance on that point, Cassiopia."

Lordy, don't I wish I could be there to hear Max not leaving Shaoming Wong in ignorance.

~ ~ ~

I swear, I don't know what's going on with Max. All he said about his trip to Vancouver was that the weather was good. As if I cared about weather. Then Godfrey Paisley called. I checked with Max to ask if it was about Godfrey's expenses. Max said it wasn't to do with expenses, but he didn't tell me what it was to do with. First time in all these years Max wasn't sharing with me what was going on.

For two days after Godfrey called, Max acted like a woman with the worst case of PMS I'd ever seen. I finally told him, if he planned on being like that all the time, I'd be looking for another job. He didn't even seem to hear me.

"You ever have a dog, Cassiopia?" He only calls me Cassiopia when he's irritated or upset with me about something, but I had no idea what I'd done to irritate him this time.

"No, never had a dog or a cat. Why do you ask?"

He turned his chair and stared out the window, like there was something real exciting happening out there. Then he asked me another peculiar question. "If you were hurt bad and were being taken to a hospital, who would you ask for?"

"Why, Melvin and my mom. What kind of question is that?"

"Just a question."

"Who would you ask for?"

He shook his head and turned back toward me. "I have no idea."

"It seems to me at a time like that most people would ask for the person they love most in the world, so likely you'd be asking for Sophie," I told him.

"No." He turned again and gave that window more of his attention. "She's in Chicago. It wouldn't make any sense to ask for her."

"You think you'd worry about her not being right handy at a time like that? No, sir. You hurt bad, you don't care. You want who you want. You're going to ask no matter what."

"Do you think..."

What was it with that window today? "What? Do I think *what*?"

"Why did you say I'd ask for Sophie?"

"It's plain as the hair on your head, Max. You love her. Course we all do. Rosie loves her, I love her. Can't help loving Sophie. She just can't love back."

"Why do you say that?"

"Girl's full of ghosts. But my momma used to say there's more than one fish in that big old ocean, Cassie."

"You're suggesting I find a fish to love?"

Max does love to kid, although, when it comes right down to cases, this was the first time he'd done it since he got back from Australia, not to mention it was a pretty pitiful effort.

"Course not, Max. You can't tell me your momma didn't say stuff like that to you."

"She still does." He rubbed his head. He looked exhausted, oh my, he did.

"So, why are you so interested in who I'd ask for if I was hurt?"

"I went to Australia because an EMT thought Jake was asking for me, but when she woke up, she claimed Max was the name of a dog she had as a kid. A blue heeler."

"And you believed that?"

"She wasn't that glad to see me."

"Humph. There's one easy way to check that story out. Talk to Jake's momma. Ask right out if she had a blue shoe or whatever you said that dog was called." I was trying to tweak Max into a better humor, but he just sat there with a thoughtful look on his face, although, right after I got back to my desk, the light on Max's line lit up.

215

Chapter Thirty-Three
MAX

Cassie was the one who pushed me to check on Jake's blue heeler story. It might seem trivial, but because some EMT guy thought she said Max, I flew halfway around the world.

Of course, the whole thing was absurd. Whether Jake had a dog or a hundred dogs named Max or Spot or any other damn thing wasn't the point. The point was why she'd acted the way she had. It didn't make sense. I'm a logical person, and it bothers me when something doesn't make sense.

I decided the first step to sorting it out was doing what Cassie suggested. I called Daniel for Mrs. Rutherford's number then dialed before I could talk myself out of it. When Jake's mother picked up the phone, I almost hung up without speaking, realizing how peculiar it was going to sound. But it was a detail that needed to be clarified.

"Mrs. Rutherford, this is Max Gildea."

"Mr. Gildea, what a surprise. Jake's okay, isn't she?"

"Yes, of course. I'm calling from the States."

"My goodness. Isn't it a wonder. Not that many years ago, we had to use our radio to call into Melbourne. Now we can talk to someone in America, just like that."

When she took a breath, I spoke quickly. "The reason I'm calling is I need a piece of information. This might sound strange, but did Jake ever have a dog, a blue heeler?"

"Oh, my goodness, no. My husband can't abide blue heelers. Besides they're cattle dogs. We've always had kelpies as pets. Wait a minute. Jake did have a dog once. A collie bitch, name of...well, fancy that. I can't remember. Shiny or Sharl maybe? Definitely something with an *S*."

So, there I had it. Jake had lied. And the most reasonable explanation? She wanted nothing to do with me. A healthy Jake would have told me straight out she didn't want me around, but as sick as she was, maybe she couldn't muster the strength for that.

I felt exhausted and suddenly old.

~ ~ ~

My most pressing problem was ensuring Jake's safety, and my only idea of how to do that long term was Godfrey's suggestion, although it was unlikely Jake would agree to it. But if I didn't make an attempt and something happened to her, it would be damn hard to face myself in the mirror every morning.

And every day I spent trying to think of an alternate solution was another day Xuefu had to plan a second attack, although at the moment he had to be distracted. His father's death had been followed by the initiation of legal actions against Helice by the states of Washington and California. It made this the perfect time for Jake to disappear, but calling her to suggest that would be worse than useless. The only chance I had of convincing her was in person.

Once again, I had Cassie make airline reservations while I arranged for the temporary transfer of my cases to other members of the firm. Last, I called Daniel to tell him I was coming and why.

"It's a long way to come for nothing, Max."

"You don't think Jake will agree?"

"Jake's not agreeing to much of anything these days. She doesn't have the temperament to be an invalid."

"Maybe it means she's recovering."

"I'm pretty sure something else is going on. Dr. Hickam said it was natural for her to be depressed, but this is more than depression."

Probably a roaring case of post-traumatic stress disorder. Not surprising. "It might be best if you don't tell her I'm coming."

"Yeah. I think you've got that right."

~ ~ ~

I called Daniel as soon as I checked into my hotel in Sydney.

"I better let Jake know you're on the way to the house," Daniel said. "It might be a bit much to find you on the doorstep with no warning."

Daniel lived across the harbor from Sydney proper. As we drove across Harbor Bridge, the cab driver pointed out the view of the opera house. I gave it a glance and mumbled something vaguely appreciative in response.

When I rang the bell to Daniel's house, a large two-story Victorian that could use some of Sophie's design magic, a man I assumed was the bodyguard opened the door. He asked for identification, which I was getting out when Jake spoke from behind him.

"It's okay. I know him."

The man stepped aside and ushered me in.

"We'll be in the kitchen." She turned and led me down the hall to the back of the house.

In spite of Daniel warning her I was coming, her hair was uncombed, and she was wearing a robe and pajamas. She walked carefully, without any of the vigor I remembered from Cairns, and when we reached the kitchen, where the light was better, I was shocked by how pale and thin she was. Her skin had the same translucence Kelly's had during her chemo and that Sophie had when I first met her.

The kitchen was an old-fashioned room with large windows overlooking a shady backyard. Jake went to the stove and spoke to me over her shoulder. "Would you like coffee or tea?"

"Coffee would be good."

I took a seat at the table, while she got out mugs and filled them from a carafe.

"This is a surprise," she said. "You being back so soon. Daniel wouldn't tell me why you're here."

I waited to speak until she turned and brought the two mugs to the table. "I'm trying to clear up a small mystery."

"Oh?"

"Yes. Matter of fact, it's been driving me nuts."

She sat and took a sip from her mug.

"Aren't you going to ask me what it is?"

"Sure, Max. What is it?"

"It has to do with what a cattle dog would be doing on a sheep ranch."

She frowned.

"Specifically, a blue heeler, allegedly named Max and allegedly owned by one Jake Rutherford."

She shifted uncomfortably. A blush started somewhere below her neck and crept up her face. She held her mug up and peered at me over the rim as if she wished it were a brick wall.

"Everyone kept pushing me about why I asked for you. I made up the dog story, so they'd leave me alone."

She finally looked me right in the eye, and I saw a flash of the old Jake in her expression. "So, there you have it. You can go home now with your mind at peace."

I waited a moment, before speaking again. "I'm also here to talk to you about your future."

"Why?"

"I'm responsible for you being shot."

"Not unless you hired the hit man."

"You know what I mean, Jake."

She bit her lip, still refusing to meet my eyes. "Sure. Okay. Feel responsible if you like. I don't see what good it's going to do either one of us."

I decided to stop futzing around and try a direct approach. "Joanna Kate, what made you change toward me?"

She was obviously startled, but she quickly overcame it. "You think just because you came all this way, you have a right to demand I answer your questions. Is that it?"

"No demands, Jake. I'd like us to be friends."

She clung to her mug, blinking rapidly. "I can't do this, Max." Her eyes filled with tears. "Go home to Sophie and leave me alone." She put the mug down and fished a tissue out of her pocket, turning away to rub at her face.

Sophie? Why was she bringing up Sophie? But Jake had asked about Sophie before. In fact, it was practically her first question after she came out of her coma, and she'd asked something similar one other time.

The pieces swung into place. "Jake, you need to know, I told you a white lie about Sophie. Like the one you told me about the blue heeler."

She didn't respond, nor did she turn toward me.

"I let you believe I was in love with her."

Her head came up. "Can you look me in the eye, Max, and tell me you don't love Sophie?"

I met her look steadily for a long beat, while I tried to think what I could say that wouldn't make this worse than it already was. "She's my...dearest friend. Of course I love her."

Jake held my gaze without moving.

"Jake, I want you to come back to the States with me. It's going to be several months before you'll be able to go back to work. You can spend that time with me. You'll be safe, and by the time you've recovered we'll have a better idea how persistent Xuefu is going to be."

"You trying to calm your conscience, Max?"

I didn't consider that worth answering.

"I'm a mess," she said.

"A comb would help."

"I didn't mean that."

"I know. It's okay, Joanna Kate. You can't go through an experience like this and not suffer ill effects."

"When do I get over it?" Tears welled. "When do I stop feeling weak and vulnerable and...not myself?" She got up and walked over to the sink, swiping a hand across her face. "They won't even let me go outside and sit under a tree. They say a sniper might be waiting. I'm in a prison, Max. Sometimes I can't stand it, but I don't seem to be able to fight them. I'm so bloody tired."

I stood and walked carefully over to her and pulled her into my arms.

"I'm a coward, Max."

"No. You're one of the most courageous people I know." Something was happening to me as I held Jake. I felt the tenderness and protectiveness I'd always felt for Sophie, but something else as well. A fierce, soaring, wondrous something.

My thoughts stopped spinning and slowed, and with that slowing, I felt a quiet certainty.

It had come right. In my arms I held the answer to everything Kelly had asked of me and wished for me.

If I had real legs, I would have been tempted to kick up my heels. Since I didn't, I contented myself with folding Jake in as close as I could get her. While she cried, I rubbed my cheek against her hair and spoke softly. "It's okay. Everything is going to be okay. You don't have to do this alone, Joanna Kate We'll figure it out together."

After a while, she stopped crying, pulled out of my arms, and said she needed to see about that comb. I sat in the quiet kitchen waiting for her, and there was nowhere else on earth I wanted to be. She came back half an hour later, her hair still damp from her shower, wearing slacks that fit loosely, showing she hadn't yet gained back any of the weight she lost in the hospital.

"How about we go out?" I said. Between us, the bodyguard and I could sneak Jake out.

Her immediate response, a smile, quickly slipped into a frown. "I don't think Ed will let me."

I hired him, I could fire him. At least for the day. "If I take care of that, will you come?"

"That's a big if, but it would be wonderful to get out. I'm going bonkers sitting here."

"Leave it to me. You think about where you'd like to go."

~ ~ ~

Jake chose to take a harbor cruise. Out on the water, a brisk breeze flipped her hair around, reminding me of the day we went snorkeling in Cairns. I took her hand in mine, something I now realized I'd wanted to do since that moment at the Thai Chai when I noticed she bit her nails. She gave me a quick, uncertain look but let me keep the hand.

After the cruise, we wandered around Sydney's waterfront until we came across a restaurant that appealed to us, one with outside seating where we could watch the parade of people. The bodyguard sat nearby keeping watch, although it was unlikely anyone knew Jake had left Daniel's house.

It was a weekday, and most people were dressed in business attire, walking purposefully, carrying briefcases, and talking on cell phones. An occasional clot of tourists, wearing the universal uniform of T-shirts and jeans, wandered by, or stood listening to the dreadlocked street musician playing out-of-place Caribbean melodies on a steel drum.

After lunch, Ed drove us to the cliffs that line the entrance to Sydney's harbor. We got out of the car and began walking on the path along the top of the cliff. To our right, we could see downtown Sydney, to the left, was an unlimited view of ocean, and below waves that shaded from deep blue to pale green were breaking into frothy white against the rocks.

Jake walked as slowly as I did now, and she stopped frequently to rest. I asked if she was tired and needed to go back. She said, yes she was tired, but she wasn't ready to go back. I suggested we sit on a bench and volunteered to be a pillow if she wanted to take a nap.

I realized how weak she still was when she curled up on the bench with her head on my thigh above the prosthesis. I sat, looking at her or at the ocean while she slept, trying not to think about the barriers still between us. For the moment, she seemed to have gotten over whatever made her standoffish when she came to in the hospital, but she'd given no hint she felt for me even a fraction of the suddenly awakened passion I felt for her. Of course, there was the not so minor detail of the man she'd met while working on the Helice story. She would likely need time to get over him.

When Jake woke up, we continued sitting on the bench talking lazily in the warm afternoon. "You thought anymore about my suggestion?" I said.

"Which suggestion is that?"

"About coming to the States."

"I'm sorry, Max. I can't afford it."

"I'm asking you to come as my guest. I'll pay your expenses."

"I can't let you do that."

"Even if the alternative is living in fear?"

"Going away is giving into fear."

"You've been in the military. You understand strategic withdrawal. That's all I'm suggesting."

She shook her head.

It was the answer I expected, but that didn't make it easier to accept, not now, when I knew without any doubt I loved her. I wondered when I started to love her. When she grinned at me the first time? Or when she held the call to her paper, so Rob McIntyre wouldn't have any warning that we'd found the diver's slate? Or was it as late as when I watched her fighting for her life in an intensive care unit? Not that it mattered. All of it had ended up in the same place.

It was way too soon to bring it up, but I doubted anything less would work. I took a deep breath. "Joanna Kate, the truth is I want you to come, because, well, you see, I seem to have fallen in love with you." *Whoa, way to go, Gildea.*

She was silent, and I didn't blame her. On a scale of one to ten, my declaration was a minus seven. I glanced at her. She was biting her bottom lip, and I wasn't sure whether she was trying not to laugh or not to cry.

"It's sweet of you, Max. Really it is. I'm touched. I really am." Definitely not laughing.

But also not saying something like, *I seem to have fallen in love with you, too.* Not that I expected that. Still, my chest tightened. Jake pulled her hand out of mine and almost had her fingers in her mouth when she must have realized what she was doing. She folded her hands in her lap instead and stared at the horizon.

I'd come too far not to make a second effort, especially when the first was so pitiful. "Daniel told me you met someone, but it didn't work out. I'm hoping, in time, you can get over him. And then, well, maybe you and I..." Words simply deserted me. Gone. All of them.

If it was one thing I'd learned to count on, it was that words didn't desert me. Just as well they had, though. Clearly, the lady wasn't interested.

"I don't understand," she said, her brow furrowed.

What was she talking about?

"You said Daniel told you?"

Right. That "Sorry, I shouldn't have brought it up." There. The words were back; I was in control.

"What about Sophie?" she asked.

Sophie? Didn't we already cover that? "What about her?"

"I saw how you were with her."

I didn't know if there was anything I could say to make her accept what had taken me so long to figure out, but I had to try. I spoke slowly and carefully. "I do love Sophie, but I'm not *in* love with her. I'm in love with you."

"I want to believe you, Max, but it's too pat."

"There's nothing pat about it." Frustration sharpened my tone, and she flinched. I took a breath and tried to speak calmly. "Look, Joanna Kate. I love you. It's as much a surprise to me as it seems to be to you. To tell you the truth, I never expected it to happen."

"I'm sorry, Max. I don't mean to question your motives."

We sat for a time, without talking. When I glanced at her, she had her hands tightly balled together in her lap, and a tear was sliding down below her sunglasses. The tear gave me the courage to try again. "We need a compromise here, Jake. Come to San Francisco. For a visit. You'll be safe, and we'll have a chance to get to know each other. Find out if we have a future together."

"And if we do, that future will be in the States, I suppose." She sounded as miserable as I felt.

"If that's a problem, we'll work something out."

"You willing to consider living in Oz, Max?" She was staring at the ocean, and tears were sliding down her cheeks, but I was starting to feel a glimmer of hope.

"Yes."

"Practically speaking, though, it wouldn't work, would it? And I'd be stuck. Isn't that the way it goes?"

"I'm no kid. I've already made a name for myself, had success. I doubt I'd miss it if I walked away tomorrow."

"You say that now, but what about later, when you find you do miss it?"

"Working on Sophie's case, I learned something about what's important. Then you were shot, and I learned the rest. I won't tell you I can give up the States and my career and come live in Australia without regrets. What I can say for sure is that without you, my life won't be a whole lot of fun."

She didn't respond or look at me.

"It's worth taking a chance, isn't it, Joanna Kate? It can't be every day you get a guy telling you his life won't be any fun without you. A month. That's all I'm asking. No pressure. I'll buy you a round-trip ticket if you like."

"This on the record, Max?"

"Yeah, as on the record as you can get."

Chapter Thirty-Four
JAKE

A huge Black man in a bright green T-shirt met Max and me at the airport when we arrived in San Francisco. He and Max clapped each other on the back and hugged. It made my ribs ache just watching the two of them.

"This is Rosie," Max said, when he got his breath back.

"A pleasure to meet you, Ms Rutherford." A smile full of strong white teeth accompanied the formal words, which were delivered in a rich baritone. My hand disappeared in his, but rather than squeezing hard, he held on gently, and I felt oddly soothed.

When we got to the car, I opted to sit in the backseat. Max sat up front, and he and Rosie talked quietly as Rosie maneuvered us through traffic. I was too exhausted to make sense of most of what they said, not to mention, the fact we were driving on the wrong side of the road was making me dizzy. I closed my eyes, and the low rumble of their voices faded as I dozed. I was still half-asleep when we arrived at Max's house.

After I said I wasn't hungry, Max showed me to my room. I needed sleep with the intensity I expect an addict overdue for his next fix might feel.

When I woke up, I could tell by the light around the window shade it was either late evening or early morning. After I showered and dressed, I went to see if Max or Rosie were around.

As I stepped into the living room, the view from the windows stopped me in my tracks. That was the first I realized Max's house was on a bluff overlooking the ocean.

The sun was low in the sky, inching toward the horizon. Evening then.

Neither Max nor Rosie seemed to be around, and the only sound I could hear was the quiet hum of the refrigerator. I got myself a glass of water, and sipping it, walked through the main rooms. Everything was open, one room flowing into the next, all of it light-filled. Pale walls, windows without curtains, and sparse furniture in earth tones: chocolate, reddish clay, tan. The tile floors, a brownish peach, were cool against my bare feet. What vivid colors there were, were found in the paintings hanging alone or in groupings.

It wasn't a large house, but given its location and its graceful, open design, it was clearly so far out of my price range I'd need a rocket to get there. I refilled my water and settled on the couch facing the setting sun, letting my preliminary conclusions settle down beside me now that I'd seen how Max lived.

I'd been scammed.

Max's big declaration that he'd suddenly discovered he loved me was revealed as the ploy I'd suspected it was. I'd almost believed it, but only because it was too awkwardly presented for it not to be genuine. But now I was a wake-up to what was going on. Max did what he needed to do to get me here. Likely he seemed sincere because he did have strong feelings. Not love, though.

Guilt.

And responsibility.

It was suddenly difficult to breathe, and I felt a deep-seated pain that a med wasn't going to dull. What a cock-up. My own fault. I'd let myself begin to believe.

"Jake. Did you get a good rest?"

I jerked around, nearly spilling the water.

Max stood in the doorway. "Sorry, I didn't mean to startle you."

"I...umm. Yes." I was shaking both because of Max's sudden appearance as well as from my anger at his duplicity.

"How about something to eat?"

"Sure. Good-oh." Food was safe. And it wasn't good form to talk with your mouth full, and I definitely couldn't talk to Max. Not yet. Not feeling the way I did. If I talked, I might start yelling. Except he wasn't the one I was really angry with. He only did what he thought was right, even if it did involve a lie. But me. I'd been a right galah to fall for it.

Max set his cane aside and began moving around the kitchen, pulling things out of the refrigerator and cupboards. He told me where the plates and silverware were, so I could set the small kitchen table. Then I sat out of the way, sipping the wine he poured for me. He cooked something he called a frittata. Eggs with vegetables, sausage, and a bunch of herbs. It was a surprise that he was so handy in the kitchen. I can cook a decent meat-and-potatoes meal over a campfire, but I'm not much on herbs and spices.

After dinner, which was unexpectedly delicious, I insisted on cleaning up, then I told Max good night and went back to bed to toss and turn most of the night, calling myself every name for drongo I could come up with.

The next morning, when I came out to the kitchen, Max was there eating breakfast. I ate cereal and yogurt, and then I went back to bed while he went to work. I finally fell asleep and slept most of the day, only getting up when Max got home. I set the table, while he got the food started, and then he poured us each a glass of wine to sip, while we watched the sun go down. I relaxed, once I realized Max liked his sunsets without talk.

During dinner, I asked him about his day, keeping away from any mention of the future or his lie about loving me. That was a discussion for when I felt stronger than I did right now. But orchestrating a conversation about nothing important made me feel like I was running along a beach, dipping my toes into the edges of the surf, ready at any moment to dash backward if a big wave approached.

~ ~ ~

I liked being in the house by myself all day, although Max didn't push at me when we were alone together. But then, he had me where he wanted me.

While he was at work, the silence and solitude were a relief. Since I'd been shot, there hadn't been much of either. After the hospital, there had been the constant sounds of the bodyguard, moving around, talking to me or not, but always just there.

When I first arrived in California, it exhausted me to walk from the terrace to the edge of the cliff and back, but soon I was walking the perimeter of Max's property several times a day. That made my appetite perk up, and I began to gain weight and feel more like myself. When Max saw I had more energy, he took me into the city for the day. If his house hadn't already clued me in that he was firmly and permanently planted in California, the visit to his office clinched it.

An assistant by the name of Cassie greeted me. As tall as I am, but she still managed to look down her Nefertiti nose at me. I felt like I'd been called in front of the principal after a prank.

I knew from that reaction, I was still not entirely myself. Usually I'd tell whoever treated me that way to rack off.

My assessment? She thinks she owns Max and doesn't like him spending time with me.

As for Max's office. Good grief. It was big enough for *The Australian*'s entire editorial board to bloody well play cricket. So, Max hadn't lied about being a success. Of course, I'd figured he wasn't hurting in the dosh department, flying back and forth to Australia that way. I'd just underestimated the amount by a considerable degree.

I went home with him that night determined to set things straight. But after dinner, Max excused himself, saying he had work to do. He left me sitting at the table, with what I wanted, needed, to say to him, squeezed together in my chest. I knew when I didn't follow him and insist on saying those words that I was more of a coward than I'd ever admitted to myself before.

It was so easy to just sit back and stay quiet. To eat Max's food and drink his wine and watch the sunset from his window. But this wasn't about just food and sunsets. I could admit that much, couldn't I?

That despite my best efforts, I looked forward to him walking in the door at night, and although we didn't talk about anything important, we did talk. He told me stories about the people in his office, and I told him about things that happened at *The Australian*. We talked about anything it seemed but ourselves.

The end of the third week I was here, Max arranged for Rosie to drive me into the city on a Friday afternoon to meet him, so we could go to dinner followed by the symphony.

Rosie arrived on schedule and greeted me with that huge smile and another careful handshake, and I found it difficult to believe he was related to Nefertiti. They're cousins, Max said, and then he'd told me about Rosie setting up the cooking school and the difficulties he'd faced.

Rosie spent the entire drive into the city talking about Max. Like enough, he told me things Max would rather I didn't know. It already hurt, being with Max, knowing when my month was up I'd go home and never see him again. I didn't need to hear more good things about him. I especially didn't need to hear how saving Sophie changed him.

It was going to be a bloody long evening.

Chapter Thirty-Five
MAX

Jake had been in San Francisco three weeks, when Godfrey Paisley called again. "Gildea, I have good news for you. Shaoming managed to do something after all. He added a codicil to his will." Godfrey chuckled.

I failed to see any potential for humor, but then I'd lost my sense of humor since I got home with Jake, and she pulled away again. I was trying to give her as much time as she needed, but it didn't seem to be getting us anywhere.

"I knew Shaoming was a clever old bastard," Godfrey continued. "But this is the clearest demonstration I've seen."

"What did he do?"

"He transferred his share of Helice, eighty percent, to a trust and named two trustees who have the power to decide who runs Helice and how."

"Won't that make Xuefu even more determined to kill Jake?"

"Not necessarily. Xuefu's getting a letter. In it, Shaoming tells Xuefu he's made this change because he loves his son and believes handing him an enormous fortune is not in his higher spiritual interest. While it will likely be a shock, it shouldn't be. Shaoming did require the boy to work his way up through the ranks at Helice, living on what he made."

"Who owns the other twenty percent?" I asked.

"Xuefu and Yimei each own the ten percent left to them by their mother."

"So, Xuefu is not exactly destitute."

"No, but Shaoming has left him no power. The trustees can force settlements of the suits against Helice, and they'll choose the CEO. Xuefu will have a difficult time convincing the two trustees he ought to continue in that role."

"How do you know all this?"

"You're talking to one of the trustees, old boy."

"And the other?"

"A woman by the name of Wanquin Liu Lin, an old friend of Shaoming's. It would surprise me greatly if she doesn't also know the particulars of why Shaoming did this."

"I'm still not convinced Jake is safe."

"No guarantees, old chap, but I did hear recently that Xuefu received a call from a certain Aussie detective, telling him there's evidence of his involvement in Jake's shooting, and if anything happens to her, Xuefu will find himself a long-term guest of the Australian government."

"And you know this because?"

"Diplomatic channels, old boy. Diplomatic channels."

~ ~ ~

It was finally over. In more ways than one.

Of course, I could put off telling Jake it was safe for her to return to Australia until her month was up. Unlikely, though, that spending additional time with me will change anything. She's been keeping me at arm's length throughout her visit. I've watched her doing it...figuring she needed time to settle things in her own mind. But deep down, I knew it wasn't going to work. Jake's not the kind of person to live with divided loyalties.

Better then to let go of her now, before I learn to miss her even more.

Chapter Thirty-Six
CASSIE

Well, if that didn't beat all. Max off to Australia again before he even unpacked from the last trip, and returning with that Jake person.

Lordy, didn't they make a pair.

She's staying at Max's place. He comes to the office, but when he's here, he isn't really here, if you know what I mean. It's clear Jake has done a number on him. I tried talking to him about it, but all Max would say was that she'd be here for a month, while they tried to decide what to do about her long-term safety. Looking at Max, I could guess what he wanted. What I couldn't figure out was Jake. She's real wary. Course, if somebody had shot me and still wanted me dead, I'd likely be wary too.

I decided that when she came in to meet Max this evening, I wasn't going to tell him right off that she'd arrived. Instead, I'd have a bit of a chat with Miss Jake. Find out her intentions, so to speak. I doubted Max was asking those kind of questions.

~ ~ ~

When Jake arrived, I told her Max was on the phone and offered her a cup of tea. Then I eased into a conversation with her. I figured I'd better start off slow.

"How're you enjoying your stay in San Francisco?"

"It's been interesting."

Well, that was certainly enlightening. I tried again. "This your first trip to the States?"

"No."

Worser and worser. I might as well forget the trying to soften up the witness part and see if I couldn't shake something loose. "You and Max figuring on getting married?"

She startled and then spoke brusquely. "Did anyone ask you to stick your bib in?"

The strange phrasing slowed me down but not for long. "Nope." I waited a beat, letting her squirm. "I'm only asking because I've been waiting to celebrate that man's happiness for more years than I care to count."

That surprised her. *Good.*

She gave me a sharp look. "You know Sophie Suriano, don't you?"

"Of course, I know Sophie. We worked on her case over a year. Sophie's a special lady. At one time I thought she and Max..." Oops. Not exactly what I meant to say.

"Did she refuse him?"

Oh my, this conversation had surely gotten onto the wrong track. My turn to squirm. "I don't believe he ever asked."

"Why not?"

Girl had a killer instinct, for sure. "You need to ask Max that."

"Since you've been with Max, has he...umm, dated...been..."

First time I'd heard her sound unsure. Interesting. "You want to know if Max has a lot of women friends?"

She nodded.

"Up until a year ago, Max was in a wheelchair. My theory? He didn't think anyone would have him, so he didn't put himself in the position to be rejected. Max may seem tough, but he hurts real easy. That's why I'm asking your intentions. He deserves to be happy. If he thinks you're the one, I don't want you toying with him."

There was a flash of anger she did nothing to hide, then her face took on a real determined look, like my Melvin when he's digging in his heels.

"You may know Max better than I do, but you don't know anything about me. I don't toy with people."

"Then what're you doing with Max?" I asked.

234

"Max has an overdeveloped sense of duty."

"And that's a problem because?"

"He lied to me. He said he loved me, just to get me to come."

Heck he did. "Well, if that isn't... you mean Max told you he loved you?" Thought I'd better double-check before I lit into her good.

She nodded, but she wouldn't look at me.

"And you told him, what? No, let me guess. When you said his name when you was hurt real bad it was actually your dog you asking for. That, girl, has got to be the sorriest story I ever heard tell of. You think Max went all that way to sit by your side while you was so sick you didn't even know he was there because...because he felt responsible? Well, maybe he did at that. But that doesn't explain why he dropped everything again, jeopardizing his future with this firm, I might add, to go off to Vancouver to meet that Shaoming person. And he topped that off by going back to Australia again to fetch you. You're right, girl. You don't know Max."

Max cleared his throat. He was standing in the doorway to his office. "Hi, Jake. Give me a minute, will you? Cassiopia, I need to speak to you."

I had no idea how much he'd overheard, but the way he looked and sounded. Oh my. And calling me Cassiopia. It wasn't good. I knew that much. I walked past him into the office, and he pulled the door shut behind us.

"Don't bother sitting. This won't take long. You're fired, for violating the confidentiality of this office."

His voice was so cold and hard I felt like I'd been socked in the stomach. Even though he told me not to sit, I barely made it to the chair. I rocked back and forth trying to ease the pain. Of course, he was right. I had no business telling Jake he went to Vancouver, but Max and me, we've been through a lot together. It couldn't end like this.

I didn't realize I was crying until Max came and poked a tissue at me.

Then Jake walked in.

We both stared at her, and she stared back at us, and nobody could think of a thing to say.

Jake recovered first. "What's going on here?"

"It's none of your business." Lord, Max sounded bleak.

She looked right at him. "I think it is."

Since I'd caused this whole mess, it was up to me to sort it back out, but God be my witness, I sure didn't know how to do it. "I think it is too," I said, taking a chance.

Max, he stood there, looking like a man who just lost his best friend. He turned away from Jake and me and walked over to his desk. He walks real good now. Still uses a cane, but I expect it won't be much longer before he doesn't even need that.

Max stared down at his desk, and I looked at him, and then I looked at Jake. I couldn't remember the last time I'd seen two more miserable people. And just like that, I knew without any doubt that they loved each other, but they were both too proud, or too scared, to say it. Or maybe, after Max said it, and Jake didn't believe him, he wouldn't say it again.

"Jake asked me a question, Max."

Out of the corner of my eye I saw her eyes open real wide, and her hand flew up to her mouth.

"She wanted to know if you asked Sophie to marry you. Seems to me that's an issue she needs to discuss with you. I'll just go on down to personnel, take care of the matter you and I were discussing. Leave you and Jake to talk about things."

"That's okay, Cassie." Max spoke without turning around. "The personnel issue can wait. You can go home."

Thank God. I was so limp with relief, it was a struggle to stand. I barely managed it. Then I did what else needed doing. "You two, no dirty fighting now. Neither one of you is in proper shape. You need to be gentle, hear?"

"Cassiopia."

"Yeah, Max, I know. I'm out of here." But what I wouldn't give to be a fly on the wall after that. *Oh my.*

I took a long time shutting off my computer, first taking the opportunity to make the backups I'd been neglecting. Lordy that alone took twenty minutes. Next I cleaned out the top drawer of my desk. It's been getting messier and messier. Comes a time a person just needs to stop and sort it out before it drives them crazy.

When they still weren't out after half an hour, I figured Max would be real annoyed if I was still around when they did come out, so I got my coat and purse and walked slowly down the hall. I took a last look back before the elevator came. Still no sign of them.

It was clear I wasn't going to find out anything else tonight. If Rosie were still at Max's, I'd pump him. Not that Rosie would ever violate Max's trust like I did.

It was going to be a very long night, and I was going to spend it worrying about Max and wondering how everything worked out.

Chapter Thirty-Seven
MAX

After Cassie walked out, leaving me and Jake at opposite ends of the room, there was a whole lot of silence. When I looked up, I found Jake had moved and was standing behind the chair where Cassie had sat rocking back and forth, moaning like I'd kicked her in the stomach. I'd let my temper get the best of me. Not something I was proud of.

And now I had to deal with Jake.

Her hands gripped the back of the chair, and I sat behind my desk, facing her across the expanse of smooth oak. She seemed to be receding somehow.

I rubbed my eyes trying to focus. "Please. Sit down."

She sat on the edge of the chair, her hands clenched in her lap.

"I heard Cassie tell you I went to Vancouver to meet with Shaoming Wong. I expect you want to know what that was about."

She nodded without taking her eyes off me.

While I told her about Godfrey Paisley and Shaoming Wong and the change in the will, she stared at me silently. "Godfrey thinks it's safe for you to go home, and I agree," I said.

"So, I was right."

"About?"

She lifted her chin, looking defiant. "You only said you loved me out of guilt. It's really Sophie you love."

"You may be one hell of an investigative reporter, Jake Rutherford, but you flunk personal communication."

"What's that supposed to mean?"

"I've already told you how I feel. About you and about Sophie. I assume you care for me if it matters so much about Sophie. But caring isn't enough. You need to trust. Obviously, you don't." A jackhammer went to work on my left temple. *Damn Kelly for starting this and Jake for finishing it.*

"It's not just a question of trust," she said. "You're asking me to give up my world, Max. Yeah, I know you said you'd consider moving to Australia, but now I've seen you here with your work, your friends, your house, and I know you can't possibly mean it. And I can't ask you to. So, I'm the one who has to give up my home and my career and move halfway around the world where you're the only person I know."

She was speaking so fast, I fell a beat or two behind.

"And if those are the conditions, I need to be sure. I love you, Max. Too much to take a chance that the only reason you said you loved me was so I wouldn't be on your conscience."

Her voice had careened out of control, and she stopped abruptly and wiped at the tears streaming down her face. She had never looked more beautiful.

I stood, walked around the desk, and stopped in front of her. "I can't kneel in these legs, Joanna Kate. You'll have to stand up."

When she did, I reached out and brushed that lock of hair back. "I love you. So very much."

Her eyes were still swimming with tears, but her mouth was beginning to curve into a smile. Then we both took that last small step into each other's arms, and for a time the movement of her lips against mine blocked out everything but a feeling of rightness and joy.

~ ~ ~

We didn't discuss it, but when we got in the car, I didn't drive to the restaurant I'd picked out for dinner or to the symphony. Instead, I took Jake home, and once there, led her to my room and my bed.

We undressed each other slowly until all that was left was for me to take off the legs. I handed them to Jake, and she laid them on the floor.

I pulled up the sheet, but she stopped me. "No, Max. Don't hide. I want..." and then she wasn't talking any more, she was touching me all over, even...

Instinctively, I reached out and gripped her wrist, holding her hand away from my thigh.

She gazed into my eyes. "It's okay, Max, let me touch you." I loosened my grip on her hand, and she brought it up and stroked my face and pulled gently on my hair.

"I'll kill her," she said.

"Who?"

"The woman who made you so unsure. You're beautiful, Max, and I love everything about you." Her hand moved down my neck, tracing a path along my chest, down to my thigh. "Everything." Her fingers skimmed over what was left of my legs.

Joanna Kate's touch...erasing the horror of my wounding, the pain of loss, the loneliness that had infused my life. I let all that float away, and in its wake came strength, certainty, and a need to smooth my hand over her, all of her. Kissing Joanna Kate, tasting, touching. The silky feel of her. All this time living, not realizing, this...this was possible.

Joanna Kate, my love. Her skin against mine, we two, moving in a rhythm as old as time that we'd made new.

It wasn't until much later that I thought about Kelly and what she said about happiness—that it existed.

Maybe she requested it for me when I had too little faith to ask for it myself.

Epilogue
New Year's 1998
CASSIE

I put in a really bad night after Max fired me, even though he did rescind it right away. Later, once I got to know Jake, when she wasn't worrying that Max loving her was too good to be true, I saw her wariness had been pure and simple fear.

The two of them, almost missing each other because they were afraid. And after what they'd both been through. *Oh my.*

My Melvin always says loving me is the most courageous thing he's ever done. Given the trouble Max and Jake had, I decided it must be true for other folk as well.

So, how it ended up—Max married Jake, on the terrace of his house. It was a small affair. Only the closest family of the bride and groom. Max said that included Rosie, Melvin, and me, and Sophie, her hand held by a man named Philip who talked a lot like Jake.

Max had his three brothers as best men, and Jake had her two sisters and me as best women. That was Max's wedding gift to Jake, paying for her sisters to be there.

While Jake and Max exchanged their vows, I cried, not caring who saw. They were so happy, those two, they were giving off sparks. Sophie and Philip were shining some too.

Max and Jake are going to live in Sydney. And in San Francisco. Jake's paper is pleased they'll have a reporter spending time in the States, and Max will establish and oversee a branch office of Stedman Richards Micelli Wermling and Gildea in Sydney.

It's a step the firm should have taken years ago—expanding into the Pacific Rim. That's what Mr. Micelli's been telling everyone who will listen. He acts like it was his idea, but I know better.

Todd is going to be Mr. Micelli's successor in the San Francisco office. Max didn't even blink when I told him. Of course, I was pretty sure he already knew.

I'm real happy everything is working out for Max, but it means I need a new job.

That turns out to be the easiest change of all. I don't even have to update my resume or pick out an interview suit. I'm going to help Rosie run the San Germano Gourmet Academy.

I'll make sure the paperwork is done right, and Rosie will do what he's best at. Cooking and helping people.

<<<>>>

A Note About DOHSA and Flags of Convenience

The Death on the High Seas Act (DOHSA) was signed into law in 1920. It forced corporations for the first time to compensate the widows and children of seamen who lost their lives due to wrongful acts occurring in international waters (three nautical miles from the U.S. coast). The compensation called for by the law was a settlement roughly equal to the expected lifetime earnings of the person who died.

Although progressive when first passed, today DOHSA dramatically limits the damages a survivor can collect for the wrongful death of a family member at sea. All that can be awarded is an amount equal to lost wages and burial expenses. No damages may be sought for loss of companionship or pain and suffering, nor may damages be sought as a punishment for negligent, reckless, or other egregious acts that resulted in a death.

A recent example of a case where DOHSA applied was the Transocean Deepwater Horizon tragedy. For legal purposes, the oil rig was considered an ocean-going vessel, and since it was located more than three nautical miles offshore at the time of the explosion, DOHSA applied. It means that although BP is paying billions to those on shore who suffered losses of income due to this tragedy, the families of the men who lost their lives when the Deepwater Horizon rig exploded have been paid as little as $1000.

Contrast that to what happened after a 2005 explosion of a rig on Texas soil. Following that, BP paid out over one billion dollars to compensate the families of those lost.

Following the crash of TWA Flight 800 off Long Island in July 1996, an amendment to the law was passed. However, this amendment applies only to airline passengers. Recent attempts to update the law have been met with intensive lobbying by the cruise ship industry. For more detailed information about DOHSA and its many ramifications, I recommend maritime attorney Jim Walker's website:

http://www.cruiselawnews.com/tags/dohsa/

Flags of Convenience

Operating under a "Flag of Convenience" refers to a business practice whereby merchant ships fly the ensign of a country different from the one where the entity that owns the ship is located. Panama, the Marshall Islands, and Liberia are three such Flag of Convenience states. Their looser regulatory structure offers many advantages to ship owners.

A Note to Readers

I hope you enjoyed *Love and Other Acts of Courage* and will want to keep in touch with me. All you have to do is go to my website (https://annwarner.net) and sign up for my mailing list.

Signing up means you will receive an occasional newsletter and notices when I have a new release.

One more thing before you go...

If you enjoyed *Love and Other Acts of Courage*, please mention the novel to friends who like to read, and consider writing a review. Having reviews enables me to reach more readers. Amazon is a very useful review site, but I appreciate reviews wherever you wish to post them.

You may also lend this book to a friend since it is lending-enabled.

I love hearing from readers. You can contact me through my website:

AnnWarner.net

About the Author

A former toxicologist and university professor, Ann Warner is the author of a heartwarming cozy mystery series, a romantic trilogy, and six single titles that have collectively garnered over 2,500 five-star reviews. During her career as a clinical toxicologist, Ann encountered many intriguing stories that have now found their way into her novels.

Ann's cozy mystery series follows the adventures and dodgy events in a not so retiring retirement community. In her trilogy and single titles the consequences of choosing to love or not to love is an underlying theme as characters face crises and complications that force them to dig deep within themselves to discover the limits of their own resilience.

Ann lives in Cincinnati with her husband. Together they have lived in or traveled to many of the settings found in Ann's books: New Zealand, Australia, Alaska, Colorado, Kansas, Boston, and Puerto Rico.

Acknowledgments

Writing is a solitary profession, and during the creation of a story, the author is alone. But once the book has taken form, one of the greatest gifts a writer can receive is a careful and thoughtful critique from another writer. I have received that gift many times over while writing *Love and Other Acts of Courage* from the following writers: Robin Borche, Jennette Heikes, Judy Carpenter, Jane Turner Goldsmith, David Johnson, Alice Barron, Meredith Stoddard, Janet Biery, Lisa Margreet, Juliet O'Callaghan, Darla Ferrara, Clair Gibson, Gail Cleare, Patricia McAuliffe, Margaret Johnson, Shelley Nolden, Lesa Clarke, and Juli Townsend. If I've forgotten anyone, I sincerely apologize.

As always, I must single out for a special thank-you my wonderful editor, Pam Berehulke. If there are any errors in this book, they are mine, not Pam's, since I have the unfortunate tendency to continue tinkering after Pam has perfected my grammar, spelling, and formatting.

Also by Ann Warner

The Babbling Brook Naked Poker Club Series

Available in Electronic, Print, and Large Print Editions
Book One available as a free download
Books One-Three Available in Audio Editions
See my website (AnnWarner.Net) for details.

A cozy mystery series with >1000 five-star reviews about troubled relationships, questionable choices, art theft, and other dodgy dealings in a not so retiring retirement community.

The Dreams Trilogy

Dreams for Stones

Book One of the Dreams Trilogy
Available as a free download in multiple formats
Indie Next Generation Book Award Finalist
Electronic, Audio, and Print editions available

A man holding fast to grief and a woman who lets go of love too easily. It will take all the magic of old diaries and a children's story to heal these two. Caught in grief and guilt over his wife's death, English professor Alan Francini is determined never to feel that much pain again. He avoids new relationships and keeps even his best friend at arms' length. His major solace is his family's ranch south of Denver.

Children's book editor Kathy Jamison has learned through a

lifetime of separations and a broken engagement that letting go is easier than hanging on. Then she meets Alan, and for once, begins to believe a lasting relationship is possible. But Alan panics and pushes her away into the arms of his best friend. Now the emotions of three people are at stake as they struggle to find a way to transform their broken dreams into a foundation for a more hopeful future.

Persistence of Dreams

Book Two of the Dreams Trilogy
Audio, Electronic, and Print editions available

Lost memories and surprising twists of mystery. Alan, Kathy, and Charles's story continues. The ending of his love affair with Kathy and an arsonist seeking revenge are the catalysts that alter the shape and direction of Charles's life. Forced to find both a new place to live and a way to ease his heartache, Charles finds much more as he reaches out to help his neighbor Luz Montalvo. Helping Luz forces Charles to come to grips with his fractured friendships and the fragmented memories of his childhood.

Luz Montalvo was a carefree college student until her parents died in a car crash. Frantic not to lose her younger siblings to foster care, Luz took them on the run. After nearly a year scraping by as an apartment manager, she's just beginning to feel safe when she discovers her newest tenant is her worst nightmare, a deputy district attorney.

Unexpected Dreams

Book Three in the Dreams Trilogy
Print and Electronic Editions Available

Murder made to look like an accident, family secrets, interfering mothers, lovers in conflict. All combine in a satisfying mix in this contemporary romantic mystery.

Phoebe Whitney-Tolliver has just ended a long-term relationship and begun a new position as the Chief Accident Investigator for the City and County of Denver. She has also fulfilled a lifelong dream—that of owning a horse. These changes bring Phoebe into contact with horse owner and attorney Sam Talbot and Luz and Charles Larimore.

Phoebe helps Charles, a district attorney, and Luz, his wife, in determining whether a traffic accident was actually murder, while Sam locates information about Luz's Chilean family. Eventually the four of them come up against Luz's murderous uncle, a man determined to maintain control of the family's large estancia in Chile. The uncle is a formidable foe, one who will require all the wiles and skill Phoebe, Sam, Charles, and Luz possess to overcome.

Single Titles

Absence of Grace

Available as a free download in multiple formats

Print is also available

The memory of an act committed when she was nineteen weaves a dark thread through Clen McClendon's life. It is a darkness Clen ignores until the discovery of her husband's infidelity propels her on a quest for her own redemption and forgiveness. At first, her journeying provides few answers and peace remains elusive. Then Clen makes a decision that is both desperate and random to go to Wrangell, Alaska. There she will meet Gerrum Kirsey and learn that choices are never truly random, and they always have consequences.

Counterpointe

Endorsed by Compulsion Reads

Print and Electronic Editions Available

Art, science, love, and ambition collide as a dancer on the verge of achieving her dreams is badly injured. Afterward, Clare Eliason rushes into a marriage with Rob Chapin. The marriage falters, propelling Clare and Rob on journeys of self-discovery. Rob joins a scientific expedition to Peru, where he discovers how easy it is to die. Clare's journey, which takes her only a few blocks from the Boston apartment she shared with Rob, is no less profound. During their time apart, each will have a chance to save a life. One will succeed, one will not. Finally, they will face the most difficult quest of all, navigating the space that lies between them.

Doubtful

Endorsed by Compulsion Reads
Red Ribbon Award - Wishing Shelf Independent Book Awards
Print and Electronic Editions Available

Doubtful Sound, New Zealand: For Dr. Van Peters, Doubtful is a retreat after a false accusation all but ends her scientific career. For David Christianson, Doubtful is a place of respite after a personal tragedy is followed by an unwelcome notoriety.

Neither is looking for love or even friendship. Each wants only to make it through another day. But when violence comes to Doubtful, Van and David's only chance of survival will be each other.

Memory Lessons

Print and Electronic Editions Available

Glenna Girard has passed through the agony and utter darkness of an unimaginable loss. It is only in planning her escape, from her marriage and her current circumstances, that she manages to start moving again, toward a place where she can live in anonymity and atone for the unforgivable mistake she has made.

As she takes tentative steps into the new life she is so carefully shaping, she has no desire to connect with other people. But fate has other ideas, bringing her a family who can benefit from her help if only she will give it. And a man, Jack Ralston, who is everything she needs to live fully again, if Glenna will just let herself see it.

Vocabulary of Light

Print and Electronic Editions Available

Living on a tropical island might sound like a dream to some people, but for Maggie Chase it's more of a challenge than she's looking for. Maggie, who has a PhD in biochemistry, agreed to put her husband's career first after the birth of their daughters, and that has now led to Mike accepting the position of CEO of the Lillith Pharmaceuticals plant in San Juan. Struggling to fit into the bilingual, Latin culture of Puerto Rico in the late 1980s, Maggie's adjustment is aided by the friendships she develops. Friendships that bring both dark and light into her life, and eventually demand of her an inner strength and resilience she didn't know she was capable of.

Made in the USA
Las Vegas, NV
23 August 2021